THE CALL OF AVALON

MARA LI

The Call of Avalon

published by

Dutch Venture Publishing

Copyright © 2023 Dutch Venture Publishing

Author: Mara Li (pseudonym of Marieke Veringa)

Cover design: Marieke Veringa

Text editor: Jen Minkman

1

THE WOLF IN THE DARK

The taste of bile in my mouth. A sticky, cold feeling between my legs. Slowly, I open my eyes. It's so dark that I seem to have been swallowed up by the earth.

I look around me, searching. I discover the only sliver of light on the floor on the other side of the room. Slowly, I crawl towards it. I grope for the source of the light. My fingers collide with the bottom of a door.

Iron.

There is a floor, and a door, and a gap.

My head is throbbing painfully. Where am I? All my memories and thoughts seem to be shaken up. What has happened to me? I can't think clearly, I only feel panic. I hoist myself up, but realise that's a bad idea. Nausea overwhelms me in intense waves and I vomit on the floor in the spot between my hands.

I'm in the Asclepius Congregation, I remind myself once I can sit upright again. *They caught me...*

No, that's not true. I have *let* myself get caught.

Yes, that's it. My thoughts clear up, but I don't have time to dwell on them for too long. I open my mouth and vomit some more. The phlegm builds up in my throat. I spit and cough and gurgle, gasping for breath.

As soon as I can breathe again, I crawl away from my own vomit and pat my neck with a trembling hand. There is a sore spot where the needle was inserted. How long have I been I unconscious for? It could be an hour, or a day... I don't know. It's so dark in this cell I can barely see my own hands. I look at the only beam of light penetrating the room from underneath the door and suddenly it dawns on me that I'm here alone. Where's my brother?

'Arthur!'

I'm startled by my own raspy voice. Groaning, I hoist myself a bit more upright and try to stand. When I lean against the door this time, it's not so difficult anymore. 'Arthur! Can you hear me?' Powerlessly, I bang against the iron door. 'Let me out!'

My only answer is silence. I grope around and find nothing, only empty corners that are not so far apart. Now I am throwing my full weight against the door. I *knew* it was a bad idea to let Arthur come along. They could've done anything to him at this point, without me being able to help him. I should've known better, protested more loudly. By Gwenhael's blood, I should've locked Arthur in the Ark!

My efforts to kick in the door takes almost all my energy; pretty soon I'm out of breath. That must be from the crap they gave me. I keep shouting and banging on the door for a while, but then I fall back on the floor, dejected. There's nobody on the other side of that door, or if there is, they don't feel like opening it. Arthur can't hear me – otherwise he would've answered.

I automatically reach for the seal pendant, but it's no longer around my neck. I have lost my talisman; lost it during those last minutes in the forest or on the way to the Institute. The discovery feels like a slap in the face.

The cold coming off the walls makes me shiver, despite my winter clothes. I wrap my arms around myself and feel something hard pressing against my chest. Rona's diary. Strange... I still have the book with me, even though they have taken my rucksack away from me. I vaguely remember groping hands all over my body, someone searching for weapons in my pockets, under my sleeves... I frown deeply as I try to piece together the fragmented images into a correct memory. I think I clasped my arms in front of my breasts to protect the diary. Then there was a woman's snarling voice, and as I lost consciousness, the hands disappeared from my body. At least one person in the Asclepius Congregation does not appreciate young women being groped by the men of Detection. I squirrel that little bit of information away, without knowing whether it'll ever come in handy. But I'm grateful. I pull out the book and tenderly stroke the torn, leather cover.

'Don't worry, Mum,' I whisper. 'We haven't given up on you.'

One day they must come and get me. I have no doubt. I'm just not sure what I'm more afraid of: being left to my fate in this dark, cramped cell or the moment that door opens and the blinding light announces my own personal hell. I remember Mirna's horrifying story: for five years she was imprisoned here. If I have to spend five years in this cage I'll go crazy.

I suspect they gave me Pax, but it's starting to wear off, since I feel wide awake and the nausea is fading. With eyes wide open, I stare into nothingness. The darkness is a fathomless maw.

'*Will you, will you follow me... breaking the waves and braving the sea ...*' My voice is no more than a breath. I shudder and flinch even more. The cell begins to reek of my vomit. I want to put on some dry trousers, see some daylight.

And where is Arthur? I have asked myself that question so often now that I'm numb with fear and uncertainty. I hope he's not in the dark like me. Or maybe that's a good thing? As long as he's locked up, like me, no one will touch him.

The oppressive silence becomes more and more threatening. I want to hear something, *anything*. As long as it's not my own breathing and anxious heartbeat.

I begin to sing softly:

'Come from Camlann, lift anchor, set sail
If death won't withhold you, then nothing else will
Hold fast the helm through the mist all those miles
Sail past the cliffs to that sweet, secret isle.'

I hear a thump behind me. I stiffen, my song smothered in a new wave of fear. I wait, without anything happening. Then I pull myself together and begin to scan the wall, but there is nothing that could've caused the sound. Did it come from the other side? After a few moments, I press my ear against the wall. 'Is ... is someone there?'

For a moment all is silent. 'Here,' I then hear. The voice sounds dull.

My heart leaps. 'Arthur?'

The voice is silent for a moment. 'You must miss him a lot.'

It's not Arthur. I sigh. 'Who is there?'

'Speak louder. Mouth against the wall.'

I press my face to the wall as close as possible. 'Where am I?' I shout. 'I don't see anything.'

'A cell.' For a moment there is silence. 'What have you done?'

'Nothing ... Not yet.'

I hear barking laughter.

'Where are these cells? I woke up here.'

'Underground,' says the stranger. It's difficult to understand him properly. 'In zero.'

'Zero?'

'Platform Zero. Underground.'

'Can they hear us?'

'Who?'

'The guards.'

'Guards don't hurt you. Doctors are to be feared.'

'I know that.' Even Rona was afraid of her own brother. 'Can they hear us?'

'I don't think so.'

I press my ear hard against the wall. He has a rough voice. Much too gruff for a young person. 'Why are you here?'

'Do *you* know?'

'I know why I'm here.' I wait, but he remains silent. 'Who are you?'

'Patient 263.'

Patient! A furious feeling coils in my stomach like a snake. If there was anything left in my stomach, I would probably have thrown it up by now. The Snake reduces us to numbers.

'Girl?'

I swallow. 'My name is Nimue. What about you?'

On the other side of the wall, I hear some scraping. Maybe he's chained and trying to get up? Will they tie me up too if I don't cooperate? I clench my fists so hard it hurts. The pain makes me even more awake. *Remember why you are here. Always keep it in mind.*

'Call me Wolf.'

I wonder if I have understood correctly. 'Ulf?'

'*Wolf.*'

I frown in confusion. A wolf, a beast of the wild ... But there are no wolves in Central Europe. At least not near Gwennec, and certainly not in the swamp near Brevalaer. 'You have a strange name.'

He says something unintelligible. I try to listen again with my ear to the wall, but falls silent.

'Wolf?'

He's quiet now. A moment later, I hear dull footsteps coming my way. I move as far away from the door as possible. For a short moment there is more silence, then a strange, squeaking sound. Suddenly, I'm blinded by bright light coming in from the corridor.

'Patient 1490,' says a soft, feminine voice coming from the doorway. 'Doctor Tangi Moal is ready for the examination. After that, I'll take you to your room.'

2

DOCTOR MOAL

She's wearing a blue dress and shiny, black shoes. Her face seems young, but the lines around her mouth tell a different story. Smiling, she looks down at me. 'Do you need help walking?'

I want to growl and tell her not to touch me, not to come near me. Mirna's warning stops me just in time. Yet, I stand frozen. I feel like a trapped animal in a cage, ready to defend myself if she pulls out another syringe.

The woman takes a step backwards. Enough to give me some space, but not far enough to shoot past her. 'Please follow me.'

It's likely that they already have Arthur upstairs somewhere. Finding out where he is must be my first priority, but after that I must focus on the reason for my arrival.

As soon as I'm outside, she shuts the door behind me. I now see how solid it is: an iron plate as thick as my clenched fist, with a massive lock.

Her fingers close around my upper arm. For a moment I try to pull away, but I notice that I'm not as steady on my feet as I thought. 'You have poisoned me, haven't you?'

'Well, no. It was just something to calm you down.' She's still smiling, though the smile doesn't reach her eyes. She has bright blue eyes, I see. Maybe she would've looked friendly, if she didn't frogmarch me away from the cell like a prisoner.

'How long was I *calmed down*?'

I see a trace of surprise in her eyes. Doesn't she often get questions like that? 'A few hours.'

6

'What was that good for?'

'Come, walk on.'

'Is my brother upstairs?'

'Your brother is sleeping,' she says, clearly impatient. 'I'll take you to Doctor Moal and then to your room, where you'll get clean clothes and a bed. You must be exhausted from all those days in the wilderness. All alone.'

What kind of story has Will told her? I decide not to correct her. If I have to pretend, I'd better play along. 'It wouldn't have been so bad if we hadn't been hunted,' I tell her with conviction.

'You can't go wandering around out there on your own,' the woman says kindly. 'It's dangerous.'

'But *you* can?'

The smile disappears. The woman presses her lips together and stares straight ahead. Maybe I shouldn't have said that. They might decide I should stay in that cell permanently, just like the strange man – Wolf.

We go up a flight of stairs. The steps are a bit too narrow for me to properly put my feet on them and there is no handrail, so I press myself against the wall.

It strikes me how long we have already been climbing. These cells must really have been built deep underground. I wonder if they were ever part of an Ark.

When the stairs end, we stand in front of a closed door. This time it's not made of iron, but it is locked. The woman uses a keycard to open it. That explains the beeping noise from earlier. Rougher than necessary, she shoves me into the corridor.

I blink against the daylight and peek up. The window that lets the sun through is too high to reach and has a long row of bars in front of the glass.

'This way,' says the woman. I follow her silently. We seem to be walking endlessly, straight ahead. I use this time to commit all the details to memory. We pass walls that seem deceptively cosy, with their soft yellow tones. It's as if they want to give the impression that the sunlight is coming in through all the windows. A lie that's immediately contradicted by the bars. The floor has been given less attention; it consists only of grey concrete and makes our footsteps sound hard and cold. On either side are dozens of closed doors, all of them numbered.

At the end of the corridor, there are three steps leading upwards. On the right, the hall fades into twilight. There are no windows and only a few lights. Here, where we stand, the lamps are fixed to the ceiling like glass tubes. It reminds me of the Ark. I feel a twinge of loss, of regret. And of fear.

At the same time, I think of Katell. She must be somewhere in this huge building, perhaps behind one of these doors. I bite the inside of my cheek, and the pain stirs up my anger again. *Remember why you are here, Nimue.*

The woman takes me to the left. Finally, we're standing in front of a large glass wall, with a glass door in it. Next to it is a sign that says: Laboratory 5.

The woman knocks on the glass door, then opens it and gestures to me to walk in. I reluctantly do so. There is a strange, sharp smell in the laboratory. A smell that I cannot really place, and it stings my nostrils almost painfully. Around me are shelves full of books and closed jars. We walk past a huge device that looks like an elongated oven. Wires are running from it in all directions, some red, some blue.

Only then do I see the man. He's overshadowed by a semi-circular wall of computer screens, which display nothing but coloured lines undulating up and down, like jagged mountain peaks.

'Doctor Moal,' says the woman in the blue dress. 'The girl.'

The doctor turns around with a little jump. He is round and balding and has thick lips. He, too, smiles at me. Why do they *do* that?

'Patient 1490,' he says warmly, approaching me with his hand extended. 'I'm Doctor Moal.'

I stare at his hand without moving. 'I have a name. I'm Ni...' Just in time, I swallow the last two syllables. *You idiot!* How many Nimues are there in Central Europe and how long would it take Benji to identify one within his own institute? 'Nicole,' I say, finishing my sentence. It's the first name that comes to mind.

The corners of his mouth turn up even more. He actually *does* look like a mole, I think involuntarily. Moal the mole.

'Well then, Nicole. Sini has already told you what is going to happen...'

I shake my head.

The doctor points to an elevated part of the room. In front of it is a white curtain. On the other side is a hospital bed. 'You may take a seat there for a moment.'

'I *may*?'

He looks at me coldly. Without a smile on his face, he suddenly looks a lot less like a mole. 'It's not a request, patient 1490. Take a seat and pull up your sleeve.' He turns to the woman, Sini. 'Those rags she's wearing can be burned later.'

I sit down on the bed. It's covered with thin, blue paper that crackles when I move. It is chilly in the laboratory. I pull up my left sleeve, but apparently Moal is not satisfied yet. He nods to Sini, and she pulls up the sleeve even further, well above my elbow. Doctor Moal takes out a bandage and wraps it around my upper arm so tightly that it cuts off my blood circulation. I clench my teeth.

'It's just for a little while.' He grabs a syringe.

'No!' I jump off the bed. 'What are you going to inject into me this time?'

'Nothing.' He shows me the empty syringe. 'We're going to take some blood for your blood test. It really doesn't hurt that much.'

'Sit down,' Sini orders me. She comes towards me.

I sit down on the crackling bed again. 'What do you mean, my blood test?'

'Nicole,' Moal says, frowning. 'I've heard that you can be quite stubborn. That's not allowed here.'

If he thinks I'm stubborn now, I'll show him. But no – fighting should come later. I'm barely inside and already I'm starting to mess up Mirna's strategy. Perhaps acting a bit dim is the best thing to do for now. I take a deep breath and humbly hold out my arm.

Doctor Moal's thumb searches for a vein and sticks the needle in me once he's found a suitable spot. I feel a sharp jab and a burning sensation.

'Blood test? What do you mean by that?'

'Standard procedure,' Doctor Moal says. 'We're working hard here at the Institute to find all kinds of solutions.' He jerks the needle out of my arm. Sini immediately presses a cotton pad against the wound. 'Personally, I don't think we'll find anything in your blood,' Doctor Moal confesses, smiling as he removes the tube from the syringe, puts a label on it and puts it in a rack with some other tubes.

'Why?' I look at him suspiciously. 'What is wrong with my blood?'

He laughs out loud. It's a high, giggling sound. 'Nothing at all. You're from the Periphery, aren't you?'

I give him "Nicole's" most ignorant look. 'How do *you* know?'

'Your accent.' He smiles broadly. 'You and Patient 1491 both talk like farmers.'

So Arthur is Patient 1491. Would he be somewhere near me once I get to my new room? 'There are no farmers in Gwennec.'

'Aren't there?' Doctor Moal looks at his equipment a little bored.

'The sea provides fish, not crops.'

'You're awfully mouthy. Your brother kept his mouth shut nicely.'

Ah, so Arthur hadn't been asleep at all. At least not for very long. 'When can I see him?'

'Not anytime soon.'

'But...'

'Lift up your jumper.'

The doctor grabs a stethoscope and puts the earpieces in.

'If I do, will you take me to him?'

'Your brother is sleeping,' Sini says clearly. 'You can't see him.'

'Your jumper,' Doctor Moal repeats.

I lift up the hem of my jumper, along with the diary in the inside pocket. They don't notice anything. The doctor presses the stethoscope against my stomach. 'Breathe in – hold – and breathe out ... Good. And again, breathe in – hold ...'

He checks my lungs, then my heart. Once he's satisfied, he takes off the earpieces of his stethoscope and steps back. 'All done. No reason to look so suspicious, okay?' His words are reassuring, but his tone unfriendly.

'Come,' Sini says. She helps me off the bed and pulls down my jumper like I'm a child who needs help getting dressed. I let her.

'Is that all? You're ... not going to do anything else?'

'What else should I do with you?' Doctor Moal already turned his back to me, clearly not interested in a chat. 'You seem healthy and strong.'

'You should rest first,' Sini says.

'And do I get food?'

Sini smiles a little condescendingly. No doubt I come across as a mutt wagging its tail at the mere thought of scraps of food. 'As promised.'

'And then? What happens next?' I wrap my arms around my chest, protecting the diary without them realising I'm hiding it there. 'Are you going to hurt me? Or my little brother?'

Sini makes a shocked and slightly disapproving sound, then purses her lips. 'Child, whyever would we hurt you?'

I frown at her. 'They call you The Snake.'

Behind me, Doctor Moal lets out another high-pitched laugh. 'Ssssnake. That *is* rather fitting. You shouldn't listen to gossip too much, Nicole.' He throws me a look I can't quite read. Is it anger? A warning? 'You have no idea what's going on here.'

I keep my thoughts to myself. If they won't take me to Arthur, I must somehow find out where they're keeping him, what is happening to him.

But I still have another priority, I remind myself sternly. Arthur at least *knew* the snake's nest he was walking into – he limped straight towards it, with his one good leg. But Katell had no idea. Nor Taran, Marci and Judikael, Arthur's friends. They have nothing to do with our uncle either. They are the ones I should be focusing my efforts on. They must be the first to be released from this building.

But by Gwenhael, the Institute is bigger than I expected. I have only seen the long straight hall and the cells underground, which Wolf called *Platform Zero*. That means there must be many more rooms, and corridors, and laboratories. How am I going to snoop around here without getting noticed?

'Move along.' Sini's voice snaps me out of my thoughts. I notice that I stopped walking a few steps away from the door. Quickly I start moving again. We walk back, down the long corridor with numbered doors on both sides. When Sini opens door 17, it reveals a room with a bed, a closet, a sink and a toilet. In the corner is a green light.

'What is that?' I ask.

'The alarm clock.' Sini looks at me blankly. 'Tomorrow morning at half past six you have to get up, shower and get dressed. If you are late, you will be disciplined.'

Silently, I step forward. Before I can even turn around, I hear the shrill sound of Sini using her keycard, closing the door behind me.

I take in the details and it doesn't make the room seem any more pleasant. The bed has rusty legs of steel. On top of the tightly made bed with white sheets is a bundle of clothes. There is no window, only a bulb on the ceiling. No light switch on the wall. I'm locked up here and I don't even control the light in my own room. This room may be a better place to stay in than the cell, but it's not exactly a victory.

Tired, I lower myself onto the bed to examine the clothes. The Asclepius Congregation apparently wants me to walk around in a knee-length skirt and a synthetic cardigan. I can hardly stand the fabric – it feels too slick on my fingers. The skirt and cardigan are both a faded blue colour, as if they have been washed too often. Have people worn these clothes before me?

There is also a woollen scarf; the only piece of clothing that feels comfortable.

Slowly, I undress myself. I take out the diary and stare at it for a few moments, before putting it under my pillow.

The skirt is too loose around my hips and the cardigan almost slips off my shoulders. I button it up to my chin. For the first time in weeks, I touch my own body and it scares me. Not because of the bruises I got from banging on the cell door; I'm used to having bruises on my skin. But I don't like how bony I am. I have never exactly been chubby, but that winter in the swamp has left me really skinny. With my thumb I can feel all the ribs, sticking out like tiny bumps. I'd better put on some weight if I want to keep my strength up, I think, as I lie back on the bed. As soon as I think about eating, I notice that my stomach is screaming for food. I had my last meal before I went to sleep and Mirna woke me up to put the plan into place. It seems like ages ago. Besides, when I woke up, I threw everything up. Anyway, Sini promised I'd get some food, so I won't pass out right away. While I wait for a meal, I try to concentrate on the positive.

I'm in. And this was day one. I snuggle into the scarf and stare at the ceiling with wide-open eyes, until all the grey specks start to look like a constellation of stars. So far, my first impression of the Asclepius Congregation only raised more questions for me: is Sini telling the truth when she says they're not going to hurt me? What does that mean for the other patients? What is that man doing in Platform Zero?

And how do I get to Benji?

3

Day Two

As I am lying on the bed with my eyes closed, thinking that they must have forgotten me, someone comes in. But it's not Sini who brings me my meal. It's a young man, dressed in the same blue colour. He doesn't look at me when he puts down the tray. Nor when he says: 'Tomorrow you'll have breakfast in the hall. Someone will pick you up.'

I wait for him to leave, wondering why Mirna never mentioned a dining room in her descriptions.

The food has little taste. There is a slice of fish on my plastic plate, mashed up potatoes and some unrecognisable vegetables. I don't care about the lack of salt or taste. The food is hot and it satisfies my appetite, that's all I want.

After I have scraped the last bits of stew from the plate, I let myself sink back into bed. My body and mind are exhausted. Now that I have been provided with food, I'm feeling overwhelmed by my next need: sleep. My pressing questions no longer keep me awake.

The shrill sound of the alarm clock wakes me. I throw the pillow at the flashing light to shut it up. It doesn't work, so I get up, swearing. I run cold water from the tap and splash it in my face. I find a bar of soap, still wrapped in plastic, and stand there naked for a full minute clumsily trying to get the plastic off. Stinging jellyfish, what a waste. Don't they know how much oil has to be pumped out of Gwennec to produce all this plastic? After I've washed and dressed myself, the alarm clock is still ringing.

'I'm *up*, by Gwenhael!' I growl. By now I'm wide awake and because of that I sharply remember where I am, and what day it is: the second day. Whatever happens today, I should, at any rate, make good use of my time.

There is a single knock on my door, followed by the beeping noise of the electronic lock. The person who comes to get me is neither the young man nor Sini. This man is tall and broad like a bull, with a shiny, bald head and bright eyes. He looks straight at me – something that seems to make Sini and the other person who appeared before uncomfortable – and says: 'You're the new one? Come with me.'

I don't have much of a choice. He leads me down the empty corridor, takes me up a few steps and around a corner without speaking to me. I strain my eyes, memorising the numbered doors we pass and guessing what might be behind them. We pass a few windows decked out with iron bars. Unless we can find a crowbar somewhere in the building, these windows do not offer an easy way out.

I'm surprised when we turn the corner and I suddenly see children standing in a queue. They're standing there, ramrod straight, dressed in white and blue – the colours of the Institute. A couple of them peek over their shoulder when they hear us coming. The man puts me in the back of the queue, doesn't say a word and walks past the children to open double doors with his key card. Behind them is a dining room with two long tables and rows of wooden chairs. He gestures for us to go inside. The children seem to know this routine. Everyone takes their seats. There is no talking. So many children together who are all dead silent – it makes me incredibly nervous. I follow their example, press my lips tightly together, and find a spot at the far edge of the table. No trace of Arthur anywhere. I notice that the second table remains almost empty. We each get a bowl of porridge, a slice of bread and an apple. There are glasses with a kind of orange-coloured juice that I cannot identify. It doesn't look like we can ask for seconds. The bull-man in his blue suit didn't come in with us, but we don't really have privacy either. At the edge of the room are three women, all dressed in blue. They seem to be keeping an eye on us while they're quietly talking to each other. I see one of them stifle a yawn behind her hand.

While spoons are ticking against bowl rims, a little boy next to me gently tugs at my sleeve. I look down at him. He can't be older than nine, I think, and has short, cropped hair. I lean towards him and he whispers:

'Don't stare at the Caretakers.'

I point at the women with my spoon. 'Are those the Caretakers?'

'When they are tired, they let us talk. But only if we do it quietly.'

I imitate his whisper as I gesture to the largely empty table beside us. 'Where are the others?'

'We never see them.'

'Never?' That's a problem if I ever want to find Arthur.

'Not often.' He has already emptied half of his bowl and eagerly shovels more porridge into his mouth. He notices me watching him, then peeks at my untouched breakfast before commenting: 'If you don't finish it, you'll have to sit here until you do.'

'All day?' The idea of wasting food is appalling, so I start eating the porridge quickly. It is lukewarm. Despite the Snakes' wealth, they can't even give their patients a decent meal? We were better off at home; even in the Ark we were eating food more tasteful.

'What's your name?' I ask the boy between my fifth and sixth bite.

'Ruben.'

'Ruben, how long have you been here?'

He shakes his head and downs his juice in three gulps. 'It was winter when they caught me.'

'What are they doing to you? Ruben, this is important.' I put my hand on his upper arm to hold his attention. 'Tell me what they did to you. Or did they say something...?'

One of the Caretakers hisses at us. Ruben collapses and seems to shrink, as if she just slapped him in the face.

I fold my lips and look at my food. Suddenly, I'm no longer hungry.

A loud bell announces the end of our breakfast. This is the only moment of chaos in this otherwise silent, timid group of children. Their chairs slide back and their feet make loud noises across the bare concrete floor.

Ruben surprises me by taking advantage of the moment. Again I feel a tug on my sleeve. 'You have to watch out for the fat doctor,' he whispers. 'Children go to him. Sometimes they don't come back.'

I nod to confirm I heard him. The bit of porridge I have eaten feels like an unpleasant cold lump in my stomach. Is he talking about Doctor Moal? I can't ask him anymore, because Ruben quickly joins the queue and doesn't look back at me either. I stand in the queue as I did before, until the muscular man takes me back to my room. Before he closes the door behind me, his gaze drills into my eyes. 'Everything alright?'

An absurd question. I don't answer it, but ask: 'What's going to happen now?'

'You're new, no schedule has been made for you yet. Wait and rest.'

I curse softly when he locks me in the room with nothing to do. An hour passes, I think, and in frustration I pace from my bed to the wall and back. Sometimes I hear footsteps outside my door, but nobody comes to get me. I don't know what I expected, exactly. That they would immediately take me to the Big Cheese within the Asclepius Congregation? Or to the place where children disappear? That wouldn't be very convenient, since I don't have a plan yet. But I'm wasting precious hours being stuck in a room, not knowing anything.

After another long, boring period where no one comes to collect me, I stop pacing up and down and drop onto my bed. I haven't seen much of the Asclepius Congregation, but I must make sure I remember everything. I close my eyes and try to remember by conjuring up the route to the dining hall. And then, from my room, the way to Doctor Moal's laboratory. I try to remember every corridor that took me from Platform Zero to the laboratory, but it frustrates me that I'm still too disoriented to recall all the details.

I get hungry. And wait some more.

When the shrill beeping noise wakes me up from my slumber, it is Sini who comes in. I prepare myself for danger, perhaps for a confrontation and an escape, but she takes me to another room, where the light is more pleasant and where, to my surprise, I hear voices talking pleasantly together. I can even hear laughter.

Inside is a playroom, one like we had in the Ark. There are a few bookshelves along the wall, some drawing materials and toy blocks and balls. The room is clearly designed for much younger children, and it makes me wonder how far Benji was willing to go. Did he ever use babies for his experiments?

Sini misunderstands the look on my face. 'You're not the only older kid,' she says. 'You'll have some company.'

'What... what am I supposed to do here?'

She seems surprised that I don't know. 'Enjoy yourself. This is your time for leisure. Normally you'll have an hour a day to yourself, but you're new and you're still under supervision. You get twenty minutes.'

I slip inside. My gaze immediately falls on the window. It's barred, but the windowsill is wide and furnished with soft cushions. Nestled in the cushions is a twelve-year-old girl with thick, blonde hair. For a moment, I think I have found Katell. The next moment, she turns and I'm disappointed when I see her face. I let my gaze wander and suddenly I get my hopes up again. On the other side of the room, I think I see a familiar face.

I wade past toys and children. 'Judikael?'

She turns around. Her face lights up. 'Nimue!'

'Shh!' I peek around, but the Caretaker at the door is looking in another direction and is too far away to hear us above the children's voices. 'Call me Nicole here.'

'Nicole? Why?'

'Just trust me. Judikael, I'm so happy to see you! Are you alright? Did they ... do anything?'

'Not yet.' Judikael speaks softly. She glances around, then takes me to a corner of the room, half out of the Caretaker's sight because a chest of drawers is blocking his view like this. 'They took Marci one day, but she came back unharmed. All they did was take her blood, she told me. But I'm not sure that's all they want. Some children are here one day, gone without a trace the next.'

'What about Taran?'

'Yes, he's here. But they know we know each other, so they have separated us.' Judikael peers at the Caretaker with a dark frown. 'What are they afraid of? An army of children?'

'Perhaps of a stampede. Judikael, do you know where Arthur is? Have you seen him?'

She looks at me. 'Arthur is here?'

'They have separated us. I haven't seen a trace of him yet.'

'He'll be fine,' Judikael says. 'As long as he's not sick.'

I look at her, surprised. 'You know about that?'

'Who doesn't? That's all they want to know. I think the Caretakers are afraid of it. They spray themselves with some kind of disinfectant as soon as they smell something even remotely weird.'

'Good luck with that,' I mutter. I lower my voice to a whisper. 'Arthur and I have come to help you. We can be picked up from Cami in eight days, if we find a way out before then.'

Judikael stares at me. I can't blame her for the bewildered look she's giving me. 'You act like it's easy! If there was a way out, I would've taken it by now.'

'It's not easy,' I admit. 'But I have a plan. At least ... I'm working on a plan, now, right this moment.'

She looks at me, waiting.

'I need paper, and something to write with.'

'If that's all, I can help you.' Judikael opens a drawer in the cupboard, rummages around for a moment and then hands me a green-coloured pencil and a wrinkled sheet of paper. I kneel down on the floor and smooth out the paper.

'This is where I start. My room, in this hall. That hallway makes a bend...' Carefully, I draw what I'm describing. Each corridor I walk through becomes a line, alternating with dots to depict the rooms and halls I have encountered. Judikael takes the pencil from me and maps out what she remembers of the surroundings next.

Once we're finished, I look at our handiwork with a critical eye. 'It's a start.'

'What are we going to do with this?'

'First we find out where Arthur and Katell are. And Taran and Marci. We'll mark the best hiding places; if there's a pattern to the Caretakers' routine patrolling the hallways, we'll make a note of it.'

'That still won't get us out,' Judikael says in a muffled voice. 'Even if we manage to get through all the corridors unseen. Every door closes with a keycard.'

'Then we'll make sure we get one.'

She looks at me in disbelief. '*How*?'

'I don't know yet,' I have to admit.

'Nimue, this is madness!' She peers at the Caretakers at the door and lowers her voice even more, until she's whispering. 'They're watching us every second of every day. That makes it impossible to slip away or steal anything...'

I follow her gaze and look at the Caretakers. 'They look tired. I bet they'll be even more tired by the end of the day. We can think of a diversion. And a complex building like this must have one or two back doors. Maybe a kitchen door, maybe a fire escape or a loading dock for goods.'

'Maybe...' Judikael looks unconvinced. 'I want to leave as much as you do. I'm terrified every day that they'll come and get me and I ... won't come back.'

Because there are no pockets in these clothes, I fold up the paper and put it in my sock together with the pencil. 'Keep your eyes open,' I tell her. 'Everything you see can be useful. If only we could pass messages to each other...' But where could we safely leave them without a Snake finding them?

Judikael guesses my idea. She shifts slightly and hooks her fingers behind a floor tile. It slides up a little. 'We can leave messages here. Just be careful the stone doesn't break by pulling too hard.'

'Excellent.' I carefully put the stone back down and note with satisfaction that the fault line is barely visible. 'If you see Arthur or Katell, please let me know.'

'Of course.'

I want to hug her, but she avoids my arms. 'If they know we know each other...'

Of course. It's safer for the Snake to keep us separate. Imagine old friends getting ideas that don't fit into the plans they have for us. I smile grimly. 'We're not defeated yet, Judikael.'

It doesn't take long for me to be collected after that. This time it's Sini who is waiting for me at the door. I find it hard not to look at Judikael over my shoulder. I carefully rearrange my facial expression to a look of bored nonchalance and follow her. The piece of paper in my sock rubs against the skin of my ankle.

I look up at the barred windows. 'Why are they all like that?'

Sini casts a glance aside. 'It was like this when we came here. This whole south complex was once a prison.'

'Before the Impact?'

She smiles. 'After the Impact, Nicole. An older building would no longer be safe. I believe the prison was built to extend one of the Arks at the time.'

'Are the cells part of an Ark?' I ask softly.

'They must be.' She looks at me appraisingly. 'Why this interest in the building, Nicole?'

Certainly not because I want to work out an escape route. I point to the next iron barricade. 'I was wondering what would happen if a fire broke out. We can't escape through the windows. What if we need to get out quickly, but we're stuck?'

'Ah,' Sini says slowly. 'Like the tidal wave in Gwennec?'

Now I'm genuinely surprised. 'You know about that?'

'I heard stories. You had to flee, didn't you? I understand why it frightens you.'

'We jumped off a roof,' I reply softly.

Sini looks at me and I see pity on her face. I avert my eyes, not feeling sure if I want her pity – she's a Snake, after all.

'At least here you don't have to fear such calamities,' Sini says light-heartedly, as we approach my door and she holds her card in front of the scanner. 'If there's ever a fire, the alarm will go off, someone will come and guide you safely through one of the firebreaks.' She waits until I enter my room and smiles at me. 'You're safe with us, Nicole. No more tidal waves and no more wilderness. Try to relax, because tomorrow you'll get your schedule.'

'Will I still get food?'

'Of course. In a few hours. Don't worry, Nicole.'

I give her a meaningless smile. Sini closes my door and I wait until I hear the beeping and the sound of her footsteps dying away.

So there are fire lanes. And in the belly of this complex is an old Ark, just as I suspected. I wouldn't be surprised if the CORE still works and the whole Institute runs on it.

MARA LI

I wonder how much chaos it would cause if that CORE broke down, just like in the Ark.

4

THE FISHER KING

From the third day onwards, I fall into the routine that the Institute sets for me. I keep quiet and absorb every detail that might be of interest. It takes four minutes to walk from my room to Laboratory 5, across a corridor that has large round drain covers every fifteen steps. Sini says that the sewer runs right under our feet. When the alarm clock wakes me in the morning, I have exactly thirty minutes to get ready for breakfast before I'm picked up by the broad-shouldered, bald staff member, twenty minutes to hastily eat my porridge, and then another hour in my lonely room before Sini takes me to Doctor Moal for examination. I pass the time by pacing around my room, like a frustrated, trapped animal in a cage.

Doctor Moal doesn't ask much from me. He even seems a bit bored, and I encourage him to find me terribly boring. He checks my heart rate, my lungs and takes some blood which he uses for later examination. It seems as if he's waiting for something. I don't know what for, until the fourth day. There is something else in the laboratory. A large device called an E.E.G. is waiting for me. I don't know what it's for, but he gestures at it as if he's inviting me to step into a playboat.

'First take off your shoes.'

I crouch down quietly to do aas he says. It is only when he whips out a syringe of white liquid that I start to protest: 'I don't want that stuff in my bloodstream.'

'It's just an anaesthetic.'

If he hopes to reassure me with those words, he is wrong. 'Not again!' When I'm sedated, they can do anything they want to me. Mirna has told me to keep quiet and be attentive, and I intend to be. But how can I pay attention if they're sedating me? I glance at the E.E.G. It looks claustrophobic.

Moal looks at me sharply. 'You do as I say. Now get on your back, girl. Lie still.'

My instincts tell me to resist. I can't keep being obedient without it coming back to bite me at some point, can I? And that terrifying device seems to be an excellent and legitimate reason to say no this once. I freeze, caught between the urge to flee and the intention to be a silent spy.

I hesitate for too long. Doctor Moal grabs me impatiently and pulls me forward. My body reacts to the touch like Corentin's wolf traps to a prey: on cue and without me thinking it through. I throw my fist in the air without hitting him.

'Hold her hands!' snarls Doctor Moal to Sini.

I lash out and the doctor steps aside. I hit Sini under her eye, hard. She gasps and shoots me a startled look. I freeze. I didn't want to hit *her*.

'Don't just stand there, grab her,' growls Moal. Sini recovers. Her fingers grab my upper arm and she forces me down. It hurts, I lose my balance and lower myself backwards onto the narrow white bed of the big machine. I sticks out like a tongue from a monstrous, electronic mouth. I don't want to be shoved in there. I don't want their filthy hands on me.

I struggle, but Sini shoves my wrists into a leather strap at the head of the bed and pulls it shut. She's much stronger than she looks. Once I have given up, the doctor approaches me again.

'This is your last warning, 1490,' he says. 'You behave during the scan, do you understand?'

But I don't hear him. With my arms tied, I feel like a fish in a net. They have only tied my arms, but sheer panic shuts down my common sense. In a second attempt to escape this tight spot, I pull my legs up and kick the doctor right in the stomach. It would've had more impact if I still had shoes on, but he bends over and stumbles backwards regardless. I let out a hoarse laugh.

Sini hurries over to him, but he pushes her away, grabbing the syringe and handing it to her. 'You numb that bitch.' His face reddens.

I'm not able to resist anymore when Sini sticks a sharp needle in my arm. The jab feels sharp and cold, like the one I had in my neck before waking up in Platform Zero.

The feeling in my arms gradually disappears. My legs become heavy. Sini waits a little longer, then ties my ankles with leather bands as well. I can't even crane my neck when she puts a third strap across my forehead.

'It's important that you lie very still,' she explains. She avoids my gaze with a guilt-ridden look on her face. Or is that just my imagination? I snarl at her by pulling up my upper lip, but even that is too much effort now.

Doctor Moal approaches me. Now that I can't hurt him, he seems to relax again. He spreads a slippery substance onto my head. I want to turn away, but the straps and the anaesthetic have turned me into a motionless lump. The doctor sticks several silver electrodes on my head. After ten, I lose count. It's difficult to think clearly. That damn anaesthetic.

'Finally,' Doctor Moal says. 'Keep an eye on her, will you? I'll be in the loft.'

With my eyes slightly open, I watch him disappear behind a glass wall. Sini shoves the bed into the maw of the machine.

'This will take a while,' she says. 'But you won't notice a thing. In a minute you'll be asleep.'

'I don't want to sl...' My eyes shut. I sink into an emptiness that imprisons me. Far away, I hear a low humming sound. Then suddenly I see a light, like lightning. It's so bright that I can see it even with my eyes closed. A few more times it flickers, then everything becomes dark again.

The anaesthetic gave me the shivers before. Now, I'm slowly starting to get warmer. The air is getting thicker by the minute. As much as I want to resist it, I no longer have control over my body. I'm sinking.

Waves break against my body. The sea sucks my legs down. I close my eyes and let myself be pulled along. I can smell the salt and know that it is glistening on my skin, like stardust. But only when the sun shines on it.

Down here, the sunlight is not important; it is no more than a reflection on the surface of the water, which is like a high ceiling above me. My body changes. Legs, arms, toes and fingers, all those helpless limbs are no match for the water and they are taken away from me. I'm slipping. I'm flying. My skin is no longer milky white. And then I hear them. Their voices, them singing the words:

Swim deeper,

Come to us.

And I am heeding the call.

The flashes come back in a series of four and then turn into a rumbling sound. I don't know where it's coming from; it seems to emerge from the depths of the machine itself. It sounds like someone is knocking restlessly on a door: *tacktacktack!* No – like one of those marshland birds. Immediately I'm standing between the trees, as if only my thoughts have conjured up the swamp. Sweet Gwenhael, how I miss the trees. And the soggy ground your feet can sink into. I would even prefer the rotting smell of humus to the sterile air of this Institute.

Sunlight and shade play hide-and-seek with the water between tree roots. I'm perfectly safe, shielded from the rest of the world by the tree dome – a living cathedral. The Asclepius Congregation is a hazy dream. This is the real world. I can feel it in the air that tickles my nose. Clear and unpolluted. Air full of life. And the colours are as vibrant as fresh paint: the leaves on the treetops, the tree bark, ferns and fens. My own clothes look like they have been bought new. I look at my hands: smooth skin, no calluses.

Where am I? Not that it really matters. This is my home. Yet I would like to know where I am. When I turn around, I recognise the menhirs beyond the stream. They look different today, as if they too are a little more elegant, a little more stately than when I was waiting for the Pale Man. Slowly I walk towards them. I feel the ground beneath my feet bounce up and down, as if I were walking on a mattress. I look at the moss growing on the stones, the ridges and rock art that the rain and some distant ancestors have carved into the surface. One image in particular catches my eye: a king with his face erased, because the stone surface has been worn away by years of erosion. But despite his missing features, his crown is still visible. He carries a staff in his left hand and holds a goblet in the other. When I reach out to touch the image, it's as if I'm being pulled away from my spot.

I struggle to get back, because I don't want to leave this marsh and my place among the menhirs. But whatever it is that pulls at me, it doesn't let go before the world has changed before my eyes again. The trees are gone, and so are the sounds of birds among the branches. The air is cold, the horizon open and wide. It is nightfall. I am looking out on a dead plain from a tower window. There is little to see outside, yet I feel that I'm not alone.

Slowly I turn around. The tower room is deprived of light. Yet I can still see something, for my gaze immediately falls on a stone throne in the middle. It is occupied by a gaunt figure – white and vulnerable as a wisp of fog. An old crown is resting on his head, faded and discoloured from years of neglect, as are his cloak and tunic.

I cannot explain how... astonished I feel. I have never seen him before... Or have I? I take a step closer, until I'm right in front of him.

I see recognition reflected on his own shocked face. The Fisher King shakes his ethereal head. 'Not you – it is him that must come.'

'I didn't know I was coming here.'

He lifts his hands from the stone armrests. Only now do I realise that he's wearing chains around his wrists. The chains are attached to riveted rings, which keep him bound to the throne. 'Give me something to drink, child of the sea.'

I look around me. Hidden in the shadows is a roughly hewn pillar, no taller than my waist, with a copper chalice on top. The cup has turned green. There's nothing in it, not even a drop of water.

'I'm sorry,' I say. 'It's empty.'

The Fisher King lets out a wispy sigh. 'Only blood from that grail can prolong my life.'

'Are you ... are you going to die soon?'

'I'm infected, child of the sea. The disease has crept into me and is making my dreams black and bloody.' With his chained hands he gestures to his lower body. A deep wound appears in his thigh. 'Now I can't travel. Soon it will crawl up and

take hold of my heart. And after my heart, my head. Therefore I have chained myself to the throne.'

My fear increases. 'I can't help you drink. There is no blood in the grail.'

'No, not you, daughter of Rona. Let the King Who Must Come enter here.'

'Arthur.' Very slowly his name comes to me, and with it the memory of who I am, and where I belong. The room seems to fade away. I have to sharpen my gaze. 'Wait! I can cure the Black Influenza ...!'

The Fisher King opens his mouth to speak, but before the sound reaches me, he fades away before my eyes. I'm left with a burning sensation in my throat and blink slowly with my dry eyelids.

I'm not sure if I'm really awake. What I do know is that I'm lying in a machine they call E.E.G. When I try to wriggle my fingers, I succeed. My toes wiggle too when I try. I swallow. My throat is as dry as sand and my tongue is sticking to the roof of my mouth like a piece of rubber. The bed is being pulled out of the machine. I recognise Sini even though she's one big blur.

'I'll untie you,' she says. 'But you have to behave.'

I blink my eyes.

'How are you feeling?'

'I can't see very well,' I say croakily. Confused, I look around me.

'That will pass.' She bends over and loosens the tight straps one by one. I groan and rub my wrists. Red scabs run across my skin where the straps cut into my flesh. When she also unties my feet and takes the electrodes off my head, I scramble upright. I feel her hand on my back. For a moment I consider hitting her again, but even though I'm in control again, I don't feel very strong. And she's only trying to help me.

Doctor Moal walks up to us from behind his glass screen.

'Is it done?' I ask weakly. 'Can I go?'

'Not yet.' Am I imagining things, or is he looking confused? 'You have unusually high theta waves.'

I rub my face with my hands. Were these the same hands I used to lift the goblet? 'I was born by the seaside.'

Sini starts laughing, but quickly stops when Doctor Moal gives her a warning look. I don't understand what's so funny. Nor do I care. Shark blood, I'm *so* thirsty! It overwhelms me. 'Can I have… some water?'

The doctor hesitates, then nods. Sini walks away and returns quickly. *Only the blood from the grail can prolong my life.* No! Not *my* life – the Fisher King's life. I have grown accustomed to the cold, chalky water that the Ark's purification plant produced. This water is lukewarm and bland. Nevertheless, I drink it greedily. Afterwards, I feel slightly better, but no less confused.

'We did a brain scan while you were listening to trance-inducing sounds,' Doctor Moal says matter-of-factly. 'Did you notice that?'

'I don't know,' I mutter. Did I hear something? 'I heard birds.'

'Birds?' He doesn't seem to have expected that answer.

'Swamp bugs.'

'You've been listening to drums.'

"Oh.' I feel disappointed. 'But I was dreaming…'

'Yes?' Doctor Moal suddenly leans towards me, as if he doesn't want to miss a word.

I blink my eyes again. 'Doesn't matter. I want to go back to my room.'

'No, no. You were dreaming.' His eyebrows go up. He licks his bottom lip with the tip of his tongue. 'What were you dreaming about?'

'Forest. Trees. Water…'

'Wilderness,' he says, as if it were something dirty.

I shrug. 'It wasn't wild. It was peaceful.'

'And then?'

'Then?'

'What did you hear? Or what did you see?' Again he licks his lips. He doesn't look like a mole when he does that, I think to myself, more like a hungry cat. 'Were the colours brighter than usual? Did your mind feel… sharper?'

I stare at him in amazement. For a moment I even forget I detest him. 'How do you know that?'

Doctor Moal smiles. 'And did you hear voices? Did someone speak to you, perhaps?'

There is not one hair on my head is thinking about telling him about the Fisher King, whether he was just a dream or real. Perhaps, somehow, I was *really* standing in front of his throne. 'No. No one.'

'Or did you experience this before?'

Gwenhael's Grave, it's as if he is seeing right through me and knows exactly what I'm thinking about. I press my lips tightly together and do my best to look back at him with a blank stare. I shake my head.

He has brown, beady eyes. Like a mole. Like a small, creepy fat animal digging through the mud. I wonder who his bosses are, here at the Institute, and whether he crawls to do *their* bidding.

'Alright then.' He shrugs almost invisibly. 'Sini, prepare a clean syringe. One milliliter of *zh15* should be sufficient.'

'Doctor?' Sini looks confused.

'Yes, you heard me right. One syringe, please, Sini.'

'Doctor Moal, the girl is *not* showing any symptom of the disease. Protocol does not allow for ...'

'That's why I am adding to the protocol,' he snarls at her. 'Pay attention, will you? The signals are as clear as daylight.' He turns to me. 'Those theta waves you produce are *clearly* a signal to somewhere. Maybe someone is answering them. Maybe you don't even know it yourself. I think you're not as stupid as you have led us to believe.' His eyes narrow as he looks at me. 'You have no idea how dangerous it is, Nicole, do you? Crying out to that other ... *place*. You might as well beg for Black Influenza to hit you. These are just preventive measures. Sini, syringe.' He holds up his hand and waits until Sini silently gives it to him. She looks pale. Unlike Doctor Moal's grin, her lips are a thin line. 'I'm just going to give you a little push, Nicole. Just a little, effective push.' He holds up the syringe. 'Give me your arm.'

'What is that? What are you going to inject me with?' I begin to tremble.

'*Zh15*. An extract from one of the victims' scabs. With any luck, that's going to have quite the effect.'

'I thought the Asclepius Congregation wanted to cure the disease,' I bark at him. 'Not make more victims with that poison!'

'Dear Nicole, we're not going to kill you.' Suddenly, his face darkens. 'Where did you pick up all this knowledge?'

I'm careful and choose not to answer. Doctor Moal doesn't know that I cannot get sick like Rona, but that doesn't mean I want any of that stuff in my body. I let my legs slide off the bed and feel strong enough to stand upright without any help. If I run to the door now, I might be able to escape the laboratory before they can stop me. But where would I hide? The hallway is long and straight and as far as I know, all those doors are locked. Back to Platform Zero? Even if I were able to get that far, there'd be two massive doors blocking the way, which only open with a keycard like Sini's.

Doctor Moal grabs me. 'Enough with the complaining,' he says. 'You better cooperate, 1490. A second dose of anaesthetic won't kill you, but I promise you won't feel so good afterwards.'

I do not resist any more, but as soon as he puts the jab into my arm, I anxiously peek at the tube. *Zh15* is colourless and thin. It quickly disappears into my vein. I expect something terrifying to happen at any moment: severe pain hitting me, or a stroke. But I feel nothing at all, though, just my heartbeat racing through my body.

'Give it a few hours,' Doctor Moal says, massaging the needle mark on my arm. 'Tomorrow we'll know what is left of her. In any case, she can be Undreamed later this week. You can take her away now,' he adds.

Sini leads me to the door. 'Can you walk by yourself?'

I nod, though I'm not convinced that I can make it to my room. 'I'm nauseous.'

'That's okay,' I hear the doctor behind me say snidely. 'Because you kicked me, you're not getting any food tonight, 1490.'

I press my lips together and slowly walk out of the lab together with Sini. When she stops to press her keycard against the lock of my room door, I ask:

'Why did he do that?'

'Because you're getting sick now.' Her voice trembles a bit. From fear or anger? 'In that case, a second procedure will follow, according to protocol.'

Right – the Undreaming. 'What are theta waves?'

'I'm not sure,' she says.

'Please.' I do not move, and lock eyes with her. 'It's *my* head we're talking about.'

Sini gives me an uncertain look. 'It means that you are dreaming while awake.'

'And what is Undreaming?'

She gets even more uncomfortable and looks away. 'I think you should rest first. That anaesthetic really took you down.'

I position myself so that she has to look at me. 'Just like *zh15* is going to take me down?'

'Nicole,' she says weakly. 'We're trying to help you.'

'Maybe *you* are. Do you really think Moal believes that too?'

'Of course. Everyone is doing their utmost best to eradicate the Black Influenza.'

'And what sacrifices we make!' I manage to smile sourly. 'If I dream while awake, the Undreaming must stop my dreams.' Suddenly I think of what Katell has told me: that she was told not to dream. 'I know that the Black Influenza is no ordinary virus,' I risk blurting out. If I want answers, I have to be able to ask the right questions. Sini looks at me without saying anything. 'I can tell you that none of this helps, Sini. I know about the Other World – yes, I know about that.' Even though I say the words calmly, my hands are sweating. I'm taking a huge gamble in telling Sini this much. What if I have misjudged her? I swallow hard. 'Whatever the Undreaming does to people, I don't believe it's the right method.'

'So.' Sini crosses her arms and purses her lips disapprovingly. 'So *you* know the right method? Are you a doctor, Nicole?'

'I know more than the doctors here. If they would only listen to me...'

'Enough.' It's almost a snarl. Sini uncrosses her arms and directs me to my door. 'Doctor Cormack and the doctors at Laboratory 12 slave away day and night, for your good. You shouldn't let things go to your head, Nicole. Now get inside.'

'So if *you* get infected, you wouldn't have a problem being treated with the Undreaming too?'

'Nicole...'

'You're not *at all* afraid that I'll make you sick tomorrow, or the day after?'

'I said, *enough*!' Her voice and face clearly show that she's afraid. Sini gives me a shove – not a hard one, but just enough to force my shaking legs across the doorstep. 'Sleep it off. And be careful with that sharp tongue of yours or you might end up on Platform Zero permanently.'

With that warning, she leaves me alone in the grim room – my cell. I listen to the beeping sound as the lock slides shut. The bed is soft and at least there is light, but it's not much better than the underground prison. I lie down on the bed. Tonight I won't have to wait for a meal to show up, if I am to believe Doctor Maul's words. And I believe him.

It's not so bad. The anaesthetic did more than just take away my ability to think clearly and use my limbs. Just thinking about food makes me feel nauseous. I put my hands on my belly, gently massaging the spot where my stomach is.

Or am I this nauseated from the second shot they gave me? Although I'm pretty sure I'm not that prone to the corruption called the Black Influenza, I can't help that I'm overcome by fear. After all, Mum never had it injected directly into her veins. Who knows what effect it will have on my body?

I feel helpless: a piece of cattle branded for slaughter. Maybe tomorrow I'll be in bed, moaning and dying, unable to control the disease. After all, neither can that Fisher King.

When I think of him, my thoughts irrevocably turn to Arthur. If they inject him too, nothing stands between him and a gruesome death. Unless he's protected by someone... or some*thing*. But who? The Fisher King, that sallow spirit from the Other World, is chained to his throne. He has already told me that he cannot travel anymore. And is he not waiting anxiously for another king to come?

I close my eyes, dizzy from all the complications. Arthur has nowhere to go until he's freed from this horrible building, I'm sure of it. I should never have taken him with me. Stupid. I'm so stupid.

A wave of nausea overwhelms me. I turn onto my side, ready to vomit. I only barely hold it in.

Mum, help me. I repeat the words until they lull me to sleep: *Give me a sign. Come and save us. Or help me to stay strong and brave.*

MARA LI

If I can still get up tomorrow, I must kick into action.

5

DARK DREAMS

I try to open my eyes. It's a futile effort. My body trembles and shivers and I'm overcome by an overwhelming dizziness. When I finally open my eyes, my bed spins around the room like a merry-go-round.

Someone puts a hand against my face and I start. Who is in the room with me?

That question is immediately answered when I hear Doctor Moal's voice. 'Give me that thermometer.' His voice sounds strangely dull.

A moment later, a gloved hand wrenches my jaw open and I feel something cold and sharp disappear under my tongue. Doctor Moal pulls my eyelid down. I try to blink. For a moment we stare at each other, him as my hunched tormentor, me confused and weak in my bed. Maybe I'm imagining things, but it seems like there is a gleam of pleasure in his dark eyes. I also understand now why he sounds so strange: he's wearing a white face mask. His hands are covered by plastic gloves, as if I'm something dirty he won't touch with his bare hands. He lets go of my eyelid and it falls shut. I don't want to close my eyes, but my body has taken precedence over my mind.

Moal says something unintelligible. A woman's voice replies. I think it's Sini, but I'm not entirely sure. They already seem miles away. I'm strongly aware of my trembling arms and legs. Is it because I'm cold? Strange. I feel *strange*. The blanket is suffocating me, but the air rushing past my uncovered head feels unpleasantly sharp. And merciful Gwenhael, my skin seems to squirm and groan in pain.

They take the thermometer from my mouth. A short conversation follows, of which I only catch parts. All the words are disappearing in a whirlpool of meaninglessness.

Someone is tapping something against my mouth. A small tube. I feel a cold drop of liquid slide between my lips. But I don't want any water. I only want one thing: 'Arthur…'

Whether they heard me, I don't know. After a long time I notice that the room's gone quiet. They're gone, left me alone with this illness that is trying to conquer me. And it takes so much effort to keep my grip on reality that I give in.

I'm sinking …

… and am back in the forest. This time the trees of the swamp are not so friendly. Here, the trees are towering over me, close together and dark. The branches cling together to intercept all daylight. Again, I have the sense that the Asclepius Congregation is a mere shadow, an echo – that this is reality. I can feel it in the air: it tingles, as if every molecule is charged with electricity.

I don't feel at ease. Wherever I am, I want to get away as quickly as possible, so I start walking. There is hardly a path to speak of, but my feet find a winding track that leads me zigzagging through wild vegetation. After a while, I become aware of faltering breathing behind me. I come to a standstill. The sound stops. I turn and peer among the tree trunks, but my searching eyes find nothing but branches and tangles of ivy.

I shiver and continue my way, speeding up my steps. Immediately, the panting begins again. It sounds as though it's coming closer. Now I know what it reminds me of: a hunter, sniffing out his prey. I start to run. It doesn't matter. Whatever it is that's chasing me, it keeps up with me effortlessly.

The track goes downhill and I get to a deep valley. Rock tips are sticking out of the surrounding hillsides like lances. If I slip, it would be the death of me. I'm forced to slow down. A high, giggling sound hits me like an arrow from a bow.

The hunter has decided to come out.

Knowing that running away is completely useless, I turn around. Fear makes me powerless as I stare at the creature that is less than an arm's length away.

You could call it a man. It has the limbs of a man, and a head, and a mouth, but that's where all similarity ends. He has staring eyes in the palms of his hands, on his forehead, even on his dark, black chest. His fingernails are long, sharp as claws. Slowly he raises his hands, so that I can see them well. His mouth is set in a huge grin, with teeth that could swallow an entire shark.

'Go away,' I stammer while flinching. Instinctively I have already recognised him: he's the shadow on the edge of my dreams. The black corruption in my mind which also affects the Fisher King.

To the rhythm of my own steps, he approaches, overtaking me.

'No,' I whisper. 'Leave me alone.'

He opens his mouth even wider. I see the pointed teeth – exactly like those of a shark – and a flicker of a blood-red tongue. All his eyes show me nothing but an insatiable hunger. No mercy, no kindness. Only darkness. But more than seeing it, I'm sensing the corruption rdiating from this creature. It roots me to the spot. When his tongue slips out and he trails it down my cheek, I come back to life.

I scream: 'HELP! HELP ME!'

For a split moment, I register a second movement behind the trees. It's so fast that I don't have time to really perceive it, but something darts towards us, hitting the many-eyed man in his side. I open my eyes, but at that moment, I feel myself being pulled away, just as I was pulled away earlier from the menhirs to the tower of the Fisher King. This time, I do not resist.

Again I'm sinking. Again I'm under water. For a moment I'm relieved: this scene is starting to be familiar. Soon, the seals will come swimming with me, their kind, wise eyes on me.

But instead of sinking down into a pleasant depth, I feel the coldness of the water sting my bones. And instead of sunlight on the surface, there is a dark abyss beneath me. The silence presses against my ears.

In that silence, a giant shadow looms over me. As it approaches, I realise how insignificant I am. My eyes get used to the darkness and I can distinguish the head and the body gliding effortlessly through the water. I have a moment to realise that it's a killer whale and, just like the creature with all the eyes, it's opening its mouth wide at me. And then I'm swallowed by its jaws, its body around mine.

Darkness. Silence.

A prison. All I can do is struggle. And if that doesn't help, I'll roll myself up, make myself as small as possible, and wait.

It could have been hours later or barely a minute. My sense of time has completely disappeared, swallowed up in the orca's belly as well. But when I wake up, I feel better. I'm disoriented and tired, but it soon dawns on me that I no longer feel pain in my body.

When I sit up straight, I don't shiver anymore. I look around me. My bed is curtained off by a white sheet. I push it aside.

I'm not in my own room, but in a sterile, hospital-like environment. My bed is the only piece of furniture in this room. I pull the blankets off me and discover that I'm wearing a long, green nightshirt. I don't like the idea of someone undressing me in my sleep. There is a band around my wrist. It says 1490 – my patient number. Next to it, in small letters, is spelled out: *Candidate F. Undreaming. Responsibility: Dr. T. Moal.*

For a moment, I consider pretending that I'm still in the grip of the Black Influenza, just to finally see what that bloody Undreaming is all about. Although my head feels a lot clearer, I still wouldn't be strong enough to fight anyone when it comes to it. I lick my dry lips. Water! Is there any water here? I look around the room, but apart from an IV drip next to the bed, there doesn't seem to be anything else. I lean closer to the IV: a transparent plastic bag containing a colourless liquid that goes into my arm through a tube and a thin needle. It could be normal fluid, but it could just as well be *Zh15*. I pull the needle out of my arm.

I throw my legs over the edge of the bed and stagger to my feet. My feet touch the floor, hesitantly and cautiously. It's alright – I can walk. Slowly, I open the door and hold it ajar. To my surprise, it isn't locked. I realise that I must have been in *really* bad shape if they didn't even think it necessary to lock me up.

But wasn't that actually true? Now that I'm awake, the memories of the black forest and the dark ocean seem to be fading away fast, but still – a shiver goes through me when I think about it. There was something about that place, and about that monstrous man; something broken, something *wrong*. I don't know if the orca was attacking me or just swallowed me up to hide me. I don't even know how I managed to come up from the depths and landed in my own body.

I shake my head to push the memory away. When I peek around the corner, the corridor in front of me is empty. I sneak out of the room and try to focus. I haven't been to this part of the building before. There are more locked doors next to mine – more infirmaries? The corridor hits a junction in front of me: on the left it leads to a staircase, on the right it leads to different rooms with wide, glass walls. Behind the walls, I see doctors in the blue uniforms of the Asclepius Congregation.

Once I'm sure that nobody is watching the corridor, my bare feet move silently across the concrete floor. I creep up the stairs, my back pressed against the wall. Should I hear any voices coming from above, I'm ready to dart off in the other direction at any moment.

The next floor is again a hallway full of doors, just like downstairs. But these doors are made of a kind of shiny wood, and there are windows with wide windowsills, that look out onto a large square outside, and for the first time in days I can see the sky. It is a grey day. Raindrops are hitting the windowpanes. But in here, thick glass protects the Asclepius Congregation doctors from any burning blisters. It makes the sound of the rain much more pleasant and the ambience of this hallway almost cosy. No fluorescent light here – they've used light bulbs in firm holders in this part. It dawns on me that an institute using this much electricity must have some sort of CORE to keep things running. The CORE in the old Ark at Platform Zero, perhaps?

With caution, I walk past the closed doors. The windows on the other side are broad, the alcoves sunk into the wall in between the windows narrow. My heart is beating nervously in my throat – I feel it grow louder with every beat.

The door to my left opens. Like a squirrel, I hide in an alcove and press myself flat against the wall. I hold my breath to make sure I don't make a sound.

A man enters the corridor with a pile of papers under his arm. He doesn't look around and cheerfully walks in the opposite direction, towards the stairs I just climbed. He's wearing a long, white lab coat over his normal clothes. It casually flutters behind him as if it is too large for him. The man has a head full of dark curls.

I wait with my heart pounding in my chest until he's gone. Only after I'm sure that I'm alone again and that no one else will emerge from that room do I dare to break free from the wall.

He didn't bother locking his door. I don't suspect any of his victims have ever entered his office. Only now do I notice the gold nameplate on the shiny wood of the door: *Dr Cormack Cairn*.

Was that him – the man who walked past me with a spring in his step? I feel a grim sort of pleasure in knowing that I have found his room. With the same feeling of joy I slip inside, leaving the door ajar. I keep my ears pricked: as soon as I hear him come back, I'll have to make a run for it.

His office is more spacious that our entire living room back in Gwennec. Opposite the door, on the right, is a broad window with protective double glazing. In front of it is an impressive desk made of solid wood, just like the door. It's not really tidy; the items scattered on top of it reveal a man whose thoughts are just as jumbled. His laptop is shut. Next to the desk, against the side wall, is a bookcase. Closer to me is a sofa facing a coffee table. Next to it is a glass cabinet in which various objects are displayed, as if they belong to Dr Cormack Cairn's special curiosity cabinet. Curiously, my eyes wander over it. There's a black mask with a strange thick tube – a kind of mouthpiece with holes to let air through. I recognise it as part of the uniform that people had to wear right after the Impact, when even inhaling the air outside meant certain death. Next to it are a number of things that I don't recognise – perhaps machine parts. On a shelf below it, an even stranger collection is displayed: a couple of fragile-looking side branches of a tree. Next to it are three dried flowers, which must once have been fresh and fragrant. Below those, in the middle of the display case, is a file containing papers that have turned yellow. The pages are bulging out.

I wonder what the doctor wants with these things, but I don't think about it for too long. After all, I don't know how much time I have here, and I have to seize this opportunity with both hands.

First, I rummage through the objects on his desk. I turn over all the papers while studying memo cards that he has stuck on it here and there. Cormack Cairn has a spidery handwriting.

I cannot decipher the sparse instructions he's giving himself on these memos. There are numbers, which I think might be patients. There are a few words: *Fever. Unwilling. Undreaming. Deteriorated condition.* None of which reassures me. None of it is helpful. I do not see my own assigned number, nor Arthur's.

The less I find, the more nervous I get. An expansive map of the building would come in handy, more than the one Judikael and I have drawn. But even when I pull open all the desk's drawers, I cannot find anything that looks like a map. There are lots of files on children without names, just numbers, a few trinkets, a broken pen, a silver key, an empty syringe. My heart bleeds for everyone who has been turned into an experiment here, but I know that there is nothing I can do for them right now. And I wouldn't dare touch too many of his things, afraid that the doctor will discover someone has been through his stuff as soon as he returns.

I peek at the computer. I bet he has all his files on *that*, and probably a lot more information. Maybe I could find out what Undreaming is, or where I can find Benji ...

Apart from the door locks in the Ark, I have never operated a computer before. At random, I open the laptop. That seems to trigger something: a blue screen appears. It says: "Password?" My fingers hover above the keyboard. *Think, Nimue.*

Undreaming? *Zh15*? Asclepius? None of the words entered are correct. I try everything related to the Asclepius Congregation, but eventually I have to admit that I have no idea. It frustrates me that I can't access Dr Cormack Cairn's files.

Angrily, I slam the computer shut. My bare feet are starting to get cold on the floor. It looks like I'll have to sneak back to my room without any results. The thought frustrates me even more. I let my gaze wander through the office.

These windows look out onto another square, with neatly trimmed trees and a few scraggly lawns. A large hedge runs around it like a screen shielding the building from the outside world, but it cannot hide the towering contours of factory chimneys. When I look up at the sky, I realise the sky isn't grey because of rain clouds. Greasy plumes of smoke are coming out of those pipes. I stare at it. What Corentin said is true – I'd hate to walk around here without a mask on.

Suddenly the grief over his death cuts through my heart like a knife. Furiously, I turn around, barely avoiding knocking over Cairn's dustbin. Corentin's death – and Anna, Josse and Alan's – are not this doctor's fault. But if it hadn't been for the Asclepius Congregation, they wouldn't have had to hide in that swamp in the first place.

I wrap my arms around myself to suppress a shiver. Something else catches my eye. On one of the shelves in the bookcase is a framed photograph. It's nothing special, but suddenly my gaze lands on a face in the picture. It could be an older version of Arthur, if the man's hair had been blond instead of flaming red. The freckles in that face are the same as mine.

'Benji,' I whisper.

He's standing next to a smiling woman – no, a girl. She has two thick, flaxen-blonde braids and she's holding an infant in her arms. My mouth goes dry when I take the frame off the shelf. I notice there isn't even a speck of dust on it. I look at the motionless faces of my family. Or the people who could've been my family.

I suddenly feel empty. What if Esoldi hadn't died? Finn could've survived his childhood ... My uncle could have chosen a different path.

For a moment I imagine a life in which Rona and Benji hadn't been separated. He would still have loved her, and Finn would have played with me and Arthur on the beach whenever they visited. Even if Dad had died, we wouldn't have been alone ...

I get a lump in my throat and try to swallow it quickly. Decisively, I put the photo back in its spot. That's just now how things played out. Benji chose sides, and so did Rona. Why Cormack would have a picture of my family in his room

– or what his role is – isn't clear to me, but that he belongs to the Asclepius Congregation is as bright as daylight.

I turn and walk towards the door. The shivers are back and I can no longer suppress them. Maybe I'm not fully recovered, or maybe it's the cold that's starting to creep up on me through my hospital gown. I refuse to believe it's because I have seen those faces for the first time. Faces that belong to the names in Mum's diary.

Before I go out, I take one more glance at the display case. The letters on the yellowish file are somewhat blurred. On a sticker, there's a single letter, written in a straight, even handwriting: *B*.

B? I fiddle with the lock on the display case, but can't open it. *Think*, I tell myself. There is a key to this lock, and Cormack must have it somewhere.

I saw something in the desk drawer: a silver-coloured key. I rush towards it and immediately pull it open. With trembling hands I try to see if the key fits.

It does.

The glass door swings open silently. I hesitate for a moment, then grab the file from the shelf. It smells musty and old, like the library books in the Ark.

I know I have to go – that every minute longer I spend in this room increases the risk that I will be caught. But my curiosity is so much stronger than my fear. Just a quick peek, I tell myself, as I open the folder and the first few pages appear. Some are printed; others are handwritten in a neat and straight handwriting.

My eyes dart across the first page.

Esoldi's fever is off the charts. Finn is glowing like a cauldron on a fire. For the first time in years I'm scared and – coward that I am – I only dare admit it on paper. A medical attendant came by. She said that childhood diseases are a regular occurrence. It's not abnormal for the mother to be affected as well. She was lying, of course. I saw it in her eyes, and when I showed her the door, she must have realised that I knew. She said nothing – she fled. There is no way to fool me. I know very well that her eyes are bloodshot, that her breathing is labored, that Finn is wheezing and gurgling. Spirits assist me. Despite all my knowledge, I am now powerless.

Shocked, I sink to the floor next to the display case, clutching the file in my hands. Suddenly I have forgotten all about my plan and how I warned myself not to risk this. The danger of being caught fades to a far corner of my mind, because I need my full attention to realise what I'm reading. There he is at last: my uncle, the black equivalent of Rona. The missing piece of the puzzle.

I swallow a few times and take a deep breath. Then, I start to read.

6

BENJI

*M*y beloved Esoldi is ill.

I held her hand for a long time, but she hardly recognised me. On her white skin the first traces of bruises are showing up. Bruises that appear out of nowhere. They'll soon develop into large, swollen subdural hematoma. The black scabs that give the disease its infamous name.

Finn is breathing with difficulty. I took him out of his cradle and rocked him as he lay against my shoulder. For hours I walked around with him, until he was so quiet I thought he'd died in my arms. Not just yet. Now he's back on his sheet ... lying underneath it seemed to suffocate him, because as soon as I tried that, he started to squirm. As if even the softest touch of the fabric was hurting his naked skin. Every hour, I dab some milk on a cloth, which I hold against his lips. Sometimes he's able to drink, but he suckles too weakly, as if he doesn't remember how to do it. As if he is off in a dream. I know it's pointless. Good spirits; I know it all too well. But how can I not keep trying in despair?

I have sent a message to Rona. She refuses to be part of Avalon any longer – well, if she doesn't want to serve her new people, I can't force her. But she will not refuse anything to her family. I know that for a fact, and that thought is my only hope in this darkness. Family is everything to her, as it is to me.

The day came to an end with difficulty and the night was like an ocean. Finally, a new dawn rises. I see the sun crawl above the rooftops of the city. It warms the apple tree in front of our house. Here in the higher districts, we always get the first light of day. Esoldi's situation has not improved. Nor does she seem any worse. I dare hope that she'll endure until Rona arrives. That bloody distance! There are no cars in the Periphery.

*

Hold on, my love. I know that Rona is already close by. I'm holding your hand and trying to take away this illness from you, as only she can. If I had the power, I would take your place.

*

Rona, my sister. Although she has inherited our mother's precious gift, she's deeply imbued with our father's cruelty. And I, fool! I didn't know – I have been blind. All she could talk about was the child in her womb.

Well, a curse on her stomach. A curse on her husband. That all spirits may leave her, that she may be left in solitude, as I am left in cold solitude.

She leaves me with imminent death.

*

Esoldi is dead. In the middle of night she slipped away from me without a farewell. She took little Finn with her. I am left behind. Hollowed out and empty.

I spent the remaining hours of the night wondering why they didn't take me with them during those brief days of their wasting illness. Why did I have to be left behind? And why am I such a coward that even now I cannot bring myself to put a knife to my throat and follow them beyond that black veil?

*

So this is the truth. My life is in the possession of others and things are torn away from me with rough hands.

First my childhood – I still remember the smell of burning wool. The heat of the falling beams. I feel my father's fists all over my body, although I haven't seen him for ten years.

My mother: silent, fair Sela. Her abandonment is an emptiness that can never be filled.

Rona, who I thought was my tower of strength. Now she has a new family, and I have no one.

Finally, my heart: my dear wife, my dear son. Will I have nothing that belongs exclusively to me?

Is this your punishment, spirits of Avalon? Is it Fergus's legacy? Am I too much like my father to be allowed to live freely?

I curse all the powers and forces that Rona loves so much. They should all leave me alone! I curse Sela's legacy as much as I curse Fergus's.

No, no more ghosts. No sacrifices. No family. I see only one path before me: the path of revenge.

Not on Rona. No, she'll help me, whether she'll want to or not. Not on our parents, who are too far away to reach. Revenge on death, that's what I'm longing for. I'm a man with nothing to lose. Turn to me, dark side. I am ready.

*

'Nicole!'

Sini is standing in the doorway, with a shocked expression on her face. A broad-shouldered guard, massive as a bull, dressed in the colours of Detection, is behind her.

I jump up and let the documents fall onto the ground. What a fool I am. Reading Benji's reports has taken such a toll on me that I forgot about the danger. Can I run away? No, by Gwenhael's blood, they are blocking the door.

Sini's gaze takes me in from head to toe and finally, she lets her eyes rest on the papers I'm still holding. Her lips tighten into a thin line. 'Grab her. Sedate her,' she orders the guard. She herself steps aside. The man comes towards me. I back away until I'm against the desk, quickly slipping around it. This messy table is my only shield.

'Don't be silly,' Sini says, clearly annoyed. 'Where do you think you can go, Nicole?'

'What is going on here?' Behind Sini, the doctor with his fluttering white coat and dark curls appears. He pushes the woman aside and steps into his office. Like Sini, he lets his eyes take in the scene: how I have been cornered, the papers that have fallen onto the floor, me still clutching some pages in my hands, as if I can somehow defend myself with them. 'Nicole...?'

'Doctor Cairn, I'm terribly sorry.' Sini wrings her hands together. 'The child had been transferred in preparation for Laboratory 12, but she's ...'

I can almost hear her searching for an explanation for my sudden escape from the hospital room.

'We must have made a mistake in the diagnosis,' she finishes weakly.

Cormack Cairn hardly seems to hear her. His gaze is still fixed on me. I see a mixture of confusion and ... something else, something I cannot identify. It makes it impossible for me to break eye contact, even if I wanted to. I continue to stare at him, my heart pounding heavily in my chest.

When he finally speaks, his voice is soft. 'You can't call that a child anymore.' He takes a step towards me and I step backwards until I'm up against the window. 'What are you doing with my father's documents?'

7

CORMACK

For a long moment I cannot speak. Doctor Cairn and I are staring at each other. Neither Sini nor the guard makes any attempt to catch me. I know that everyone is waiting for my response.

I try to think straight. 'But Finn is dead.'

A bewildered look slips across Dr Cairn's face. For a moment he's speechless, then he makes a brief gesture with his hand towards Sini and the other man. 'You're dismissed.'

'Sir?'

'Nicole and I have something to discuss.'

I see that Sini is hesitating. Her gaze goes from him to me and it is clear that she's trying to make sense of what is going on. I don't even quite get it myself. Apparently, she finally seems to decide that she can't ignore Cairn's order. She silently retreats from the room, with the guard on her heels.

Cormack Cairn closes the door softly. I'm still standing at the window, clutching the file to my chest, and I have no intention of coming any closer. The doctor must see my distrust. 'Don't be afraid. You're not in trouble.'

That confuses me even more. He steps towards me and looks at me. We are both silent for a while. He has a pensive look in his eyes and I'm nervous, my hands are sweaty.

'You are Nimue.'

Again, I'm shocked. 'How ...?'

'You look like him. Like my father.' He holds out his hand to me. 'I'm Cormack. Your cousin.'

I look at his hand, then at his face again. 'You can't be. Finn is dead.'

When he realises that I'm not going to shake his hand, he lowers it. He's looking at the floor between us, his voice soft. 'Yeah, that's true. And that picture in the cabinet is all I've ever seen of him. You seem confused. I'm sorry, I need to be clearer.' He pauses, as if he hopes I'm going to say something. I remain silent. 'My real parents are a blurry memory. Struck by the same disease Benji was trying to fight. He took me in. Brought me up as his own son. I believe he loved me... At least I loved him. Won't you sit down?' He gestures towards the desk.

Slowly I let that information sink in. 'My uncle is your foster father.'

'You're right; though I've never considered him as anything but my real father. Please, Nimue... sit down,' he says, almost pleadingly. He takes a seat on the other side, leaving a place open for me at the head of the desk.

Slowly and still on my guard, I lower myself onto the chair. I place the file in front of me on the desk between us, my hand protectively on top of it. 'How do you know my name?'

Cormack Cairn nods at the file. 'I can't remember how many times I've read that. He mentions you several times. You and your brother Arthur.'

I stay silent.

Cormack sighs. 'Actually, I've wanted to find you for a long time. Time has never been kind to me. The fact that you have come here now can only mean one thing.' Am I imagining it, or is he turning a little white? 'You've added things up and you've come to the conclusion that Benji knows where your mother is. Am I wrong?'

'We came here as prisoners.' It takes some effort to hold his gaze, because I am cold and the room seems to spin around me. Yet I persevere. 'We were seized and sedated and separated. Gwenhael knows what they're doing to Arthur at this moment.' My own words stir up my anger.

'I had no idea.' This time I'm quite sure Cormack is turning white. 'Believe me – if I had known you were here...' Maybe he understands how lame that excuse sounds. He remains silent and I stare at him defiantly. Cormack clears his throat. 'Is it really a coincidence that you're here?'

'No. We let ourselves get caught on purpose, but that doesn't make it any less bad. And I made a mistake. I shouldn't have taken Arthur with me to your snake's nest.'

I might as well have called him a murderer right away. Cormack cringes; it's a small gesture, but I notice it. 'I suppose you were hoping to find Benji. To hold him... accountable.'

When I don't reply, he sighs deeply. 'I'm afraid those reports are the only way to get Benji to speak for himself,' he says. 'My father is dead.'

Perhaps I should've known, but still it comes as a shock to me. I automatically look at the photo in the cupboard. At the man with crimson curls and freckles in his face. The black sheep of my family, that's how I see him. With his written words of despair and grief still fresh in my mind, I now see him as a vulnerable man – someone who looks so much like me that it is almost spooky. 'Did he really hate her that much?' I hear myself asking after a while. 'Did he still hate Rona at the end of his life?'

'I'm not sure. I don't know if he ever really hated her.'

'He hated her.'

'He loved her too.' Cormack's voice is soft.

I pull down the sleeves of my hospital gown as far as I can to protect myself against another attack of shivers. 'How did he die?'

'Alone, in his lab. I found him sprawled on the floor. That was nine years ago.'

Something in his voice makes me look up. There are no tears in Cormack Cairn's eyes, but the pain is clearly visible in his pupils. I decide to give him a piece of information, just to see what I'll get in return. I say: 'My mother disappeared nine years ago.'

'Benji didn't know where she was.'

'Maybe he didn't tell you anything.'

'I think he would've told me,' Cormack says softly.

He honestly believes it, I conclude, while silently taking him in. That doesn't mean he's right. Benji must have known things that he withheld from Cormack – or did he really love his foster son? Nothing in his documents suggests that he had room for such feelings after losing Esoldi and Finn ... But I haven't finished reading all of it. Perhaps the years were kind to his wounds, turned them into scars.

However, this poses a whole new problem, one that worries me almost more than the thought of Rona as Benji's prisoner: if my uncle wasn't able to find Mum... what happened to her?

'Nimue?' Cormack's voice pulls me out of my thoughts. 'You look a little pale. Would you like some tea? Something to eat?'

'Tea.' I scoff. 'Nobody gets tea here.'

'When was the last time you ate?'

'Sometimes I don't get anything. Doctor Moal doesn't like me.' I shrug. 'I'm used to hunger. We were never rich in Gwennec.' How different it must be for Cormack, I think to myself. Raised in Central Europe with a powerful foster father who made sure he never lacked anything. He even had him trained to be a doctor. There are miles between us in more sense than one.

'That will stop immediately. I'll make sure you get a decent meal. And warm clothes.'

'I want my brother.' A meal sounds appealing, but as long as Arthur's wellbeing is still a question to me, I wouldn't be able to enjoy anything. And I remind myself that Cormack is also a Snake, whether he's my cousin or not. Again I shiver, more violently this time.

'Of course. I can assure you that nothing bad will happen to him. And I would like to meet him, if that is ...'

'I want to see him alone first.'

He sighs. 'I know you're angry, Nimue. But I beg you not to be angry with me. If you give me a chance, I think we would get along just fine. All three of us.'

'Why?' Actually, I should throw this kindness right back in his face, along with his tea and a dose of *zh15*. But it's getting harder and harder to keep my head clear. This is no ordinary cold I am suffering from.

Cormack seems a bit perplexed by my question. 'You want your family. I want that too, Nimue. When Benji died, I had no one left. He left me this clinic, along with his dream. That's what kept me going all these years. But I knew you were out there somewhere. Far away, in Gwennec. Believe me, seeing you now, in that hospital gown, I regret that I never came to visit you before. Not as Head of the Asclepius Congregation, but as your cousin.' He is silent for a moment. 'We could close the gap between Rona and Benji.'

In recent weeks, I have imagined a thousand different things happening at the Asclepius Congregation, house of the Serpent, but never hearing *those* words. I came to find out the truth about Rona, to look Benji straight in the eye... to fully understand my heritage, yes, but also to free dozens of imprisoned children. All for different reasons – but reconciliation was never one of them.

I swallow hard and try to think of what to say. Cormack looks at me expectantly. 'I don't know,' I say. 'I feel...'

Something in his face changes. He gets out of his chair in a hurry. 'Forgive me! I shouldn't leave you sitting there like that. You have been very ill.'

His worried face coming towards me is the last thing I remember.

When I wake up, I look into a face that's framed by blonde curls. I gasp and get up too quickly. The world is shaking around me. I don't let it stop me. 'Arthur!'

He wraps his arms around me. He smells of the Institute, the chemical detergent they use for our clothes and the acrid smell that pervades Laboratory 5. But underneath it all, he still smells like my little brother.

'You're fine,' I finally mutter, leaning back to cup his face with my hands. 'You *are* alright, aren't you?'

He nods.

'And your leg?'

'They patched me up.' To demonstrate, he wiggles his ankle for a moment. 'But walking is still difficult.' His blue eyes look at me with concern. 'Oh, Nim, they say you've been terribly ill! And then Doctor Cairn came and he said... Nim, is it true?'

My mouth feels as dry as when I woke up in the infirmary. Now I'm in my own room; room 17. 'That's what he says,' I say wearily. 'Cormack is Benji's foster son.'

'And the Black Influenza?'

He looks scared, I suddenly realise. Maybe he's taking a big risk by being in the room with me, hugging me. I touch my own face and feel the bags under my swollen eyes. Slowly, I run my fingers through my tangled hair. Finally I lower my hands and look at them: they're trembling incessantly. I can't stop it. 'I don't think I'm contagious,' I say hoarsely. 'But they injected that stuff directly into my blood.'

'Can't you cure yourself?'

'I think that's what I'm doing.' I cough. 'My body is fighting. It's a veritable battlefield in my head... I dreamt of this hunter...'

Before I can tell Arthur about my disturbing dream, the door to the room opens and Cormack Cairn steps inside. He's still wearing his oversized coat, but he no longer has a skip in his step. His dark eyes take us in; for a moment I think I see him hesitating. Then he regains his posture and closes the door.

'Good that you are awake; I was worried.' He casually comes towards us and sits on the edge of my bed. I hear Arthur hissing softly between his teeth. I don't know if Cormack notices. He turns to my little brother and an endearing smile appears on his face. 'Arthur. I'm sorry everything went so chaotic earlier. Let's try again.' He holds out his hand.

Arthur moves back a little. Not far – he doesn't want to desert me – but far enough to make it clear to Cormack that he doesn't want a peace offering. Cormack's smile fades. He lowers his hand. 'I mean it,' he says softly. 'I want nothing more than to get to know you.'

'*Snake*,' my little brother hisses.

I cough again, harder this time. I gasp heavily. After a few moments, the tightness in my chest subsides and I can breathe again. My little brother and my cousin are both staring at me. 'I'm fine, really,' I mumble.

'I hope so,' Cormack says. 'I don't know how else to help you.'

'I thought you had your ways,' Arthur says venomously.

Cormack's jaw tightens a little, and it looks like he's getting a little pale. But when he speaks, he says calmly: 'Undreaming works for ordinary patients. Your sister has the blood of the Other World in her body. What it will do to her is impossible to say. I would rather avoid it.'

'Yes, you'd better!'

'What?' I ask, confused. 'What are you talking about? Arthur?'

He opens his mouth to say something, but Cormack makes a repellent gesture with his arm. 'Your sister needs to get a lot of rest. Let her.'

'Let her? LET HER?' Arthur jumps up. He looks furious. '*You* better let her, filthy snake! Who plucked her out of the swamp like a fish on a hook? Who put that poison in her veins? And now she's not allowed to know the truth because *you* want to use her for your nasty experiments! Leave her alone, you bastard!'

Arthur's explosion of anger is so violent that Cormack takes a few steps towards the door, a disconcerted look on his handsome face. Arthur himself is red with anger. He's trembling on his legs as he gets to his feet, catching his breath to shout some more. I look at him with my mouth open.

'I don't understand any of this...' Pain lances through me and I gasp for breath again. Only after a few seconds do I hear the groaning sound in the room, which silences both Arthur and Cormack. A few seconds later I realise that the sound is coming from my own throat. The room spins incessantly, like a fan in the wind. And it's not just my hands that are shaking; my whole body is.

'What is it?' my little brother asks timidly. All his bravado has disappeared. 'Nim, are you in pain?'

I can only nod. Flames are licking my insides – a hot, greedy kind of pain in my heart.

'Do something!' I hear Arthur scream. Two hands grab me as I almost fall forward. Someone calls my name. Cormack.

But the pain demands all my attention. And behind that pain, a black presence is hiding. Something that feels *wrong*. It forces itself onto me, seeping into my bones and nerves and up to my head.

They're not here to help you, a voice whispers in my head. The Hunter. *They want to use you, all of them.*

Surely not all of them...?

The charming young doctor – your cousin? He is the living legacy of Benji, and equally corrupt. And Arthur? He can't live without his big sister. When will he ever make his own decisions? When will he ever become sensible – a man? He would have you choke on Gwennec to stop you from travelling the world on your own...

No!

With all the power I have in me, I resist the black presence. The corruption will not get me – neither in my head, nor in my heart! I am Sela's granddaughter, daughter of Rona, and I. do. not. surrender!

She pushes me up from the depths as if I weigh nothing. She has come to protect me, I know this instinctively. I see her slender body, her large, dark eyes. The smooth seal skin is pleasant against my own naked skin. I cling to her. That's the only thing I know how to do: hold on. She carries me away from the vertiginous depths below.

She lays me down on the beach. Her black fur slips off her and reveals two white legs, a belly, breasts and shoulders covered by a mass of black hair. I stare at her. I want to say something, but I'm out of breath.

The seal woman bends over me and smiles. 'Calm down. Return to your body. You're fine.'

I extend my hand to her and gasp, 'Sela!'

8

THE GUIDED TOUR

I sleep for the rest of the day and the following night. When I wake up, the pain is gone and I remember little of my restless dreams.

Sini comes in and helps me into new clothes: no longer the washed-out skirt and blouse, but a pair of woollen stockings, a fire-red, warm skirt that comes down to my knees, and a dark blue cardigan of such good quality that even Yannick could never have been able to afford it. She pushes me down onto the bed and starts running a comb through my wild bunch of curls.

'You'll scalp me!' I complain.

'Then sit still. You can't attend breakfast like this.' She mercilessly combs the tangles out of my hair.

I grimace, but obediently remain seated. Sini keeps quiet. I feel a bit embarrassed. Nobody has ever dressed me before, nobody has ever even done my hair.

'Sini?' I ask cautiously, when the silence becomes so thick it makes me itch.

'Hm?'

'Are you angry?'

'I'm not.' She remains silent even longer. 'Doctor Cairn has officially reprimanded Doctor Moal.'

'Reprimanded? For what?'

'For improper behaviour towards his cousins, what else?' Her fingers grab my hair a little harder than they should.

Ah, and Doctor Moal took it out on Sini.

She braids my hair back and ties a ribbon around it. As soon as she lets go of me, I turn around. 'He's a shark. Don't let him rile you up.'

I see something soften in her gaze; for a moment I think she's going to smile. Then she regains control of herself. 'It's not for me to make such statements, Nic... Nimue.' She pronounces my name awkwardly. 'And not for you either.'

'Ha. I *am* the niece of Doctor Cairn.'

'And therefore not Doctor Cairn himself. Are you still shaking?'

I look at my hands. They lie still in my lap.

'Good. Get up then. We don't want you to be late.'

Sini, in particular, doesn't want me to be late. She takes me through the corridor and then up a few stairs to rooms that I haven't yet come across during my exploration. If I get a moment, I should add these sections to my makeshift map. I notice that Sini is watching me from the corner of her eye the whole time. Normally, I'd find that annoying, but now I'm rather grateful, because I cannot fully rely on my own legs yet. At the moment, however, the rest of my body seems to be doing alright. I'm just starving, but that, too, is a feeling I'm used to. I watch her walk. She's limping to take pressure off her right ankle. Does she always do that? I have been so occupied with getting to know the building that I haven't paid enough attention to the woman I spent most of my time with.

Sini knocks on an oak door and then pushes it open to lead me inside. The room behind it is set up as a kitchen. A thick rug is on the tiled floor. In the corner by the window is a big dining table with polished chairs. There is a bar, and an old-fashioned furnace with a steaming kettle on it.

I realise that these must be Cormack's own quarters. He lives above the institute that he inherited from his foster father.

Voices drift in from an adjoining room. As soon as they realise I'm there, my brother and cousin enter the kitchen. Arthur looks relieved. Cormack is smiling.

'Good to see you up and about.'

'Good to be up,' I mutter. 'What are we all doing here?'

'I thought you might like some breakfast.' Cormack gestures to the table.

I glance at my brother. He has exchanged his look of relief for a sullen expression. I suspect he was like that before I came in. I'm too hungry and too tired from all the pain to care much about his mood, or the strange family we have found within the Asclepius Congregation. Besides, I suspect there will be time enough to discuss that. I sink into one of the chairs and inhale the scent drifting towards me from the furnace. Cormack is busy laying out bowls, spoons, mugs and a tray. He pours me and Arthur a fragrant kind of tea, which I have never tasted before. He scoops some porridge with apples and sultanas into my bowl, prepares coarsely cut bread and pushes honey and jam towards me. There is a basket of boiled eggs on the table and just before Cormack takes his seat, he brings another pan filled with fried bacon from the stove. It's making me dizzy.

Cormack must see the expression on our faces, because he hesitates. 'Isn't this what you want? I didn't know what the two of you like for breakfast, so I made a little bit of everything.'

Slowly, I take a piece of bacon from the pan. I burn my fingers, but the smell is so tempting that I ignore it. 'I have never seen so much food together. And what is this?'

'Butter. To put on bread.'

I run my finger through it experimentally. It is yellow and soft, but not as soft as the lard we use at home.

'We do that with a knife.'

I withdraw my hand and turn red. 'Sorry.'

Cormack pushes a knife towards me and hesitates again. 'You really never saw butter? What did you eat back in your village?'

'Fish. Seaweed, bread and milk. A bit of cheese sometimes, but that was usually too expensive.'

'And in the wilderness?'

Next to me Arthur makes a sharp movement. I think he's about to say something, but after a few moments he just picks up his spoon and starts eating his porridge. I swallow a sip of tea and try to answer as casually as possible. 'Some turnips and other greens. We were able to hunt in the forest and fish in the stream. Until it became winter.'

'What happened when winter came?'

'Then our friends died.' Arthur looks up from his bowl. I'm startled by his face twisted with anger. 'And some children!'

Cormack looks at him in bewilderment. 'That ... I'm sorry to hear that, Arthur.'

Arthur makes a hissing sound.

'I'm really sorry! But you can't blame me for that, can you?'

'No, maybe not.' My little brother throws down his spoon. 'Maybe it's Benji's fault.'

'Arthur…'

But Arthur pushes his chair back. He throws me an accusing look before stomping out of the kitchen.

Cormack and I fall silent. He sighs, while fidgeting with the spoon in his own bowl. I look at my hands: they're trembling slightly. Am I going to have another attack, or am I just startled by Arthur's outburst?

'How am I supposed to make peace with him?" Cormack asks suddenly. He looks unhappy.

'We have seen what you do,' I say bitterly. 'The mutilations, the fear, the abductions.' I hold up my arm, the arm into which Doctor Moal has shamelessly injected a dose of *zh15*. 'All in the name of the common good. But there is nothing good about it. How can you ask us to forgive you?'

'You see us as executioners. Both of you. Do you think we chop off limbs while laughing maniacally?' As I continue to look at him silently, he turns pale again. He whispers: 'Those few times it did happen were terrible accidents. It was never meant to turn out like that.'

'A viper might also say that it didn't intend to bite.'

'Is that what Arthur thinks?'

'That's what we *all* think!' I growl. I bend over my porridge and shovel it down in silence. I don't know whether Cormack is keeping quiet because he's angry too, or because I've hit a nerve. He doesn't speak again until he has cleared away the plates on the table.

'I want to show you my handiwork today. If you feel well enough.'

I look at him, flabbergasted. 'You know what I think of that.'

'That's exactly why I want to show you. Maybe I can change your mind.'

'Maybe.' I stand up. 'Don't count on Arthur to change his, though.'

Cormack Cairn opens the doors to the laboratories for me, and lets me look behind the large glass walls. I discover that the doctors and assistants in each lab are busy with different things. Laboratory 1 is studying dozens of blood samples – from the captured children, I assume. Cormack beckons one of the doctors, who makes an attempt to explain the process to me. I nod and try my best to understand.

She surprises me by saying, 'Your uncle was a specialist in this department.'

'Did you know Benji?' I ask.

The woman nods. 'I dare say he was fascinated by blood.'

'That's – nice,' I mutter.

She smiles. 'Not in that way. He was a quiet man, not cruel. No, your uncle was looking for innate qualities, which might be found in the blood.'

Sela's gift. 'Has he ever found such a thing?'

She shrugged. 'He died before he could. But maybe…'

I peek at Cormack. He's talking to someone in the laboratory, and I can see that he's doing his best to pay attention. But his eyes dart to me. He makes an almost invisible gesture at the woman. The doctor then smiles and turns away from me.

'Are you keeping things from me?' I ask him as he leads me away from the laboratory.

'Of course not.' Cormack looks at me sideways. 'I just think she wouldn't have been able to tell you anything you didn't already know.' There's a question hiding in that statement.

'I've read Rona's diary carefully.'

'You've done more than that, I think.'

'You *think*?'

'You have recovered quite well from the Black Influenza.'

'It's not a disease,' I say, as we go through a narrow, windowless hallway and enter an outbuilding. The door is securely locked and guarded by two men from Detection. Cormack nods his head at them; they step aside and unlock the door with the keycard that all employees here seem to carry.

'I know that too. Come on, Nimue. You don't have to look so anxious.'

'Where are we going?' I don't like the hall in front of me. The air is stuffy, and the few windows I see are barricaded with bars, as usual. Something occurs to me. 'Is this where you Undream people?'

'No.' His gaze volleys between me and the guards. 'Not exactly. Are you coming or what?'

I hesitate for a moment. I'm torn between my thirst for knowledge and my instinct to be careful. Arthur wasn't conflicted in the least: he silently and sullenly disappeared into his room when Cormack invited him. I sigh. Curiosity wins out and I follow Cormack across the threshold into the stuffy hall.

'Do you know what it is, then?' asks Cormack, as if our previous conversation was never interrupted. 'The Black Influenza – do you know the cause of it?'

I remain silent for a moment as we walk. 'Do you?'

'I have a hunch. Benji had his suspicions ... and so do you, I think.' He looks at me from the corner of his eye.

'Well?'

'There is a world beyond ours.' He draws a circle in the sky with his finger; around it, he draws another one. 'That world overlaps ours. Your mother, your uncle and their people believed in it. Elderly people of Central Europe remember such folk beliefs, from before the Impact. There are fairy tales that speak of certain ... beings.' He hesitates. 'Do you know anything about that?'

I could tell him about the things I have seen. About the Pale Man, who is actually the Fisher King who chained himself up. About my dreams, in which my mind slips to that other place, without me having any explanation for it or control over it. And about the Hunter, who scares me more than I'd be able to express. But I just shrug.

Cormack doesn't seem to believe me. He licks his lips. 'Once that second world merges with ours, those beings will be able to come here. But there are also people – many people, in fact – who accidentally reach out to that Other World with their... their minds. Like they're antennae.' He points upwards, as if he imagines that this Other World is right above his head. 'Through that antenna, the beings can reach into their minds and bodies. Benji had a theory that the Black Influenza, which people wrongly call a disease, leaks out of that Other World and into ours. Like an oil slick on the sea. I assume you understand that.'

I nod, more as a response than to agree with him. So that's Benji's conclusion, after years of obsession. I grit my teeth when I must admit that I feel a new kind of respect for my uncle's intelligence. Even if he's not quite right, he was thinking along the right lines; that I can't deny.

'It's not the spirits' fault,' I say.

'What?'

'The spirits don't come in through our antennae. They *themselves* are affected, and it distorts them. Twists them. I think ...' I lick my lips nervously, not quite sure if I want to reveal my theory to Cormack. I haven't even talked to Arthur about it yet.

Cormack stops mid-stride and looks at me intently. 'What are you thinking? Nimue, this is neither the time nor place for secrets.'

'I think it's because of the Impact,' I admit. 'And all the poison that was released then. It got into the sea, got trapped in the rain and was absorbed into the soil. We almost died from it, Cormack. And we weren't the only ones... The Fisher K – ehm, an inhabitant of the Other World has made it clear to me that we cannot live without each other. The damage inflicted in our world can be felt on the other side ... and vice versa.'

Cormack looks at me with an unreadable expression on his face. 'You mean the Black Influenza came from the meteorite?'

'No. But I think that's how it started, and then we made the world even sicker. All this...' I gesture around me, hoping he'll understand that I mean all of Central Europe. 'Maybe it's destroying more than it's restoring.'

Cormack looks annoyed. 'Your uncle gave everything to contribute to this world. Without Central Europe, we would never have made it. You wear these clothes because of *our* labor, you eat the food and you sleep under a roof and in a heated home, all thanks to Central Europe.'

I bow my head. 'The spirit told me that we forgot who we are. And that we forgot who *they* are. And so our worlds are being torn apart. The more cracks there are, the more room there is for corruption to leak out or in, if you want to call it that.'

'The *spirit* told you this.'

I don't answer. Cormack stares at me and his dark eyes seem to pierce my soul like a knife. Once he realises that I don't want to reveal anything else, he shrugs impatiently. 'Alright, then. But this doesn't explain the disease yet.'

'I told you – the spirits are affected too. But instead of dying, they change. They ... are breaking inside. At least I think they are.' I interlock my fingers. 'It's possible that poison breaks a spirit, and then it ... begins to hunt.' I suddenly feel uncomfortable.

Cormack frowns. 'Starts hunting what?'

'Us. And other spirits.' I think about the Hunter in my dream. I have the feeling he wasn't so picky about who or what he wanted to sink his teeth into.

'And then? Will all spirits go mad? Will we be left with a broken world full of evil creatures?'

'I don't know about that, Cormack.'

'It sounds far-fetched.'

'It's just a theory.'

'Hm.' For a while he refrains from commenting further, but then he says: 'The question that my father took to his grave is how to kill a spirit.'

I feel shocked. Did he really just say that? 'He wanted to *exterminate* the spirits?'

'Can't you see why?'

'Gwenhael's grave! Has he found the answer?'

'I don't know. Do you believe it can be done?'

I'm still staring at Cormack. 'I think it's the wrong question to be asking. What do *you* think, Cormack?' I need to know if he's entertaining the same dangerous delusions. I'm a little terrified at the thought that he could have the same destructive power as his foster father. I almost came to believe that Cormack is different from Benji.

Cormack smiles; it makes his face even more handsome. And with his dark eyes and hair, and his charming appearance, he suddenly reminds me a little of Will.

'You look upset,' he says. 'Of course it's the wrong question. After all, we could hardly tackle all those creatures one by one, *if* we even knew how. Here we are.'

He switches to another subject as if turning on a light switch. He pulls on a heavy lever on a door to open it and pulls me gently into the room. We're standing in a space that reminds me of the main hall in the Ark. There are rows and rows of beds, all neatly arranged. The two medical attendants who are walking between the beds are wearing the same clothes as Sini. They make little noise as they walk around, as if they're doing their best not to wake up any of the patients. But I think it would've made little difference, because the children lying under the sheets are staring at me with blank looks on their faces. When they do move, they do so slowly, uncoordinated. Like sleepwalkers.

There is a stinging, sour smell that pervades the room. Urine. Slowly, I let my eyes wander the scene. One of the medical attendants bends down and lifts a four-year-old child up under the armpits. The girl is slumped against the pillow like a rag doll. The medical attendant takes off her hospital gown and starts washing her without saying a word. The girl briefly flinches when she feels the cold water on her body, but meekly lets it happen.

No, not meekly. Disinterestedly.

I turn to Cormack. 'What is this place?'

'This is just the infirmary. They can't keep themselves clean anymore.' Cormack clears his throat. 'Even children who have been potty-trained for years seem to forget that... Anyway, it's a rather unpleasant sight. I'd rather show you the playroom.'

The only reason I follow him silently through the hall is because I can't utter even a single word. What he calls "the playroom" is further up ahead. We get there by going through another door. The room is indeed a lot more pleasant and resembles the recreation room where I first saw Judikael: the walls have been painted a pale yellow, there is a thick, fluffy carpet on the floor and there are various toys for the children to play with. In one corner are shelves filled with books; a precious treasure.

But the children don't seem to care. Like the patients in the infirmary, they all stare ahead with hollow eyes. A few toddlers are playing with toy blocks, but when I come nearer, it's as if they're doing it more out of habit than for fun. They hardly look at what they're doing.

'The rest are outside,' Cormack says. 'They're being aired at the moment.'

'I don't understand.' I make a helpless gesture around me. 'What is wrong with them? Are they sick?' But if they were, I would've recognised the symptoms. And then Cormack wouldn't be so comfortable walking amongst them.

'Most of them have colds, the flu ... just a normal flu, mind you. They get contusions and some bruise easily. As you can see, we are short of workers to take care of all the children.'

'There are medical attendants walking around everywhere...'

'Yes, but there's work overload. These children are bored.' His gaze bores into mine. 'I was hoping you could entertain them a little bit.'

So *that's* his intention? To use me as a glorified nanny? I lick my lips, confused. These kids don't look like they're bored. They look like they're *dead*. 'Are they orphans?'

'All of them. That's why I'm asking you, Nimue. Otherwise I would send every child back to their families, no doubt about it. But they have no one. They have nothing. We try our best, but ..' He helplessly holds up his hands. 'We are doctors, not the leaders of an orphanage. And some children are old enough to go to school. You can read and write, can't you?'

I can't manage more than a nod.

'Then it's decided. You don't have to spend more than a few hours a day in here.' He puts his hand on my shoulder. 'And you don't have to come to the infirmary, if you don't want to. I understand that something like that can be unpleasant.'

I shove his hand off me, frustrated. 'I tended bleeding wounds and pulled hooks out of flesh on a daily basis,' I snarl. 'Do you think we had enough doctors in the Periphery to patch us up? We didn't have them close by, and they usually showed up too late anyway.'

'Excuse me. I'd forgotten about the great tidal wave that hit Gwennec.'

Oh, he'd *forgotten*. I look at him for a moment and feel my gaze become as hollow as that of the children around me. It must be so easy for him, here in his bulwark of iron and stone, high and dry in Central Europe. 'Well, I don't have that luxury,' I say softly. I turn around and start walking away.

'Oh, Nimue, wait. I'm sorry. You're right, I don't know what I'm talking about.'

'Obviously not.' I keep walking. 'I need to think.'

I push the door open and rush out through the infirmary. Cormack lets me go.

9

THE TRUTH

'I need to speak to you.'

I'm just buttoning up my spotless white doctor's coat when Arthur comes to stand in front of me. He looks at me sharply. Since the accident at the Ark, the light in his eyes has disappeared. His mouth has become a grim line, there's nothing boyish about him anymore. He is now as tall as I am.

'Cormack has asked me to help with the children. I have to go.'

He makes a hissing sound that I've come to associate with his distaste for our cousin. 'I need to talk to you about Benji. But not here.' He pulls on my arm. 'Somewhere we can talk in private.'

I hesitate. Benji or the children, which is more important?

'Nimue, are you coming?' Cormack appears in the doorway, his hair tousled and looking charming. He smiles at me.

Arthur lets go of my sleeve and accuses me with his eyes, as if Cormack's appearance is somehow my fault. I slightly shrug my shoulders. 'See you tonight,' I say, hoping he can hear in my voice that I intend to hear him out then. Arthur, however, keeps giving him an angry face as Cormack and I walk away.

Cormack takes me back to the infirmary wing of the Asclepius Congregation, where the children listlessly allow themselves to be fed, clothed and taught. Despite the apathy, the few staff members manning the infirmary have many chores, which they could never do in one afternoon, and my presence is immediately welcomed. First I make myself useful in the infirmary, a place that seems more familiar to me than a classroom. There is a limited supply of herbs; not nearly enough to treat all the coughs and ailments I come across. The Asclepius Congregation relies on pills and ointments with long lists of instructions that I don't understand. I prefer to rely on my old methods, which were usually good enough in Gwennec. I pound, mix, brew, and wash vomit or mucus from faces and clothes. I pull tangles out of the bristly hair of quiet girls, I scrub, polish, do the laundry and in the meantime I'm pondering what Arthur wanted to say about Benji. We're here to find out the truth; that's our job and we haven't got much time for it. Anything that helps us track down Rona, any little clue, is important. But would Mum just stand by, unaffected by the imprisonment of childless parents? Never. I don't need to question that. No, our mother would find a way to ease their suffering, and now that she's not here, that task is ours. That's why I take up everything, I notice which children can walk by themselves and which probably need help getting anywhere.

After a few hours, Cormack shows up to see how I'm doing and takes me to the recreation room where a few desks and outdated textbooks are gathering dust. I gather the older children around me. They are all pale, skinny and quiet. They can't be more than ten years old. Despite my best efforts to teach them some writing and reading, the results are limited. It's not that they're stupid, or that they don't understand what I want them to do, but they seem to have trouble concentrating on the letters or their pens.

At the end of the afternoon, my head is throbbing painfully. I rub my face in an attempt to keep my focus. One of the older girls, Sophia, draws pointless doodles on her sheet of paper, spilling more ink than actually using it. It's as if she's still asleep. As if she can't really wake up and reality is only slowly sinking in. I know; I myself have often felt this way in the past few days, after that strange trip to the Other World, and once through the Pax. But these children are not drugged like I was.

When it gets dark outside, I help putting the children to bed. The empty walls and concrete floor don't make it a very cozy place to sleep in. I think about my old room with a tinge of melancholy: the dusty wooden beams under the loam and thatched roof, the window with its rattling shutters, the sheep wool rug between my bed and Arthur's. The warmth and security of that room, which used to be our parents'. All those things are gone now. They exist only in my memories.

The feeling of loss threatens to overwhelm me. I bite my lip to hold back the tears suddenly welling up. Sophia drops back onto her pillow. I take a deep breath and pull the sheet over her. She obediently closes her eyes. Still, I don't think she's sleepy. Or awake. She looks more like a living doll in a large dollhouse that belongs to Benji. His power should've been buried when he himself was put in his grave, I think angrily. With Gwenhael's bones, if only I could do more than carefully tuck Sophia in.

'Sweat dreams,' I say hoarsely.

She squeezes her eyes shut even more, as if trying to remember something difficult. For a while I observe her, until suddenly Cormack puts his hand on my shoulder and I startle. 'You seem exhausted.'

'This was more tiring than I thought,' I mutter.

'I can see that. Come, a hot meal and a quiet evening will do you good.'

I follow him.

He glances at me. 'You have been working with herbs.'

'I did that at home. You don't have much. Most of it is gone now.'

He surprises me by asking: 'What do you need? No, wait, make a list later. I'll make sure you get supplies.'

'The medical staff didn't look convinced before,' I comment.

Cormack shrugged. 'You have inherited Sela's special qualities, haven't you? I hope you can help those children in a way we're not able to.'

I frown. 'Fever and colds, a few bedsores, that's all they have. I think it can all be solved by dressing them warmly and sending them outside every day.'

'They can't. Not as they are now.'

'Cormack – what is really wrong with those children?'

He gives me a fleeting smile. 'Fever, cold and a couple of bedsores, like you said. You've had a long day, Nimue, and I have some things to take care of in the west wing. Please go upstairs. And if you are able to put some food on the table, I'll make you our new mascot.'

I smile back, briefly and insincerely.

Halfway down the corridor, Arthur approaches me. He looks even grimmer than earlier this morning and stops me with a gesture.

'What are you doing?' he hisses softly. 'Have you forgotten where you are, Nim?'

'Not even a second. I'm looking for a way to help those kids.'

'There is only one way to help them. Take them far away from here.'

'I can't do magic,' I snarl. 'Do you have anything that can help?'

'Maybe not for our plan,' he whispers. 'No escape plan. But it's important. I know what happened to Sela...'

The door nearby opens and Doctor Moal steps into the corridor, a stack of files in his hands. Arthur immediately shuts up. I turn around with an unpleasant feeling in my stomach. Seeing that smug smile of his is the last thing I need right now.

'Look at that, Cairn's new favourite toy.' Moal's beady eyes first skip over Arthur before his gaze comes to rest on my face. 'Come around to our way of thinking yet, *Nicole*?'

'Screw you,' I growl. 'I know Cormack reprimanded you.'

'Well, if you two are so close, surely you don't mind handing over these files to him.' He pushes the stack into my arms before I can refuse. 'An apprentice doctor must know her place. That's how we all start.' Moal smiles without kindness. 'Have a nice evening, 1491. *Nicole.*'

We both watch him with equal disgust, until he has disappeared from the corridor and out of view. 'I'd rather eat jellyfish than be alone with *him*,' Arthur mutters. The oppressive silence that follows makes it clear that we agree with each other without exchanging any more words.

The files in my arms are heavy. 'You know something about Sela?'

'Yes. And it's really important. Come with me, we can go to my room...'

'Not yet,' I decide, however frustrating it may be to wait. 'Wait until tonight, Arthur. I'll take this to Cormack's office first and then he'll be expecting us upstairs.'

He wants to protest, but swallows his words. Maybe because he sees how pale I am, and that my hands are shaking from the tough day.

I leave him and take the files to Cormack's study, where I throw them onto his desk. I look around. Apart from me, there's nobody else on this floor at the moment. Most of the doctors have already gone home and the staff have their own wing, where they eat and sleep. After making sure that Cormack isn't going to walk in at any moment, I open all the files, one by one.

I look at the contents, not sure if I'm understanding what's there. The rising and falling peaks of these graphs must have been made by the brain machine – the same machine that made a scan of the inside of my head. Are these theta waves? Do these children also dream while they're awake, and do they call out to the Other World, the way Doctor Moal believes they do? I can only guess.

Each file has been given a number, just like Arthur and I were given a number, and most numbers are accompanied by a photo of poor quality. Pale children, all of them. I wonder what became of the teenagers and adults in District 15. The Asclepius Congregation must have taken them... Undreamed them... And then?

Each child has a short biography, typed in the typical square font that computers generate. Strange letters, so neat, and stripped of any human emotion. Not much is said about these children. Only their name, if known, their approximate age, their general health, blood type and origins. A lot of children have red stamps on their files. Ink that has clearly printed a single word onto the white paper, sharp and cruel and inevitable: *Undream.*

I stare at those red stamps for a while. Then I carefully fold up the papers and flatten them so they become a kind of parcel, until that's small enough to hide between my skirt and my long cardigan. I stack up the rest of the files and open Cormack's enormous cabinet, where he keeps all his things.

As driven and intelligent as Cormack may be, he is also chaotic when it comes to storing his things. Loose sheets of paper and haphazardly-closed folders tumble left and right as I attempt to put the files away in an orderly fashion. I push them aside and a whole pile of paper flutters to the floor. I sigh and bend down to pick up the papers when a drawing of corridors and rooms catches my eye.

I stop and take a good look at it. It is a map of the Asclepius Congregation, much better than our own poorly drawn map. My gaze flits from top to bottom. Platform Zero is the lowest level of the complex, but there aren't just cells hidden there. A narrow corridor leads to a control room. The CORE, I think. And at the very top, Cormack's own quarters. His office is one floor below.

I look for exit points. On the west side of the complex is the main entrance, but it opens onto the large square that I can see from the window here. It's too out in the open, too wide to be able to escape unseen. The east side seems to feature a smaller exit, perhaps for staff or to be used a loading dock. But Cami is to the west of the building. We'd have to make our way around, and with half of the children ailing and apathetic, it would create a daunting extra obstacle.

I hear footsteps in the corridor. They're coming closer. I quickly fold up the map and hide it within the files that are already tucked in my clothes against my belly. Just in time. Cormack peeks around the corner. When he sees me, he flashes his charming smile again. 'Arthur said Doctor Moal is using you as a messenger.'

'Only to deliver these files to you.' I sound a little hoarse. 'You're making a mess of your drawers.'

'A bad habit, I must admit. You don't have to let him boss you around, by the way.' Cormack gestures at me to step out of the office, and I follow him, hoping he won't notice the slight bulge under my jumper.

'You should fire him,' I hear myself say. Cormack looks down at me in surprise. 'Moal. He's childish and cruel – I'm sure you can see that too.'

'I can't fire Moal, Nimue. He is our only neurologist.'

'Yes, his "help" is much appreciated.' I lift my arm for a moment. 'Or have you already forgotten about this?'

'Of course not. He was reprimanded.'

'I'm sure he wasn't the least bit contrite,' I growl. 'That man is a rotten fish.'

'That's quite enough.' Cormack says it mildly, but I hear a strong undertone of disdain in his voice. It's clear that the subject is closed. But he knows I'm right. Everyone knows it, even Sini. But now is not the time to confront my cousin. First I must get these files to safety and make sure he'll never set eyes on them. I don't know if it will save the marked children from the mysterious process called Undreaming – jellyfish and sharks, I don't even know *what* happens to the Undreamed – but I firmly believe that anything that makes Doctor Moal this happy can't be anything good.

'Change your clothes before you come to dinner, Nimue.'

Without protest, I hurry to my room. Room 17 has become a little cosier since it became known that I am the boss's cousin. There's a new rug on the floor, and a desk and a table lamp were added. I suspect Sini is behind this. Besides, nobody locks the door anymore.

I close the door as I come in, pull the files from underneath my jumper and spread them out on my desk. After a moment, I change my mind and put them in my pillowcase, where I still keep Mum's diary hidden. I won't be able to hide all this stuff for long, I realise. Sini will come and change my sheets at some point. Before that happens, I need a better hiding place.

I'll think about it tomorrow. How long have we been here? I try to count the days, but because of my long sleep I lost track of time. Seven? That means we'd only have three days left before Will is waiting for us at the rendezvous point. So far, we haven't achieved much. We only have a semblance of a plan and a rudimentary map. I haven't even had a chance to look up Judikael again or see if she left a message for me. Arthur or I should give her a sign, I decide, as soon as we can.

My thoughts flash to Cormack for a moment. No doubt he thinks he's achieved a great deal with us. With me at least, since Arthur is still too unwilling. Cormack knows what I want. For the first time in my life, all these opportunities are being dropped into my lap. If I asked Cormack, he would immediately choose me to be his doctor apprentice. Arthur and I are safe in his care, he constantly tries to make that clear to us. We will never again feel gnawing hunger, never again be at the mercy of the capricious sea. We can live here safely and comfortably, as long as we accept Cormack as the hero and saviour of the story.

Then he would make me his instrument, of course. Benji's wish would come true, nine years after his death.

I remember Cormack's order and quickly change into some clean clothes, brush the tangles out of my curls and tie them back. When I turn around and look at my reflection in the full-length mirror – another one of Sini's presents – I shake my head at myself in pity. The illness and lack of fresh air have left their marks on me: my cheeks are white, making the freckles stand out more, and my eyelids are swollen. All I can do is wash my face with cold water coming from the tap. I give myself a few gentle slaps on my cheeks. They turn a light red, vivid, like the life returning to me after the injection that made me so ill.

Dinner is quiet and tense. I listen to the clatter of the cutlery on our plates. Arthur stares ahead sullenly; whatever he has discovered about Sela must be bothering him. I want to know what it is. Cormack looks relaxed, but I notice that every now and then he casts an annoyed glance at my brother. Arthur either doesn't notice it, or he ignores it. The latter seems more likely.

My excuse is that I'm too tired to have a proper conversation. At least they both seem to accept that, and so the three of us remain silent.

Finally, it's Cormack who breaks the silence. He turns to me and asks, 'How are your hands?'

I look at them. 'They're not shaking anymore.'

'Do you think you can heal people?'

The question is so direct that I'm thrown off balance for a moment. 'I... I don't know. I'm very tired.'

'Then go to bed early. Tomorrow, I want to test to what extent we can employ your powers. There is much to be done here for someone with your gift, Nimue.' He makes it sound almost satisfying as he leans back in his chair. 'Benji's experiments are just the beginning. With you, we'll begin our victory march. Nimue, I hope I'm not catching you off guard...'

He is, though. I stare at him and notice that Arthur is doing the same. I open my mouth to say something, but Arthur beats me to it. 'She can't do that. Nim, say you won't!'

Confused, I look from him to Cormack. 'Of course I have to do it.'

'He's using you,' Arthur snarled. 'Have you forgotten how Benji used Rona?'

'This is not the same!' Cormack gets up. He is tall and towers over us. 'You don't have to worry about exhausting yourself with an endless stream of sick people, Nimue. No, I'm only talking about the people who are already infected. There will be fewer and fewer of them. Think about it! With our Undreaming and your gift, we could eradicate the Black Influenza within a year.'

'Nimue has been ill,' Arthur snarls. He too rises to his feet. 'She needs rest and some fresh air, not the dreary, sterile air of your Institute. This place is bad for her. It's bad for *everyone*!'

Cormack's face flushes red as he turns to my little brother. 'Your sister has a very special gift. Don't you think she should use it to pull Central Europe out of the abyss? She cannot shun her responsibilities. She has a duty.'

'Exactly what Benji said.'

'And my father was right! Your mother selfishly put aside her duty for the sake of her own life. Our country cannot afford to do that a second time.'

'Mum protected Nimue.'

'And now it's Nimue's turn to make the right choice.'

'Stop,' I whisper. Cormack's words brush over me like whisps of ice. I clasp my hands together in my lap. They're starting to tremble again. I clear my throat and say more loudly: 'Stop! Shut up, the both of you. It's *my* gift.'

Arthur looks as if he wants to say something, then holds back. Cormack swallows. His jaw tightens and a storm brews in his eyes. But eventually he nods, albeit unwillingly.

I slowly raise my shaking hands. 'I never asked for this gift. But Cormack is right. I have a duty... or a responsibility, at least. I was too late to help Katell. What choice do I have, Arthur?' I turn to him. 'I can't let all these people die, can I?'

'Katell,' he repeated bitterly. 'She's here, you know? I found her.' His blue eyes bore into mine and I see his disgust.

'Arthur.' Cormack's voice sounds like distant thunder. There is a warning evident in his low tone.

My little brother looks at him rebelliously. 'You mutilate them all.'

'Enough already, Arthur!' Cormack bangs his fist on the table. It's like a thunderclap that shakes us. I cringe. Arthur shuts his mouth. After a few moments he turns around and disappears, without even slamming the door.

I glance at my plate. My food is now as cold as the icy silence around us. Cormack is looking at me, a tense expression on his face. I can't make out what he's thinking, but my own thoughts are racing through my head like a storm.

'What have you done with Katell?' I ask.

'We helped her. Arthur is shocked, but I assure you that the girl is alive. She's alive because of us.'

'Right.' I look at him and save my anger for a later moment. The half-lie easily passes my lips. 'I'll do whatever you want, Cormack. I'll heal everyone. But don't be angry with Arthur. He's just upset, nothing more.'

He nods. My promise softens the lines around his mouth. 'I don't know how to convince that boy.'

'Let me talk to him.' I get up. 'He'll listen to me.'

'You think so?'

'Of course.' I actually manage to smile. 'I'm his big sister. Trust me, Cormack, Arthur means nothing by it.'

He sighs as he sits down again and leans back wearily. 'Try it. You have my blessing.'

I leave him alone with the cold food. I find Arthur in his room, three corridors away from my own. The door is unlocked, but I knock softly before stepping inside.

There is a desk in the corner similar to mine, and a mirror hanging on his wardrobe. Next to his bed is a pile of worn-out books. I take a look at them: travel stories, a book with pictures of people with tall feathers on their heads. I wonder what else Cormack keeps in those archives of his.

Arthur is sitting on his bed. As soon as he sees me, he crosses his arms in front of his chest, giving me an angry look before demonstratively turning away from me. I decide to ignore it and make sure the door is closed properly before I drop down next to him on the bed. 'Tell me what you know.'

His eyes shoot back to me, surprised. 'Are you sure you wouldn't rather hear *Cormack* talk?'

'Don't be an idiot,' I bark, giving him a stern look. 'Cormack is keeping things from me, you think I don't know that? Now, tell me about Katell!'

His face becomes even more dejected. It's as if a shadow falls over the entire room. A cold feeling forms a lump in the pit of my stomach.

'It's as if she's been chopped in two,' Arthur says. When he sees my shocked face, he quickly adds: 'Not literally! But she might as well have been. There's something missing from her, Nim. I don't get it. She understands everything, but she's not *there*.'

'Sweet Gwenhael...' Everything suddenly becomes clear: the orphaned children in the Asclepius Congregation, the painful expression on little Sophia's face as she tried to sleep, Doctor Moal's belief that I'm calling out to the Other World with some kind of antenna that can make me sick ... 'Undreaming,' I groan. '*That's* what Undreaming means. Removing the antenna to disconnect them from the Other World.' Part of me already understood it. I just didn't want to accept it, because how can anyone do something that insane? Now I have to face it: this is what our uncle has set in motion and what Cormack is carrying on with, without a second thought. Yes, Arthur is right – the Snakes might as well have mutilated their victims with a butcher's knife; that would make me just as ill.

I grope for something to hold myself upright. It is Arthur's hands that steady me. I sit still while the world is spinning around me. When I calm down, my hands still tremble like leaves in the wind.

'I should've known,' I whisper. 'The Fisher King said everything will be destroyed when the two worlds are torn apart.'

'The Fisher King?'

Arthur is confused, but I pay no attention to it. 'Why wasn't she there? Why didn't I see Katell in the infirmary, with the other children?'

'Cormack is lying to you, that's why.' Arthur trembles, but not because of the disease and not because he's filled with dread. His blue eyes are the colour of ripe berries, that's how angry he is. 'When I found Katell, she could only say one thing: Nimue, Nimue. As if she had been hypnotised. I think she wanted you to heal her so badly that part of her still clings to that idea, no matter what she is like in her present state. Cormack knows that you know her, that you know what she was like before.'

There's a sob stuck in my throat. 'Where is she?'

'In a room, in corridor C-12. Far away from you, and from Cormack's precious orphanage.'

'How did you know... How did you find her?'

'I've been looking for her. Did you think I was just bumming around while you were running errands for Cormack?'

I feel ashamed and keep quiet.

'I stole a key off Sini when she wasn't paying attention. One of those keycards, you know. She didn't have permission to go to that many places, but she did have permission to visit Katell. Someone has to take care of her. Sini gets to do all the grunt work.'

'If you have a keycard, you can also go see Judikael, Taran and Marci. And look what I've got hidden under my sleeve.' I show him the map of the building. I mark the exits with a pen. 'Our best option would be this exit on the east side, but I don't like it. It'll take too long before we're completely out of sight.'

Arthur points to the map. 'This is a fire lane.'

'Yes, but it's dangerously close to Laboratory 5. You know that Moal always works late. There's another fire lane on the west side. The Orphanage and the rooms are further away, but we can try...'

'That's no good,' Arthur says with a sigh. 'I've been there. Detection is right next to it.'

'Gwenhael's grave.' I chew on the inside of my cheek. 'We could drug them? A big hit of Paxshould give us a few hours to get away.'

I don't really mean it, because how would we ever manage to inject all the Snakes? But Arthur frowns and points to a small room on the map. It's more like a booth. 'Isn't that a storage room, right next to the Orphanage?'

'What, you seriously want to drug them with Pax? Arthur, that's asking for trouble.'

'We drug Cormack.' He looks at me, dead serious. 'Just him, and Sini, if she gets in the way.'

'Okay, fine. But then what?'

He shakes his head. He's clearly just as frustrated as I am. 'We'll have to take the exit on the east side. If it's dark *and* if we move quickly, we might be able to make it.'

''Might' doesn't sound like a good idea,' I say gloomily. 'We can't risk our lives and hope we'll be lucky. There are a lot of locked doors and other obstacles to conquer before we'll get there. You said yourself that Sini's keycard doesn't have access to all the rooms.'

'Take Cormack's card, then.'

Of course. If anyone will have permission to go anywhere he likes, it's Cormack himself.

'There is something else,' Arthur says. 'Sela. We can't leave until you know the whole story.'

He pulls something from out of his pillowcase: Benji's files. It's obviously not the whole pile of papers that I found in the display cabinet. Arthur has hidden a few sheets in the same place I was hiding my own secret stash. My little brother shoves them into my hands. 'Read it all the way to the end.'

I look at him for a moment before turning my gaze to the typewritten words.

10

SELA'S DESTINY

*T*oday I spoke with Peregrino. These constant disappointments are like coals on the fire of my frustration. But all these failures, all these unsuccessful cures for the Black Influenza, make me want to win this fight even more.

The years have also embittered me, he told me. I have no idea if that's true. 'I don't see myself anymore,' I told him.

'Look again, closely,' he instructed me, with his usual smile. 'What do you see?'

'Anger.'

'I see strength, Benji. The problem is that you're shying away from all the possibilities that you have. Are you afraid of the fire that your father and sister have fueled in you? Are you afraid of your own anger?'

'No. I fear neither. I long for it.'

He stared at me for a long time. Peregrino's gaze pierced right through me. If I hadn't known him for so long, it would've made me uncomfortable.

Finally, he spoke again. His words were like stabbing daggers. Damn him – always touching me where it hurts the most. He said: 'The source of your anger isn't Rona herself. The problem is that she inherited all your mother's virtues, while you were left with all the sins of your father.'

'Maybe I'm afraid of the destruction he could've caused,' I had to admit. 'Maybe that stain has become mine.'

'You are so much more than what your father once was,' Peregrino said.

'You never met him.'

'I have seen your ambition. Your suffocating rage, your paralysing grief. I see that the memories of everything you loved almost poisoned you. Turn it around, Benji. There's more than revenge.'

'I don't think there is more for me.'

'With ten thousand New Euros a year in your pocket, I daresay there's more waiting for you.'

And then he explained his plan to me: he has founded a small institute, still in its infancy. Asclepius, he calls it. Peregrino has been monitoring Avalon's results for years. Together we can do more – he is convinced of it. Asclepius can be a place where brilliant minds gather, starting with him and me. I said yes.

'Fight for the lives of those who still have a chance,' he said to me, looking at me determinedly as we shook hands on it.

'Isn't that revenge, too?'

'No, it's war. But for all the right reasons.'

*

Peregrino tells me to write down more. He says writing does me good. It keeps my thoughts in order in a way that talking and pacing the room do not. He's probably right.

Is there any way of getting to the heart of my nightmares when I describe them? I often dream of fire. Of fists. I dream of narrow, enclosed spaces from which I cannot escape. But more often, I dream of vast, empty plains, where I stand alone, crying out for answers that never come.

I understand that these dreams of fear and loneliness are a reflection of what my life has been like so far. Perhaps it is time to write things down: maybe I should get on with my life and hope that from there, I can unravel the tangled mess in my mind. So here goes nothing.

My life, like all lives, begins with my mother. I suppose we did share some years of happiness, however badly she took on the role of caregiver and educator later on. I remember Rona describing her laughter once. She said it sounded like music. But from my earliest memories I only remember her white face. Skin like whalebone, hair like the dark of night. I never heard her laugh. I don't think she could, anymore.

I have clearer memories of Fergus, my father. Why he hit me and not Rona, I'll never fully understand. I didn't wish my sister any harm – not back then – but that kind of isolation made me even lonelier. I remember the pain, searching for a way out of there in my mind. Sometimes I'd drive a blade into my arm until blood welled up. That brought me some relief.

Our mother only whispered, if she spoke at all. In the last few years before our departure, she would sometimes not speak a word for twenty-four hours. She would just sit and stare, her big black eyes fixed on an invisible horizon.

I have sometimes wondered if we were being foolish by not seeing who she really was. But I'm getting ahead of myself.

I remember the fire in the shearing shed near our house. Who knows, maybe Fergus dropped the lamp on purpose that day and then silently watched as the flames burst from the roof in an uncontrolled attempt to burn away the Other World forever. I already had very low expectations of him as a father. From that day onwards, I completely erased him from my memory. It's only thanks to Rona's efforts that I'm sitting here now, writing this story, unharmed. Mother didn't raise a finger. She just stood there looking, dazed, pale, and trembling like a twig in the wind. It was as if she could break so easily, by a mere gust of wind, but what I came to realise is that she would have let me burn in that shed. It was not she who broke, but my heart.

Not long after that, my sister took us across the sea. I know she struggled with the decision. I could see that the new world overwhelmed her. I myself never regretted it for a moment; all the drab-looking cities of the new world were like a liberation to me.

But there was another matter to settle before we could leave the island and its inhabitants behind us for good. That day, Rona told me the whole truth, with trembling hands and unwilling lips. I remember that it looked like she wanted to cry. She didn't. Everything she told me sounded clipped and formal. I don't know if I would have described it in that same matter-of-fact way. This was not like a medical report – a thing that I've become so familiar in recent years. This is the very root of my family tree, which has dug deeper than I suspected until that day.

Mother. Sela. Whenever she was staring ahead, did she see the sea? When she didn't seem to hear us and sat there motionless in her chair, did she hear the rushing of the waves? The suction of the water currents below?

Sela was a woman who did not belong in our world. How Fergus managed to capture her is a riddle I won't be able to solve. The key to her freedom – her true shape – lay hidden in a cave in the form of a shriveled-up fur.

But perhaps I'm telling this story from the wrong perspective. Will it be useful if I first write down the common knowledge that every child who belongs to the people of Danu grows up with? Oh, it's strange to call myself that, even in my own handwriting. For long years I have been just Benji Cairn, Head of the Asclepius Congregation. Avalon and the Danu – my island and my people - are oceans away.

The common knowledge, which is more like a myth, describes the seal people as one of the gentlest inhabitants of the Other World. As soon as the moon rises to its highest point in the night, they will shed their furs on the beach and turn into young women. Every man who sees them, finds a womblike warmth to rest in. But at dawn, they put their furs back on and slip away underneath the waves. They may never become brides to human men. That's how the story goes.

From this I can conclude that Fergus made Sela his hostage. By stealing her seal skin and hiding it in the highest cave on the island, he made it impossible for her to return to the sea – to freedom. So she had to allow him to come to her, night after night. She had to carry the children he conceived with her, give birth to them. First came Rona, slender and dark as Sela herself. I imagine it was a kind of comfort to our mother that her daughter was so like her, and even inherited her magic. But then I came, looking so much like Fergus that the delicate balm that Rona had been was obliterated. Sela retreated into silence. Her silence was her only armour, even when Fergus's fists began to fly, and he turned more violent. I'm not sure if he ever hit Sela. Even in her withdrawn, languishing state, she had something about her that made it hard to be enraged with her. Maybe it was a remnant of magic from the seal people. Perhaps that same magic kept Rona safe from father's abuse. But I can only speculate, for the truth will never be found.

Finally, it was Tamsin who told Rona the whispered stories about Sela. "There is a cave somewhere," she said, "and in that cave lies the true form of your mother".

How Tamsin came by this knowledge is yet another mystery. Perhaps she got Fergus drunk one night; he always loved strong berry wine. Whatever the case, Rona must have felt she had nothing left to lose. However much we grew apart, to this day I admire her courage to climb up into that deserted cave and give Sela back her seal skin.

Sometimes I wonder what our mother was thinking in that moment when she was standing naked on the beach and was finally released. Did she cry when Rona hugged her? Did she not want to say goodbye to me? I was her son, too, wasn't I, despite my resemblance to Fergus? But who knows how an inhabitant of the Other World thinks or how they reason. Who knows, she may not have thought of us as her children, but only as the guards of that prison she'd been living in all this time. If she ever did return to the island to come see us, we certainly never found out. Because by then, Rona, Esoldi and I were far away, in the heart of Central Europe.

And that's the whole truth, as far as I know, about my life and Sela's fate. A strange history from a mysterious world, that I am both connected to and cut off from. So did it help me to put all this on paper? I don't know. The pain still feels like a dull wound: covered, but not forgotten. At moments like these, I miss Rona. My sister is the only one who still knows where I came from, who I was born to, and what the journey to freedom has cost us all.

Will we ever embrace each other again?

I don't know that either.

11

WOLF

Speechless and appalled, I sit there with the papers in my lap, long after I have let the final words sink in. Sela's secret has finally been revealed. Cormack must have known it all along.

Everything seems blurry and yet things are clearer now: my dreams of the deep sea, the swimming seals calling out to me... And didn't I already know this, somewhere deep inside? I struggle to remember my last dream vision. The woman who carried me to the beach and reassured me... she now has a name. In my mind I recognised her, even though I have never seen Sela in real life. And Rona's seal pendant, which I have carried like a talisman ... I reach for my chest, then remember again that I lost it.

I look up at my brother, who has sat motionless in front of me the whole time. 'It doesn't say anything about the Undreaming.'

He shrugs. 'Maybe Cormack has put those files away some place else. You said these were in some kind of display case.'

'Like the relics in Saint Gwenhael.' Perhaps it's not so strange that Cormack keeps these records on display. The origin story of his foster father, whom he admires above anyone else. I lick my lips, suddenly aware of how dry they've become. 'I think Benji really didn't know where Rona went. But I think I *do* know.'

'What are you trying to say...?'

I look grimly at Benji's handwriting. My embittered uncle. My *dead* uncle. He can neither help nor stop us, but our journey into the heart of the Asclepius

85

Congregation has not been in vain. 'If Mum had been anywhere in Central Europe, he would've found her, I'm pretty sure of that.'

Arthur suddenly looks at me strangely – a mixture of fear and hope. 'Are you saying she went back to the island?'

'Avalon,' I mumble, tasting the word in my mouth. 'Either she's dead, or she's there. Even Benji wouldn't have suspected she'd want to go back to Avalon. And even if he had, I don't think he would've followed her. Not back to Fergus.'

'Then all we have to do is figure out how to get to Avalon.' Arthur grins. 'As soon as we break free.'

'Whatever happens we have to take the children to Cima. But they are small, sick, or they've been Undreamed...' I feel my fatigue grow. 'We need to create a diversion, one that lasts long enough. Pax isn't going to be enough. And we need help. Arthur, you pick up Judikael, Taran and Marci. Then we'll split up. They'll have to get the children from the orphanage. Tell Judikael to get Katell.'

'And what about me?'

'I need you on Platform Zero.' In my head, the plan rapidly begins to get shape. 'To go to the CORE. If you turn it off, the power will cut out. The doors will open, the alarm won't go off, the lights will go out.'

He's already nodding before I've finished my sentence. 'But there may be some kind of backup system in place. This is not the Ark. And even in the Ark, an outage didn't last longer than an hour, usually.'

'But that should be enough. We need all the time we can get, every minute is precious. But you're right, time is of the essence. And you must understand precisely what you're supposed to be doing.' I look at him. '*Do* you know what you'll be doing?'

'Nim, I'm not Corentin.'

'But he's explained things to you. *Can* you do it?'

He nods. 'I think so.'

'Then we have to make do with that.'

'What about the children? Do we leave all those Undreamed with Will?'

I lick my lips again. 'I don't like it. You know what he did to Katell.'

'A mistake,' Arthur says, a little too reasonably for my taste. 'He will be able to protect the children better than us, Nim.'

It don't like to admit that he's right. I heave a sigh. 'Get to work then. I'll get the Paxout of the storeroom, you find Judikael and the others.' I get to my feet.

'Are you going to do that right away?'

'There's something I have to do first. I have files with the names of children who need to be Undreamed. And this report on Sela... Cormack has had it in his possession long enough.'

'Where are you going to hide it?'

'Somewhere they'll never look, I'm sure. Give me that keycard.'

After a moment of hesitation, Arthur takes the thin, plastic pass from under his pillow and hands it over to me. I slip it into the pocket of my skirt.

'Nim,' Arthur says softly. 'What will you do when Cormack wants you to use your powers tomorrow?'

I think for a moment. 'I'll say I'm too sick. I know I need all my strength for our plan.' Yet it feels wrong. Mum used Sela's gift for good and I feel like I should do the same. But Arthur nods.

I lean over to him and do something I haven't done since we were children: I kiss Arthur gently on his forehead. 'Goodnight, little brother.'

'Be careful,' he says, looking at me with a worried frown on his brow.

No one is standing guard at the bottom of the long stairs leading to Platform Zero; only the iron door is there to stop people from leaving. The Asclepius Congregation apparently believes that escape from the other side is impossible. I don't blame them – a bull wouldn't manage to break through that solid obstacle, not even using his full strength. I smile as I effortlessly enter with Sini's keycard. I wonder if Sini realises yet that she's been robbed, or if she just thinks that she misplaced it in a moment of absent-mindedness. Either way, this is not the time for reckless behaviour. We must remain cautious, Arthur and I.

The light comes from the bare fluorescent tubes on the ceiling, just like in the Ark. The walls are bare and grey, as is the concrete floor. My eyes pass over the rows of closed doors, all as thick and solid as the one at the top of the stairs. Platform Zero is the most desolate place I've ever seen, even more sad-looking than the wing I have come to call the Orphanage.

All the cell doors look alike. I can't tell where exactly I was locked up or what the prison next to mine was. My footsteps sound hollow as I approach. I whisper into the eerie silence. 'Wolf?'

For a moment, a frightening thought flashes through my mind: what if he is no longer here? Or what if he is dead?

'Wolf!' I shout more loudly.

A bang against one of the doors almost makes me jump.

'What?'

It's the raw voice I remember. He sounds suspicious, almost angry for being disturbed. I approach his cell door, which is easy now because I can locate him by the sound he made. Hesitantly I ask: 'Wolf ... do you remember me?'

'Girl?'

'My name is Nimue. I need your help.'

For a moment he remains silent. When he does speak, he sounds duller, as if he's moved further away from his cell door. 'What kind of trick is this?'

'It's no trick,' I say quickly. 'I want to ask you if ...'

'Do those *daikus* think that they can make me talk by deception and trickery? *Helviti!*' He must bang his fist against the other side of the door, so hard is the pounding noise that follows his strange curse words.

'Sssh! Do you want them to hear us?' Anxiously I look over my shoulder, but the underground facility is still as deserted as ever. No footsteps on the stairs. I press myself against the cell door and lean with my head against the cold steel. 'My brother stole Sini's key, and nobody knows I'm here. You can trust me. Can I trust you?'

'Do you have a key?' he growls. 'Then let me out of this cursed cell.'

'Give me a second.' I pull out the card again and hold it against the lock. Nothing happens. I wipe the plastic with my sleeve and try again. The door remains shut. 'I'm sorry,' I say in frustration. 'I don't think Sini is authorised to let you go.'

I hear a resigned sigh. 'What do you want from me, girl?' he says.

I pull out Benji's files and Rona's diary, which I've kept under my jumper. 'I have to hide something. If I slip it underneath the door, will you keep it with you until I come back to set you free?'

'To set me *free?*' I hear a sound resembling a laugh, but it's so painful and raw that it chills me to the bone. 'No one escapes from the Asclepius Congregation.'

'I will,' I say. 'We have a plan and we have the means. Besides, I know someone who once escaped this place.'

'Do you think they'll let that happen again?' Again I hear him bark out a short laugh. 'Donkeys and stones, dear. Fool them once, shame on them. Fool them twice and you'll have a big problem.'

'Believe me. As soon as the CORE stops working, all doors will open. Can it really get any worse than rotting away here in the dark, Wolf?'

He waits a moment before answering. 'You shouldn't use doors,' he finally says. 'If you really want to escape, you go underground. Where they won't see you.'

In the brief silence I let his words sink in. Underground, where they won't see you... The wells, I think. The sewer runs right under the building's corridors. I can't believe I didn't think of that before! Nobody from the Asclepius Congregation would think of crawling through the sewers. I can already see Sini pulling that disgusted face that seems to be her permanent facial expression, and Cormack with his flapping, neat coat doesn't strike me as the person to crawl through the excrement of his prisoners either.

'Girl?' Wolf's voice brings me back to reality. 'You're quiet.'

'In three days we'll come back and get you,' I say. 'I promise.'

'I want to believe you.' Again I hear him sigh. 'What do I need to hide for you?'

I kneel down and push Benji's files through the crack under the door first. Despite my intention to trust this man, my heart is pounding nervously. I hesitate when the diary is next. Mum's precious memories, her last words to us... if anything happens to them now, I may never see them again.

I pull myself together and push the diary to the other side of the door. It barely fits, the old leather rubbing the floor. From the other side, Wolf grabs my dearest treasure and pulls it further into his cell. Strange to think that his hands are holding it now... I don't even know what he looks like.

'What is this? Why do you want to hide this?'

I sigh and close my eyes for a moment. 'You'll find out, if you can read.'

'I've learned your alphabet. A bit of it.'

'Wolf? When will they pick you up?'

'Not today.' He is silent for a moment. 'Not for a long time.'

At least that gives me time. I dare to relax and lean my back against his door, my knees pulled up. 'Why are you here?'

'I could ask you the same.'

I almost laugh. 'I'm here because my family is one big mess. Or maybe those damned ghosts have always been leading us here, with their whispers and half-answers. Maybe the Fisher King has put us here, like pawns on a chessboard. Wouldn't that be something? And maybe he's just waiting for me to somehow stop Cormack, as if I could... And for Arthur to come to him, to make him drink from the grail.' It is surprisingly easy to speak those truths aloud to someone I can't see.

I hear him inhale sharply, but don't know whether it's from surprise or confusion. 'The Fisher King?'

'Forget that,' I mutter.

'He talks to you? You speak to the Others?'

I turn around and stare at his door. 'You know him?'

He suddenly sounds feverish. 'They spoke to *me*. But that was years ago. I had a friend on that side. A helper. But he too has been silenced since I got here. No matter how many times I've called out ... It's this triple-damned place, I'm sure. *Helviti.*' This time he pronounces the curse softly and with a hissing voice.

'How is that possible?' I ask softly. 'Do you also have blood from the Other World?'

'It's not in your blood, it's in your mind. Why do you think I'm here, girl? Why do you think they're holding me?'

I shake my head in silence. That's a riddle I haven't found the solution to, not even in Benji's writings.

'I'm *Hura*, not a Central European. You a" think there are no countries outside this sick continent. You think you are the only people. You are wrong.' The anger in his voice suddenly ebbs away, like water on dry sand. 'At least, you were. There is little left of my people now, unless a few have managed to cling to the edge of life. In any case, I'll never seen them again.'

'Wolf…'

'I was a boy, still a child. The fever overtook me for days; I was at death's door. It brought my *nani* to despair. But she wasn't surprised that I crossed the border of the Other World during my delirium. They were not gentle.'

Is it my imagination, or do I hear him laughing bitterly and softly?

'They came to me, the Others, in the form of predators. I was torn apart and made anew. Until the flames and blood made me a new boy – then I was recreated as a man. But the trappers came one of those nights and left none of my people alive. A whole tribe wiped out. Can you imagine that, girl? You, in this huge Central Europe? All members of the *Hura*, swept away like trees after a forest fire. I returned to the smoking silence of the camp. Imagine the smell of smouldering flesh – imagine the unrecognisable faces, when you know you should know every one of them! So I fled.'

In the oppressive silence of Platform Zero, I can hear him breathing with difficulty.

'Loneliness and fear are bad counsellors, girl. Instead of using the safety of the old camp, I let myself be driven into the forest, where I struggled to survive. Every night I heard the wolves. That howling … it penetrated my flesh, settled permanently in my mind. They hunted me. Protected me. I don't know; I don't remember. But I do know that they kept driving me forward, for months or years. Until *they* found me, that fat doctor and the man with hair red as fire. And they thought that I could give them easy access to the Other World. That I would be their bridge, willingly or forcibly. And then I would exterminate the Others. Hah!' His laughter, resounding again, is cold. 'Even after I learned your language so I could understand what they wanted, I wasn't willing to participate in such perverse projects. I cut my mind off from that world. To protect them, those Others, my old friends. I'm not a toy. I'm the last shaman of the *Hura*. And what kind? A shaman with no ears, no voice. I'm a broken bridge. And I'll stay that way, even if it means death.'

I only notice my tears when they start rolling down my cheeks. 'I'm sorry for you,' I whisper, just loud enough for him to hear.

'That's easy to say.'

'I have not encountered any trappers, Wolf. But I have encountered a terrible storm by the seaside. I have seen too much death to ever forget.'

A silence follows my words and I make no attempt to break it. Silently I sit against his door, my face in my hands. The tears slowly dry up. No new ones appear.

When he speaks again, it is with a quiet voice. 'I'll help you, Nimue. Though I'm afraid I can't do much for you.'

'Keep those papers hidden for me; that'll be enough for now.' I stand up with stiff limbs. The coldness of the ground has seeped through my clothes. 'I have to go, before they notice I'm gone. Trust me, Wolf.' For a moment I rest my forehead against the iron plate of his door, almost kissing the hostile barricade. 'Three days. Wait for me.'

12

ESCAPE

'I went to the recreation room.' Arthur sat cross-legged on my bed, a huge atlas resting on his lap. 'Judikael wasn't there. But I found the stone, like you said. She left a message.'

I hastily unfold the piece of paper that he hands over. I can see Judikael has scribbled down the words in a hurry:

Found Taran and Marci. We're all fine. Unfortunately, no sign of Katell yet. We're waiting for you. Gwenhael's blood, hurry up with that plan of yours. This place is like a barrel of rotten fish.

J.

'At least they're unharmed.' I let out a sigh of relief before flashing a grin. 'Rotten fish, indeed.'

'They won't have to wait long.' Arthur almost completely disappears behind the atlas when he puts it up to read in it. Only his blond curls are peeping out above the edge. We stop talking while Arthur browses the atlas in silence. I sit at the end of the bed, resting my back against the wall. Deep thoughts furrow my forehead. I stare at the grey ceiling without actually seeing it.

After dinner, Arthur leaves Cormack's kitchen as soon as was possible without being offensive. I excuse myself soon after, saying that I'm not feeling well. I didn't really have to lie: my hands are still shaking, even when I clench my fingers, and the room regularly rolls around me, up and down like a barge on high waves.

We have been planning and thinking and whispering. And now the plan is firm in my mind, after having considered every detail. The only thing I worry about is the state my own body is in. What if the trembling doesn't pass? We have only one chance to smuggle the children out of the Institute and hand them over to Will. I'm not very happy about that prospect – I still haven't quite forgiven Will for what he did to Katell. But there is no other option, Arthur has reminded me again and again tonight. The children are too small to walk from here all the way to Brevalaer. It will be a long, tough walk for us too, even though the view from the barred windows reassures me that the weather is getting better.

Besides that, I worry about the actual number of children we can take with us. I counted ten in the infirmary, maybe ten more in the recreation room – all of them Undreamed, too listless to move on their own without constantly spurring them on. And then, there are the others, not yet Undreamed, but locked up in rooms like mine and Arthur's... how many are *they*?

'We can't take more than ten,' I hear myself say. Arthur looks up.

'That means we'd leave a lot of children behind, Nim...'

'I know.' I feel like a traitor. 'But we don't know exactly how much time we have. We can't make much noise. Each child added to the group means more risk of getting caught. More than ten is *too* many.'

Arthur looks at me in silence for a while, until I lower my gaze. But then he says slowly: 'I guess you're right.'

I try to ignore the burning guilt. Of course we will also bring Wolf, and I have no idea of the shape he's in. Wouldn't his body be too weak and emaciated after all those years of imprisonment?

I blame myself for not asking him, but now there's no way around it: tonight I'll have to pick him up. The plan is as complicated as it is nerve-racking: while Arthur will use Sini's stolen key to free Taran, Marci and Judikael, I'll sneak into Cormack's office. I retrace the steps in my mind and try to remember all the details: where the Detection guards are, where that one floorboard is that creaks when you step on it, where I saw Cormack hang up his coat this afternoon. I close my eyes and concentrate on the images of the corridor and his office. After visiting Cormack's office, Arthur and I will head for Platform Zero; he'll disable the CORE, I'll free Wolf. Finally, we will all assemble in Corridor C-1, where the manholes to the sewers are located.

'Nim!'

I start. Arthur doesn't whisper this time, but almost shouts. He points to a page in the atlas, then turns the heavy book over so that I can see what has made him so agitated. Arthur excitedly taps on the map. 'It's not far from here. It's located near a harbour.'

'Camlann!' I lick my lips and taste the word in my mouth. 'If Mum did go back to the island, she must have left from there.'

'We don't know that for sure,' Arthur says reasonably. Yet I can see the excitement in his eyes. My heart is pounding in my throat.

'They arrived in Camlann. Plus, it's a point of departure. Arthur...' I stare at him. 'What do we do?'

His gaze drifts back to the map, to the small harbour located in a deep bay that gradually opens out into the ocean. 'We'll take the children to Will. Then we'll go to Camlann. Agreed?'

'Yes,' I confirm. 'Agreed.'

'Are you sure this is the right stuff?' Arthur whispers to me in the kitchen. 'Is this Pax?'

'I'm sure,' I reply mutely. 'It's the powdered version.'

That makes it easier to mix it into Cormack's food. The white powder forms a thick layer on top of his soup for a moment, but then dissolves into the meal. I know he won't notice the taste, because the children in the Orphanage are given the same in their food.

I put our soup bowls on the table just as Cormack is entering the kitchen. With a weary sigh, he drops down in his seat. I smile at him.

'I've had to chase down Moal all day,' he says unsolicited. 'You have a point, Nimue. That man is a loose cannon.'

That sounds good. I hope he'll do something about it as soon as he wakes up. 'Have some hot food. It helps after a hard day.'

Cormack chuckles for a moment and blows into his bowl. 'You look tired. Have you experienced any fatigue?'

'I think I'm getting stronger every day,' I say. 'But it's a slow process.'

'Don't put too much pressure on yourself until things really improve. Leave chores to others when they become too much. No one will blame you.'

That sounds tempting, but tonight I can't afford to rest.

'How about you, Arthur?' Cormack takes his first bite of soup.

'I read a lot,' my little brother says.

'Great. Reading sharpens the mind.'

'Quite,' Arthur says softly.

I have to force myself to eat my own soup. It would be unwise to escape on an empty stomach, but nervous jitters are racing through my body. I think I can see the same nervousness on Arthur's face. Cormack doesn't notice; he's chatting away about his day while eating the meal I prepared for him. Every time he lifts his spoon from the bowl to his mouth, I tense and stare at him to see if the Pax is beginning to take effect.

Maybe I didn't give him enough. Those doses are meant for young children and Cormack is a full-grown man. I might be able to mix some more of the powder into his second portion of soup, or into his wine when he's not looking. I lean forward across the table, the little bag hidden in my hand.

Cormack rubs his face. He mumbles something unintelligible.

'Is something wrong?' Arthur asks innocently.

Cormack blinks his eyes. 'Ah, I'm such a fool. I know I should lay off that heavy wine after a day like today.' He gets up and for a moment I think he staggers. He recovers, but doesn't look exactly awake anymore. 'I'm going to lie down for a while. Leave the dishes if you guys are too tired.'

'No problem,' I kindly tell him.

'I mean it, Nimue. Don't force yourself too much...' He interrupts himself with a yawn. '... yet. Excuse me.' He disappears into the sitting room, where he plops down on the couch, his long legs sticking out over the edge.

Arthur and I look at each other tensely. After a few minutes of deadly silence, Arthur tiptoes forward to peek at Cormack and whispers: 'Like a baby in a cradle.'

I stretch my muscles and roll my shoulders. 'Ready ... set ...'

Arthur grins. 'Go.'

Like shadows, we slip into the corridor. He smiles at me in the dim light that's still on in the building. It's just bright enough to make out where I put my feet as we descend a flight of stairs. There, I wrap my arms around Arthur in a brief embrace before he turns left, heading for Judikael, and I quietly and quickly make my way to Cormack's office.

The corridor seems longer than usual. I stick as close to the wall as possible, while my trembling hands are getting sticky with sweat. I have a right to be here, I tell myself. I could tell them that I forgot something. Yet I prefer to avoid any confrontation.

I go around the corner. Up ahead, I see the bright light of a torch before I hear the quiet footsteps of two guards wearing the colours of Detection. Their voices are just above a whisper. I hide in an alcove and make myself as small as possible until they have passed me by and disappear behind a couple of wide pillars. I break away from my hiding place and, with a few large strides, I reach the polished wooden door giving access to Cormack's office. I know it won't be locked. I carefully push down the door handle. It gives off a small, plaintive sound that almost sounds human – fortunately not loud enough to bridge the deserted corridor and alert the two guards. I slip inside the room and close the door behind me.

Cormack's office is plunged in darkness, because the faint corridor light doesn't get inside and he hasn't left any other lights on. I decide not to take any chances. I'd rather search in the dark than alert the guards to my presence. I cautiously walk towards his desk and open the drawers. The key is not in there. I do find some new files, barely making out Dr Moal's telltale red stamp on them. With a grim feeling, I tear the papers up into three or four pieces. None of these children will be Undreamed; not tomorrow, not ever.

I throw the shredded papers into the bin next to the desk. Let Cormack find them tomorrow. We'll be gone by then. I turn around and reach for the coat rack near the window, where he has hung his white coat. My hand first slips into one pocket, then into the other, and my fingers touch the flat piece of plastic I was looking for. With a sweet sense of victory, I slip the keycard into my own pocket.

On the way out, something makes me pause. In the dark, the large bookcase on the wall is little more than a shadowy object. My gaze goes over it and lands on the photograph that shocked me so much before. I know we're on a tight schedule. Every minute counts if we are to meet Will on time tonight at the assembly point outside Cima. Still, it's as if my arm moves on its own accord to pick up the picture frame. I hold it close to my face so I can see it. The faces of Benji, Esoldi and Finn are blurry, pink spots. Benji's hair stands out because it's so red. I look at it and feel my heart become strangely empty, as if all the emotions I had intended for this man are quietly washing away. I'll never get to know him; he'll never make peace with Rona. There, in the darkness of a room that once belonged to him, I let him go.

The moment is there, and then it's gone. I put the photograph back in its place and slip out of the office. Dizziness overwhelms me as I hurry along the corridor. I try not to take any breaks, even though the shadowy world is sometimes dancing before my eyes like odd pieces of a puzzle.

Deep breaths. Stay calm. Stay on your feet. My hands are cold. They're still trembling.

I have to hide two more times when guards cross my path. When I reach Platform Zero, the long staircase leading downwards lies before me without any apparent obstacles. The cold light in the corridor illuminates every speck of filth on the walls.

'Wolf,' I say quietly, knocking on his cell door with a trembling fist. 'Are you awake?'

A sound on the other side. 'You came back.'

'Of course.' Without wasting any more time, I take out Cormack's card and press it against the lock. I have to try three times before I can keep my hands steady enough to open it.

The beeping sound breaks the silence too loudly, just like the clicking of the iron lock. I hope no guard was just passing by at the top of the stairs. I resolutely shake off the thought and with a dry mouth, I pull on the heavy door. It opens almost reluctantly, as if the cell wants to keep its prisoner hidden inside.

I hear Wolf's voice as he makes a faint sound, perhaps of surprise. Maybe even in disbelief, temporarily stopping him from speaking.

I take a step back as his silhouette hesitantly comes forward. He stands on the threshold for a moment, then steps over it. The cold light falls on his lean face, his jet-black eyes. I see skin that is darker than mine, long and dull-looking, long hair touching shoulders that once must have been broad and strong. He has sharp features, like a predator. But he's a predator in a cage. Although he's not old, the years of imprisonment have taken their toll. And yet, despite all the traces of neglect, I can see that he was a strong, young man – that he may still be one, for the shadow of his youth is still apparent in his face. And the longer he stares at me, the more clearly I see the smouldering fire in his pupils. Words get lodged in my throat.

'Nimue,' he says hoarsely. He holds out his hand and for a moment, I think he wants to greet me. Then he stumbles forward, as if he has been pushed. I catch him and prevent him from falling onto the concrete floor. At the same moment, the world shifts before my eyes again and I almost fall, too. With effort I manage to keep myself upright. Underneath his clothes, his body feels lean and wiry. He puts a hand on my shoulder, digging his fingers hard into my flesh. I don't protest. After only a few moments, he gets up on his feet. This time he seems be more steady on his feet.

'The light,' he mumbles. I understand: when Sini took me out of my cell, the strip lights on Platform Zero were quite disorienting.

Hollow footsteps are coming down the stairs. 'It's me,' Arthur hisses. For a moment he stops at the bottom of the stairs, staring at Wolf.

'Judikael and the rest?' I ask.

'Ready to go.'

'Then *go*!' I hiss. I push Cormack's key into his hand and Arthur slips past us towards the door leading to the control room. I hear a shrill beeping but decide not to linger any longer. Arthur is probably moving a lot faster than Wolf.

'Come,' I say softly. On impulse, I hold out my hand to Wolf. 'We haven't got much time and we'll have to run.'

He takes my hand without a hint of hesitation. His hand is surprisingly warm, his fingers stronger than I had expected by looking at that skinny body. It helps to suppress my own shivers. We leave and I don't bother closing the iron doors behind us.

Arthur works faster than I thought possible. We're only halfway down the first corridor when the twilight around us changes to an even deeper darkness. Only pale moonlight is coming through the windows. The low humming sound coming from behind the walls is barely audible, and then, that sound dies out too. Against my better judgement, I slow down to allow Arthur to catch up with us. It doesn't take long before he comes running in our direction. His face is slightly visible in the moonlight, and I see his shining eyes.

'And now we *really* have to run,' he whispers.

I try to make as little noise as possible. We leave the first corridor behind, round a sharp corner, when suddenly I hear hurried-sounding voices.

People are coming our way. I hear their footsteps before I see them appear around the corner. The power cut is doing its job. The Caretakers and the men of Detection are emerging from their rooms, all of them confused. The dancing lights of torches appear in front of them.

I yank open the nearest door, but I'm too late: Sini comes around the corner and we are just underneath a window, where the pale moonlight mercilessly betrays our presence. It's as if all my limbs turn to stone.

Her eyes scan Wolf and then bore into mine. I'm shocked when she suddenly comes towards us. She pulls open a door and pushes me inside. I stumble, but Wolf catches me. Arthur rushes in behind us, his mouth hanging open in surprise. The door slams shut.

I'm dizzy and keep still in the empty room, pressed close to Wolf's wiry body. He stares down at me with his large and bewildered black eyes. I slowly shake my head. Even if I dared to make a sound, I wouldn't know what to tell him.

My heartbeat thunders through my body and I have to swallow hard a few times. On the other side of the door, I can hear more footfalls as well as Sini's voice, but I can't understand what she's saying. After a few moments, everything seems to quiet down again. That's a good sign, isn't it? Should I risk taking a peek? I don't have time to worry about this strange turn of events, to even consider that this is some kind of trap. Somewhere in this building, Judikael and the others are also heading for corridor C-1, with a horde of frightened children in tow. With sweaty palms, I pull the door ajar and peek around the corner, into the corridor. They're all gone, undoubtedly on their way to the control room.

'We only have a few minutes,' Arthur warns us, and those practical words pull me out of my musings.

'This way,' I say.

'What is your plan?' Wolf asks.

I look around. We may even have less than a few minutes, and we still have a long way to go before we'll reach the assembly point. Even Sini's unexpected help won't protect us for long. 'There's a sewer running underneath the building. Like you said, we're going underground.'

A grin appears on his weathered face. 'We'll make it.'

I nod, but halfway to the assembly point, I stumble and come to a halt. I notice that I'm out of breath from all the running. I'm incredibly dizzy, even. With a soft groan, I lean against the wall. I close my eyes for a moment, even though I know I shouldn't.

'Nimue.' Wolf growls my name quietly and insistently, like a wild animal.

I shake my head and force myself to open my eyes again. 'I'm fine.'

'Are you ill?'

'Not in the way you think.' I shake my head to clear my vision. It helps – a little. I pull myself together and stand up straight again. 'We're almost there.'

We are just rounding a corner when Marci comes running towards us. I can't help coming to a stop for the second time, this time to peer through the darkness at the small procession of children following behind her. I can make out Taran and Judikael, who are closing the rank. Each of them is pulling three children with them, holding their hands. Children with empty stares, who are walking, but don't seem to realise that they are running for their lives. And then I see Katell clinging to Judikael's arm. Her lips are trembling. She looks thinner than I remember, and she already was so skinny.

I embrace her, trembling with fatigue and relief. She hardly moves. I let go of her and for a moment, her eyes meet mine. I dare to hope that she sees me, *really* sees me, but what I see when I look at those blue irises makes my body temperature drop to a level that's dangerously low. I can't say exactly what's wrong with her, but there's something missing. Something seems to have been drained out of her, and with it, the light in her eyes has completely vanished.

I turn my face away, suddenly ashamed. If I had cured her before, she wouldn't be here now.

'Nim. Nim?'

Startled, I look at Arthur. 'What?'

'You're as white as a ghost fish.'

'Nothing we can do about it.' I rub my cold hands down my cold face. 'It's time to go... is this everyone?'

'Everyone we could bring.' Judikael's face expresses her frustration. 'It's not enough...'

'I know.' I just can't make it better. I look from Katell to Wolf. Now that he's been out of his cell for a bit, he seems to be slowly regaining his strength. He's steadier on his feet. I meet his gaze and again I'm struck by the fire burning in it. 'Turn right. Corridor C-1.'

Arthur pushes Katell towards me and I grab her with my left hand. My little brother lets the other children go first and closes up the rank, like a sheepdog pushing a flock of sheep forward. I fold my fingers around Katell's hand and run down the corridor as fast as I can. Our footsteps are making too much noise. The thought flashes through me, but so be it. C-1 is only two more corridors away and so are the manhole covers. My head spins and spins... Oh, Gwenhael, if only I could rest for a moment.

Wolf roughly grabs my arm. It jolts me out of a kind of trance and to my surprise I slow down. Now he's pulling *me* along, while my other arm is still supporting Katell. With his longer legs, Wolf runs faster than I do and soon I struggle to see anything in the dark surroundings.

'Wait' I squeak, stumbling to a halt. 'I'm falling...'

'Concentrate.' He tightens his grip on my wrist.

I'm trying. We run into corridor C-1 without being bothered by anyone. I'm confident enough to believe that we're going to make it.

I stop at the first manhole cover and bend down to lift it up, but I fall on my knees, groaning. Wolf grabs the edge of the lid and pulls it hard. The manhole opens like the mouth of an iron monster, revealing a deep, dark hole below.

'Jump,' Wolf says.

I'm too afraid. The pit is too dark and too deep – who knows how long the fall will be? If I land wrong, I might break my neck.

Wolf makes an impatient noise, pushes me aside and lowers himself into the hole. A second later he has disappeared.

I push Katell over the edge, then squeeze my eyes shut and slip into the dark behind her. Faster than I was expecting, I feel two arms catching me. Wolf and I roll onto the ground, me panting from all the excitement. I'm still alive. My hands touch something soft, cold and wet on the floor. The stench almost makes my stomach turn. I get up. It's slippery.

From up there, I hear Arthur giving orders, followed by some adamant words from Judikael. I wipe my hands on my trousers and get ready when the children come tumbling down, one by one. We are able to catch most of them, but some take a hard fall and start crying. I drag them up. I have neither the energy nor the time to console them. Finally, Arthur and his friends drop down. They're all mere silhouettes in the dark.

'Keep walking,' Wolf says. I look up. The hole above our heads is like a floating moon. But I don't know how fast I can go. That damned body of mine – that triple-cursed Doctor Moal and his *zh15*! Why do I have to suffer so much from these tremors right *now*? I feel around for someone to support me and find Wolf. Arthur gives new orders: Taran in the middle, Marci and Judikael in the back, us in front. All this takes less than a minute. The children who are not Undreamed crowd around us and force us forward in our wild flight into the sewers. Not far behind us I can suddenly hear loud voices. It won't be long before they realise what has happened.

'Where should we go?' asks Wolf.

'To the west, if you can,' I say. 'These pipes must lead somewhere. Once we're outside, we need to get our bearings and proceed to Cima.'

I listen intently to all the sounds surrounding us. Our own agitated breathing, Wolf's footfalls right next to me, the swampy sound we're making on the floor. I don't want to think about what we're currently wading through.

Without any light coming from above, it is so pitch black that I can't even see my own hands, but I do notice that the tunnel is narrowing.

'Slow down,' I say, slowing my own step. Disgusted, I reach out to the wall of the enormous tube. Everything is round, below as well as above us. 'Not even a yard in width now. We have to duck down and crawl after each other in single file.'

I can tell from the sighs and vomiting noises that the others are following me. The stench of the tunnel is almost too overwhelming to bear. It penetrates all my pores. With difficulty I hold back the acidic bile bubbling up in my throat. 'Arthur?'

'Everything's fine.' His voice sounds reassuringly steady.

'Taran? Marci and Judikael?'

'Present,' whispers Marci.

'So are we,' Taran says. He sounds further away and not as confident as my little brother. 'How long is this corridor?'

I have no idea, and since the rancid smell seems to invade my lungs every time I open my mouth, I make no attempt to tell him. After a while, I realise that I haven't heard Wolf in a while. 'Wolf? Where are you?'

'Here.' His voice comes from the darkness in front of me. 'There seems to be some kind of junction up here.'

By touch, I find the place where he's standing. He's right: around me, the space suddenly widens.

'Do you hear something?' That's Arthur.

Like an alert heron, I stand still and listen. Voices... They can't be coming from above in the Institute. And I think I see a flash of light. It's gone as fast as it came. And then a screeching sound breaks the silence, through the thick sewer walls.

'The CORE is back on,' I conclude.

'Lockdown,' Wolf growls. 'They'll be here soon. Or they'll lock us down.'

'Oh, Saint Gwenhael.' Already I am so sick of the stench and the darkness. I couldn't bear it if they actually locked us in here. I'd rather be in that cell in Platform Zero.

'Think about it,' Wolf says. 'After the junction, they can't know for sure where we went. Right or left?'

'I don't know! Left – go left.'

I feel like we're wandering around the tunnels for days. Sometimes they are wide and high, other times they are so narrow that we have to crawl behind each other on hands and knees. A couple of times, I feel something move and get scared, but it's only rats scurrying away from us. Meanwhile, the smell has become unbearable. It's no longer just urine and excrement – there's also the rotting carcasses of dead animals lying around. The filthy goo is sticking to my hands and clothes. I have never felt so dirty in my entire life.

'Let's rest for a minute.' Arthur breaks our long silence. I welcome the idea. My trembling hands are still not steady and every now and then I stagger as I'm hit by waves of dizziness.

'Here. Lean on me.' Arthur crawls forward and finds me in the darkness. Gratefully I cling to his arm. 'Cormack was right. Exertion isn't good for you.'

'Not now,' I pant. What use is Cormack's advice in the middle of this sewer?

'I'm beginning to fear that there is no exit,' Marci whispers.

'Quiet. Don't scare them.'

Somewhere ahead of us, a couple of rats are running away. I can hear their high-pitched squeaking.

'*They* get in and out of here,' Wolf says. 'There will be an exit. But not a clean one.'

'Come on then,' I sigh. 'Let's try to follow a group of rats.'

Again we plod through the filth and darkness, until I bump into Wolf. 'Quiet,' he hisses, before I can say anything.

Immediately I freeze because I can see it too: behind us, a light flares up in the darkness. It slides across the curved wall of the enormous sewer pipe like a blinking eye.

Detection is living up to its name.

13

SEPARATED

I lunge for my little brother. Without saying a word, I pull him away from the light – left, right, I don't care, as long as they don't see us. I can hear the footsteps of our ragged parade of children following us.

'Light,' I gasp. A few steps ahead of us is a faint glow breaking through the dark. Not the bright glare coming from the searchlights of our pursuers, but pale daylight. We duck down and cautiously crawl towards it. At the end of the tunnel I see a crack in the wall, an opening. I smell water coming through it.

'Where is it coming from?' Wolf asks hoarsely.

'I can't see.' I shuffle forward a bit more. The gunk on me makes me feel like one of the sewer rats. 'I don't hear anything.' I stick my head through the crack. The daylight hurts my eyes. 'There's no one here.'

'You first,' Wolf says. 'Quick!'

'It's very narrow.'

'Squeeze through. They're close.'

Fear grips my heart with its cold fingers. When I look back, I think I see the flickering of searchlights again. In the grey daylight that shines through the crevice, I can see Wolf's face. He's covered in dirt and his dark hair has become even duller than before. I look from him to Arthur. My little brother doesn't look much cleaner, but he somehow finds the strength to grin. 'If you won't go, I will,' he says.

He crawls past me and slips out effortlessly. His soft voice reaches back to us: 'Coast is clear.'

'What are you waiting for?' Wolf growls. He shoves me.

I don't linger any longer and slip through the opening into daylight. I end up in a ditch full of grey water. Dripping wet, I wade over to the bank and pull myself up by long blades of grass. Arthur grabs my hands and helps me with his last bit of strength. All my clothes are covered in stinking goo, my hair is sticking to my face. I have no time to wipe myself clean. I hear a splash behind me and the next moment I find Wolf next to me, just as dirty and unrecognisable as I am. I look at him and start laughing. He and Arthur look like street dogs.

'You should see yourselves,' Arthur says. 'Judikael, over here!' Without paying attention to all the filth, he wades through the ditch again, back to the opening. I follow him. We help the children to climb out one by one. We carry the little ones through the shallow water. Wolf pulls them all up and puts them on the sloping bank with both feet. I marvel at the strength he has in his arms.

As if he senses my gaze, he looks in my direction. In the light of day, he seems more vital than before, driven not only by anger and survival instinct, but spurred on by something else – something that glows deep within his piercing eyes.

I don't have time to wonder about what I'm feeling at that moment. Taran is the last to emerge from the opening. He pushes Katell forward. The Undreamed children let themselves be dragged along without complaining, but don't lend us a hand to make things any easier either. With Arthur's help, Taran hoists Katell up onto the riverbank. My arms and legs are trembling from all the effort and from the anxiety I have experienced in the past few hours. Wolf takes me by the arms and lifts me out of the mud-grey water. My clothes are soaked, the wind howls against my shivering body.

We hear voices coming from the tunnel. Suddenly we find ourselves in a sea of bright lights. Not only do men in uniform emerge from the sewers, but behind us I hear the heavy growling of jeep engines. Headlights illuminate the landscape with a grim light, from which we cannot hide.

'Run,' Arthur whispers. He catches hold of three children. Taran, Marci and Judikael do the same. I slip my arm around Katell and dig my fingers deep into the fabric of her jumper. These cars will be unrelenting, we're exhausted and nerve-racked from all the scrambling through slippery tunnels. But the jeeps can't move fast enough through this stony, hilly landscape that we need to navigate. Arthur runs past me. I'm glad that he has so much energy left, and that he's taking the lead. The children follow him like a flock of runaway sheep. Arthur chooses the most dangerous route: steeply downhill, with sharp turns. When I risk glancing back, I see that some of the jeeps are turning around. A group of men jumps out of the cars. They carry stun guns and follow us on foot.

My head is pounding. Everything seems to be constantly shifting: Arthur ahead of me, Taran somewhere behind him, Katell next to me with her rasping, tired breathing. I stagger. My foot catches behind a stone, I almost fall over, but Wolf grabs me by the collar. That brief moment helps me to catch my breath. Not too far away from us, the Institute seems to be stuck to the hill like a cancerous growth. The pipelines made a slight turn, apparently. I suppress a shudder when I see the barred windows, which look like luminous stains in the early twilight. I look away. I can already see outlines of buildings in the distance, blurred by a blanket of mist or vapour.

And then, unexpectedly, we're torn apart, like a school of fish broken up by a shark. Two jeeps pop up between us, separating the vanguard from the rearguard. I press Katell against me and, without thinking, jump backwards to seek shelter under a meager, protruding rock on the ridge. Ahead of me, I see how Arthur glances back. His face is lit up by headlights. His curls look like a halo. For a moment he looks shocked, before a grim expression appears on his face. He barks out a few orders that I cannot understand. Judikael and Marci go backwards to pull three children away from the jeep just in time. Arthur gestures. He points to the city, which already seems a lot closer. Without missing a beat, Taran takes the lead.

'Nimue.' Wolf is beside me, pressing me closer to the stone and sheltering Katell with his body. 'We're cut off.'

'No.' I frantically search for a way around the cars. Three more jeeps join the two that were already there. The children disappear behind the second ridge. Only Arthur remains, nervous, ready to flee at any moment. I know he's looking for me.

'Let go of me,' I hiss.

Wolf's arms slip off me. I push Katell towards him and drop to my knees in order to crawl up until I reach the top of the hill.

'The girl!' someone shouts. A man from Detection yanks on the steering wheel and the jeep is coming my way. Arthur gestures frantically that I should run in the other direction. I freeze. I'm rooted to the ground. He points to himself and raises his thumbs. Then his head quickly disappears behind the hill.

I have no choice. The jeep is coming at me like a hungry predator. From behind the overhang, Wolf rushes towards me. He roughly takes hold of me and I let him take me away.

We're running. I don't even know how I can still summon up all this strength. Somewhere in my body, I must have some source of energy that I can draw from. Every step hurts my body. Wolf makes us zigzag through the landscape, but the jeep cuts through it like a ship through waves.

Suddenly he pulls me aside. We fall down. I roll over and end up against some rocks. My head lands in the water. I struggle, cough and then sit up, gasping for breath. Wolf presses his hand against my mouth, his fingers pinching my cheeks. I look around and take in our whereabouts. We're in a deep ditch, a dirty stream running through it. Maybe it's natural water, but chances are that it's an extension of the sewage system. The foul stench coming from the water seems to confirm my suspicions. Wolf presses me and Katell against the ground. His dark clothes and black hair form give us at least some shelter in the darkness surrounding us. I stare upwards, frozen in place. The headlights pierce the dark as the jeeps go past us. I can't believe they've lost track of where we are. I pant against Wolf's hand and feel his breath against my cheek. Katell is like a frightened little bird, motionless and silent.

The lights disappear, leaving me with dancing spots in front of my eyes. I don't risk moving yet. The same goes for Wolf, for he's lying heavily on top of me. My belly is starting to get cold in the mud, but where he is touching me, my body feels warm, almost hot. I wonder if he's taking notice of the awkward position we are in. Not that it matters – not if we get caught.

After a while, his hand slips away from my mouth and he rolls off me. I suppress a painful groan. Stiff and aching, I get up. I help Katell to sit up too and take her head between my hands. She's so dirty that she's taken on the perfect camouflage, wearing all the colours of this landscape.

'Are you hurt?' I whisper. 'Do you feel pain anywhere?'

She looks at me with wide, broken eyes and remains silent. That gaze is like a knife through my heart, a poisonous pain fuelling my anger for the Asclepius Congregation. I quickly examine her from top to bottom. She doesn't seem to have broken anything – I only see some bruises and scratches. No, the real damage is *inside*. I'll never be able to heal it.

'They might come back.'

Wolf's practical words snap me out of my thoughts. Of course they'll come back. As soon as they notice that we're no longer on the road ahead of them, they'll turn those damned vehicles right around. I grab Katell more roughly than necessary. 'We have to get to that town.'

'No. That road is now full of Detection.'

I look at him, shocked. 'But that's our only way out!'

'They're hunting us. If you want to help yourself and that little girl, you'll be smart and flee in the other direction.'

I swallow. Maybe he's right. 'But my brother is there. I can't leave him.'

'If he is both fast and smart, they might not catch him. The others had a head start. Nimue.' He puts his hand on my shoulder and I look at him in the faint light of the crescent moon. 'You can't help him now. Make sure you don't get caught yourself.'

I nod, suddenly exhausted. 'I don't know how much energy I have left.'

'You'll have to use every last bit of it. We won't be able to rest tonight.'

14

A Lullaby

For the next three days, we flee from the green jeeps with the silver snake emblem. Three exhausting days that blend together like a haze, broken only by moments of darkness and sunrise. At night, we are too afraid to make a fire. I lie shivering, both from the cold and from the remnants of the illness simmering in my limbs. At the same time, I feel a dark presence pressing against my mind, looking for a weak spot to get through. The constant struggle to shut out its poisonous voice wear me out and weaken me.

I let Wolf guide me. I feel him staring at me regularly, with those eyes that are sometimes more animal-like than human-like. They flick back and forth at every sound, and narrow like a predator spying on its prey. His whole body moves like a vigilant animal. He drives us forward through a barren landscape of hills. The few trees that grow here are sparse and don't look as if they'll be growing leaves any time soon, even though the weather has become much milder. It dawns on me that spring must be near, and that it has been two whole seasons since that terrible night brought the tidal wave to Gwennec.

Two seasons. It feels like an eternity, and yet so recent. I don't feel like there is much left of the old Nimue. I feel sick and defeated. We have escaped the claws of the Asclepius Congregation, but what has it gotten me? A handful of secrets that will only hurt me, the loss of someone who could've been family, children whose souls can never be mended and, on top of all that, I lost track of Arthur. At least I finally know what happened to Sela, but even that knowledge doesn't cheer me up.

You aren't a single step closer to Rona, the Hunter whispers in my mind. *Why don't you just give up?* The spot we have chosen to spend this night is a stony slope with sharp, tall grass. It gives us a bit of shelter against the wind. *You could lie down here and simply not get up. Wouldn't that easier?*

I wrap my arms around Katell, like I have done the last few nights. I feel her shivering a little bit, but she doesn't complain.

'Wolf.' I hold out my hand to him and he comes to lie down against us, his arm resting on my waist. The embarrassment of sleeping like this wore off days ago. This is the only way to keep warm and I'm grateful for the protection against the wind in my back.

I run a hand through Katell's tangled hair and mumble: 'Goodnight.'

I know she won't sleep. She hardly ever seems to; at most she'll slumber in my arms, her eyes closed as if trying to convince herself it's a real sleep. During the past few days she has only grown paler, dead white. That, and her blank stare, worry me more than I have cared to admit to Wolf, but I think he knows. His hand is stroking my arm soothingly. I smile wearily in the darkness descending upon us. I wonder if I might be able to heal Katell – If I might be able to find the missing fragment of her soul somewhere and return it to her, like a missing puzzle piece slotted back into place. Maybe the Fisher King can tell me how. But I haven't dreamed of the Other World for a while now, and I lack the energy to go look for it myself.

'Wolf,' I say again, more quietly than before. I don't want to wake Katell from her little slumber.

He remains silent. He doesn't talk much, I have discovered. He only speaks when he wants to change our route, or to warn us. Usually, he only answers my questions; he doesn't ask many himself. I have realised that I like it. His silence isn't sad, but reassuring. As long as he remains silent, I feel safe.

But now I want to hear his voice, so I insist. 'We need a plan.'

'Are you afraid?' There is no blame in that question, but no compassion either.

I nod. 'Yes, I'm scared.'

'As long as we stay out of the cities we'll have a chance.'

'We can't stay out of the cities forever. I'm hungry. I know Katell is hungry, even if she doesn't say so. And we can't keep drinking rainwater. It's not good for us.'

'You are still alive, right?'

'I have to find Arthur.'

His chest moves against my back and his warm breath brushes against my skin. It makes the hairs in my neck stand up. 'You want to go back to Cami.'

I say nothing. He's right – I regret that I didn't follow Arthur into town every moment I think of it. If we'd been quicker, we might have caught up with Will. We could've been in the Ark right now, hidden and safe, with food and clean water. 'I can't just let him go. We belong together.'

'Then you should look for him,' Wolf says softly. 'He'll probably be looking for you too.'

'With all those jeeps around? He'd be lucky if he made it to Cami.'

'Your brother didn't stay there a moment longer than necessary. Not if he is smart.'

'Of course not,' I mutter. 'After getting to Cami he went with Will.'

'Are you sure about that?'

'It seems like the logical choice to me.'

Wolf seems to think for a moment. 'Brevalaer is too far to walk.'

'That's why it's smart. It's far away.'

'He knows that you can't walk that distance. Would he really have gone without you?'

Now it's my turn to be silent and think. 'Camlann. There's a port nearby called Camlann. We wanted to give the children to Will and travel on to that harbour.'

Wolf shakes his head; I can feel it. 'You shouldn't go to the cities, Nimue.'

'If Arthur has gone there, I should go too.'

Wolf stays silent.

'You don't have to come with me,' I say. 'You've been through so much already. Go the other way. Claim back your freedom.'

'And where would I go?'

'You can go to the Ark. I can't think of a safer place in Brevalaer. And it's in the middle of the swamp, among the trees. I think you'll like it there.'

'Where is Camlann?' he asks reluctantly.

'To the west.' I lift my arm from Katell and carefully pull my backpack towards me. I have to dig around for a moment before my fingers locate what I'm looking for, and I pull out Jodoc's compass. I can't see the needle in the dark, but I know it will spin and spin and then find north. As sure as the arrow on the compass, I must find Arthur, I decide. And as true as the north star that never wanders, we must continue on our way until we reach Rona.

For a long time, Wolf and I are both silent. I think he's fallen asleep. I still feel cold, but it's a distant enemy that I can put out of my mind for a long moment.

Suddenly his head whips forward so that his mouth brushes against my ear. 'I know what you are.'

Tired, dizzy and sick, but he probably doesn't mean that.

'I have read your book. The whole story.' He doesn't even sound apologetic.

I swallow. 'That was bound to happen when I gave it to you for safekeeping.'

'I understand why the Others speak to you.' There is a longing kind of desire in his voice – it almost sounds like jealousy.

'I hardly understand it myself.'

'You don't? You don't understand that there's something inside you that is not human?'

I smile vaguely and shake my head. 'I'm as human as you and Katell.'

His soft laugh vibrates against me pleasantly. 'I'm not sure I'm quite human anymore. Not after everything that happened.'

'Is that why you call yourself Wolf?'

'Hm.' It's a soft sound, neither a denial nor a confirmation. Then he's silent again, his arm gently pulling me closer to him, and I envelop myself in his warmth. I stop asking questions. My eyes fall closed. In the darkness, in the silence, I lay my head to rest.

He's getting much too close. He's touching you in an inappropriate way. Get rid of him quickly, or you will find yourself in danger.

I ignore the dark voice and fall asleep, exhausted.

For the first time in days, Katell speaks. Her face twists into a unsatisfied grimace and she clamps her hand down on her nose. 'The air smells.'

'That's Camlann.' Wolf pulls up his frayed jumper to his nose to protect himself from the suffocating smoke.

The sky looks cloudy and it's like fog is clinging to the ground, but it must be fumes from the factories. It makes it difficult to breathe -even with my jumper in front of my nose, it still seems to be entering my lungs.

'A friend told me that you need a mask to walk around here safely,' I say. The fabric of our clothes only seems like a wafer-thin shield.

'It's not healthy,' Wolf says. 'But needing a mask is an exaggeration.'

'I miss the sea.'

Katell surprises me by saying: 'Me too.' Her voice sounds reedy.

Wolf puts an arm around me, and takes Katell's hand. A little roughly, I notice, but she doesn't flinch and willingly lets herself be pulled along. As for myself, the spot where his arm rests against my body feels pleasant. Katell and I are getting weaker and weaker, but it seems as though Wolf has been gaining strength over the past few days. The freedom and the open air – however polluted – are doing him good.

'It'll take us the whole afternoon before we get there,' he says. 'You'll get fresh water, Katell. And food, and a sheltered place to sleep.'

'I thought you didn't want to go to town,' I remark.

He looks down at me. His scruffy beard is as dark as his hair. 'I see now that we have no choice. The girl has grown weak.'

And so have you, I hear him think. I can only imagine what I look like in his eyes: shaky, with rings under my eyes and the remnants of the sewer still stuck in my clothes and hair. Too many times I have to pause because an attack of dizziness and nausea will overwhelm me.

He thinks you are weak. He'll leave you when it suits him.

'Maybe Arthur is waiting for us there,' I say loudly, to silence the voice in my mind.

We enter Camlann from the east, along a poorly paved road with houses that lean against each other, built of grey stones or corrugated iron and wooden planks that barely slot together. Shutters are closed against the falling dusk. A bit of moss grows on the roofs here and there, and the wooden doors are painted green or red, without any paint peeling off. This neighbourhood must be new, probably built after Rona, Benji and Esoldi first docked in the port.

Everything tells me that this is a harbour town, and despite the unfamiliar, dark alleyways, I feel more at ease than I have in weeks. Houses are decorated with strings of shells and starfish; the oil lamps lighting the main streets are the same large glass bulbs we used as ship lanterns in Gwennec. Fishing nets are strung between the roofs when in need of repairing. Despite the lingering, acrid smell of the factories, I catch more and more familiar scents of home: the smell of fish, which can penetrate almost anything, the salt and brine, the tar smeared on boats, and the iodine-like smell of seaweed.

I'm so busy taking in all the smells that I don't realise I'm slowing down. It's only when the world suddenly jerks to the right and I start to shake that I realise that Katell and Wolf have stopped in their tracks. Wolf is looking at me with a worried expression. I look down at my hands. I can't hold them still; they're trembling like reeds in the wind.

'It's the hunger,' I say weakly.

We both know it's not true. Still, he puts a reassuring arm around my shoulders as he takes me along.

'First shelter, then food.'

He finds us an old barn, far away from the town centre and even further away from the harbour. Here, the sea air barely reaches me. I can only smell rotting wood and damp hay that's piled up in bales. Meanwhile, I'm leaning heavily on Wolf's arm. He lowers me against the bales and lets Katell sit down beside me. I want to embrace the girl, but my limbs suddenly seem to weigh a ton.

'Keep still,' he says.

I have little choice. As soon as I try to focus and look around, the barn starts to spin like that yellow kite on the beach, so long ago in Gwennec. I seem to have no anchor left and helplessly twirl along.

To prevent myself from falling, I close my eyes and take a deep breath. That seems to steady me a little.

'I'll be back soon,' Wolf says.

I want to say that he shouldn't go out alone. There might be cars from Detection nearby, something else may happen – after all, what do we know about this city except the few details my young mother wrote down about it? I hear the sound of his footsteps moving away from me, the door creaking. Katell and I are alone.

I open my eyes. The world finally stops spinning. *For now. Aren't you too weak to travel? You are infected, admit it. Let him look for scraps of food in the bins; even a full meal won't cure you. Worthless. You are worthless.* I look at my hands in the twilight of the barn. *Can you still help people with those hands? Rona has failed, but you – you are even weaker than her.*

The Hunter has discovered that my body doesn't succumb so easily and now he's trying to influence me this way. As long as I don't know how to get rid of him, I must ignore him. My throat is dry. I swallow and get up. My gaze wanders through the small room. On the wall is a tattered fishing net. I notice that I look at it as if I'm inspecting it. You don't just throw nets away and this one looks unused. But the ropes are thin and probably rotting. Beneath it is a grey bundle of something. When I pick it up, a damp stench emanates from it. The underside is dry and soft. It is sheepskin, large enough to wear on my shoulders like a cloak.

The more I look around, the more traces of habitation I see. There's a small fireplace, hardly what I'd call a hearth, with a low pile of firewood next to it, and a ship lantern that has turned green from algae. I open the lower compartment and discover a little bit of oil. There is even some oil left in a barrel next to it, just enough to fill the lamp again. Under a layer of dust I find a matchbox. There are still three matches in it, not very dry anymore. Whoever was using this shelter hasn't been around for a long time. I squat down on the ground and wipe the ashes and dirt from the fire pit with my bare hands, which I then wipe on my trousers. It takes a long time before I get the damp match to ignite. Only when the fire is strong enough so it won't be blown out by a random gust of wind do I turn to the lamp. The second match makes it light up a little bit. The dirt gives the light a mysterious, green colour, as if it were glowing seawater. I put the lamp next to the door. Now that we have light and warmth, the barn is starting to feel like a pleasant refuge. There is no chimney, but smoke escapes through the many holes and cracks in the roof.

Tired from the small effort, I return to the hay bales and hold out a hand to Katell. 'Come here.'

She obeys without any enthusiasm. I pull her towards me so that the flames are near enough to warm her up. 'Katell, you can still understand me, can't you?' I ask softly.

'Yes.'

I stroke her messy hair. 'How are you feeling?'

Her skinny shoulders go up and down in a shrug.

'Surely you must feel something?' I insist. 'Are you cold? Are you tired, hungry?'

'Hungry.'

I nod. 'Hopefully Wolf will do something about that.'

'Nimue ...'

I'm surprised when she utters my name. 'What is it?'

Although she doesn't look at me, I notice how she hesitates. As if searching for words that are difficult to grasp. 'I remember Gwennec. I remember ... I remember everything.'

I stay quiet, afraid that one word from me will silence her again.

'I think there was a room. And a knife. They injected something in my arm ... Then it was gone.'

'What was gone, Katell?'

She seems unable or unwilling to say. It looks like she's confused. I find a trace of fear on her face as she turns towards me.

'It's alright,' I mumble, putting my arms around her. She presses her face into my dirty jumper, but I can't feel her crying. I want to promise her that things will be alright. That she's safe. That this time, I'll really make sure no one can imprison her or hurt her ever again. But the words get lodged in my throat. How can I promise any of that? Instead, I say hoarsely: 'You're going home, Katell. You, and Arthur, and me ... one day we'll all go back to Gwennec.'

Katell is silent.

I wake up from my slumber when the door of the barn creaks and Wolf enters. His gaze immediately goes to the fire. 'They might see tha.'

'I had to,' I groan as I'm getting up. 'We can't get through another freezing night. We need warmth.'

The smoke makes him squint his eyes. Despite the many holes and cracks, it has now filled the entire barn. After a moment, he nods, before he pulls out a bundle of something from under his jumper. 'I took what I could find.'

My stomach gives sort of a triumphant growl and I look at what he is laying out on the floor: some slices of bread, and three salted fish. A plastic bottle full of clean water. Katell surprises me by crawling forward, faster than me, and snatching the bottle.

'Watch out,' I warn her, when I notice that in her utter thirst, she almost rips the cap off the bottle and spills the water onto the floor. I quickly take off the cap for her. 'Drink slowly; otherwise there won't be any left for us.'

I don't think she hears me. Her throat is bobbing up and down and water is dripping down her chin. I know she's dehydrated.

'Enough. Katell, that's enough.' Carefully, I grab the bottle and pull it out of her grasp. She makes a desperate, almost feral sound. 'I'm sorry,' I say sincerely. 'Here, eat. That'll make you feel better too.'

With the same eagerness, the girl looks at the piece of bread and the fish that I hand her. I put the bottle to my own lips and close my eyes. The water feels cool and healing against my cracked lips. My bone-dry palate becomes moist again. I do understand Katell – once I'm drinking, I don't want to stop. My body seems to absorb the water like dry earth sucking up rainfall; it's gone far too soon. Far too soon I have to force myself to stop. Grudgingly, I give what is left to Wolf. He drinks the rest and then we eat the bits of food he managed to scrape together. For a moment I'm only focused on that. I lick the fat of the fish from my lips, stuff the bread into my mouth so fast I almost choke on the dry crusts, and when it's all gone, I still stare hungrily at the spot where all that fantastic food just was. As if my desire is strong enough to magically conjure up more of it.

'In the morning, I can find more,' Wolf promises.

'How did you even get this?'

He smiles wearily. 'I can be a stray dog, if need be.'

Slowly, my body begins to relax. The gnawing hunger has dulled somewhat. Now that I'm getting sleepy, I even begin to forget the feeling. The warm light is making the barn look cosier and more comfortable. It has been so long since I last felt like this. The CORE in the Ark was unreliable and always spread this unpleasant, dry air. The rooms and corridors of the Asclepius Congregation were pleasant enough, but neither cosy nor comfortable, and Cormack's own quarters were nothing like the house I was used to in Gwennec. Now, with that old net on the wall and the ship lamp by the door, I can pretend to be home. I even imagine that I can feel the eternal tides of the sea again. I'm called by that sea to go to the harbour, I can feel it in my blood. *Tomorrow*, I think sleepily. *Tomorrow, I will come to you.*

Even the damp hay, which made me nauseous at first, is starting to smell good. At least it's drowning out the factory smell outside.

Katell is napping on the sheepskin. The scraps of food seems to have satisfied her. For a while, I just lie there listening to her breathing, which is quiet and regular. 'I believe she's actually asleep.'

'She's exhausted,' Wolf says.

'All the better. I have a feeling that the Undreamed can no longer find real inner peace.'

Wolf gets up and moves around some hay bales, so that we are lying in the middle of some kind of bed, protected by a low wall. I let out a sigh.

'You say that the Undreamed have lost their connection with the Other World,' he states.

I nod, sleepily. 'As if the connection has been cut. Moal talked about an antenna. Katell said...' I hesitate. Thinking about what happened to her still makes me nauseous. 'I think she had surgery.'

He lowers himself next to me and hesitates for a moment. His hand is close to my face, as if he wanted to stroke my cheek, then thought better of it. My heart suddenly skips a beat when I look at him. In the warm light of the room, his face seems smoother. His eyes are as deep as a moonless night.

'This world and the Other World are like two trees.' His hesitant hand moves to mine, which is lying on my stomach. He raises my arm in the air. His skin feels rough. His fingers intertwine with mine. 'Two trees, leaning into each other, with roots and branches that keep them balanced. People like you and me are standing on the far edge. We balance on the branches, where the shift takes place, without always knowing where one tree ends and the other begins.' His fingertips touch mine. 'Those are the branches – that's where we both stand. Can you see it?'

'I see it.' I'm desperate for more water, because my mouth is so dry again.

'Everyone is part of a branch, and one branch takes hold of the other. If one tree falls over, we'll all fall.'

I nod. That's what the Fisher King said.

'This girl is a cut-off branch,' he says, sounding defeated. He lowers our arms without disconnecting his fingers from mine.

'Can't we help her?'

He shakes his head. The hay rustles. 'You can't nail a branch to a trunk and hope it will grow back...' He pauses. 'I'm sorry, Nimue.'

I'm too exhausted to cry. Still, my eyes squeeze out a few tears. He notices, because this time he finally puts his hand against my cheek. I roll towards him and bury my face in his neck. We're surrounded by the smell of sweat and fire. Strangely enough, it's not unpleasant. He holds me close and does not try to comfort me with words. Soon, sleep wraps itself around me and pulls me down like an anchor towards the abyss.

The grassland is almost completely bare – the rocks and hills, sharp peaks and valleys shrouded in shadows, where no life stirs. The few crops that grow there have an unwholesome colour. There are some trees up ahead with scaly trunks, the branches like bone-like claws.

It's not these surroundings, but the sound that makes the hairs on my arms stand on end. A hissing sound at regular intervals, as though the air is escaping from a closed vessel somewhere. I feel heat under the soles of my feet – my shoes have disappeared. I look down and see vapour rising from the ground.

Sssssss

All around me, the same cloudy damps rise up.

I cover my nose with my hand and start walking. In the distance, I think I can see the outline of a tower. Is that where the Fisher King lives? It occurs to me that this could be the same valley. The same surroundings, but unrecognisable. Desolate areas that now exude a vicious ambience. I don't feel welcome here; every time the shattered soil forces up a new vapour and scorches my feet, I'm forced to run faster.

I don't know exactly when I first became aware of the prying eyes. When I turn around, I see nothing. My eyes search the valley. The protruding rocks might hide all sorts of creatures, but no matter how hard I strain my eyes, the entire landscape seems to be frozen in a single moment of time. Only the vapours break the silence with their unpredictable outbursts.

I walk on towards the tower. That's my only point of reference. I remember the dull beauty of the Fisher King, emaciated and chained to his throne. If I can reach him somehow, this desolate wasteland might not hurt me. I have to be fast ...

The moment I start to run, I feel it: a sweltering breath in my neck. I scream and turn around again. Finally, I see it – a flash of a creature in the corner of my eye. It has disappeared too quickly for me to see it clearly, but I recognise the pointy teeth set in a wide, grinning mouth. I recognise those fingernails that could tear through the leathery skin of a whale.

I flee without thinking. I no longer care that the fumes are scorching my flesh. I clamber up, stumbling across stones and ridges, sharp edges cut me open and make me bleed. Instinctively, I know that it's my blood that he's after. The Hunter knows my scent and he has dozens of eyes with which he can trace me.

I stumble. I curse. Fast as lightning, he lands on my back. He emits the stench of rotting flesh. I gag and struggle against him with all my strength. He bends down and plants his arms on either sides of my face. The eyeballs in his hands roll up and look at me without blinking. I gasp in fear.

'Run like a wolf, flee like a fish. Up or down, your scent is mine.'

It's shocking to hear him speaking out loud, after hearing his voice in my head for days.

'I will eat you, child of the sea. I will rip the flesh from your bones with my teeth. I will toss your bones aside like fish guts. I will gobble up your salty blood and I will

fortify myself with it. Fast though you may be, I will catch you in the dark crevices of your sleep eventually.'

He lowers his head towards my neck. His smell now fills my lungs completely and I'm unable to breathe. Everything is rotten; it seems to seep in through my nose and destroy me from within. His breath is scorching hot. Without any more warning, he sinks his teeth into the flesh of my shoulder.

I can breathe once more, and scream.

'Nimue!'

I shoot up. Where am I? There is a faint glow of fire, not enough to help me find my bearings. After a few panicky heartbeats, I remember that I'm in the barn, that it's night, and that I'm here with Wolf and Katell.

'The Hunter! He had me.' My jaws clench together. 'He was going to tear me apart ...'

Two arms embrace me from behind. 'It's alright.'

Instinctively, I cower, as if it were the Hunter who wants to sink his teeth into my body again. Wolf doesn't loosen his grip. 'There is no Hunter here. You are awake and you are safe.'

I let his words sink in. Finally, I let myself collapse in his arms, exhausted. 'There *is* a Hunter there. He's waiting for me on the other side.'

'Forget him. He can't do anything to you.'

'I think he can,' I say, shuddering with fear. 'As soon as I close my eyes.'

'You are a shaman, Nimue. So tell him to go away.'

I laugh nervously, without any joy. 'You don't understand. I can't... I won't be able to sleep anymore.'

'You have to. You must gain strength for tomorrow.'

'But...'

'Sssh. Hush now, *lille bekk. Skogen har gått i seng, og i mørket hyler ulven...*'

His warmth, his arms, his voice murmuring unfamiliar words in my ear – for a while, these are the only things that shield me from the terrible images of my nightmare.

After a while, he falls silent.

'Don't stop,' I mutter. I calmed down a little, but I'm still too afraid to go back to sleep.

He loosens his grip around my waist. I hear him breathing and feel the warm air on my neck as he rests his chin on my head. His voice is still hoarse, probably from all those years in Platform Zero. But he keeps talking softly to me and it starts to sound like a melody. A simple song, simple words. I close my eyes and concentrate on the sound.

Hush now, little creek,
the forest slumbers light.
And the wolves cry,
cry out in the night.
Be still, do not be afraid,
of the night, so deep and dark and blue.

In my arms you are protected,
no animal will harm you.

His arms around me and his warm breath in my hair feel nice and familiar. Slowly, my body seems to warm up, until I feel like I'm burning inside. And I want more than just his embrace and his song. I turn around and steel his voice away with a kiss.

His stubbly beard feels as rough as sandpaper when I rub my cheek against his. He breathes my name against my skin, sending shivers down my spine. The way he says my name... I have never heard it before. His one hand slowly moves to my face. His rough fingers tenderly trail my jawline, touching me as if he were a blind man feeling a sculpture. I feel his other hand finding its way to my waist, but then, he stops. His mouth falls away.

'We can't do this.'

The air is sweet and dark, the fire extinguished and leaving only red, smouldering coals. I let myself fall backwards into the hay. 'We *can* do this.'

'You are young.'

He lowers himself onto me and leans on his arms. We're so low to the ground, the darkness turns him into a mere shadow.

'You're not that old.' I open my arms for him. I want to pull him closer and feel him tremble. It conjures up a smile on my lips, a smile he probably won't have seen.

'And Katell?'

'She's asleep.'

And it has been so long since I could think of anything else but the many complications of my journey – the Asclepius Congregation, and my confusing family history. The barn is a shelter that keeps all these things out, at least for tonight. And I'm filled with a sudden desire that I don't want to fight. When I try to pull him closer again, he doesn't resist. His mouth finds mine.

I see the gleam in his eyes. I hear and feel him when he gasps against my neck.

Something is happening between us, in the blood that rushes through our bodies. In our hands that touch and explore. I'm vaguely aware that the small amount of lamp oil we've got left will burn up sometime during the night. That the barn will then be swallowed up by total darkness. And I know that the sea is beating with her waves against the shoreline. Pushing and pulling. A deep, dark primal sound that I can feel in my deepest, darkest places.

15

CAMLANN HARBOUR

A cold draught wakes me up. Wolf is still asleep and I look at him. The set of his mouth is relaxed. One hand is on his stomach, the other propped under his head.

The hay is prickly against my bare skin. Slowly, so I don't wake him, I put on my T-shirt, jumper and trousers. I sit down on one of the bales that form a wall between us and the rest of the barn, and put on my boots. In the morning light coming through the cracks in the wall, Wolf looks very pale. His dark hair stands out against his white skin. He has been so strong these past few days whenever I was weakened, exhausted and drained like a leaking barrel. I hope he can sleep away the circles under his eyes.

I kneel down by his side and tenderly slide my lips over his warm, rough cheek. His eyelashes flutter. I withdraw silently and take a moment to pull the sheepskin up over Katell, which she has shrugged off in her sleep. Without Wolf and Katell, I might not have had the motivation to walk all this way to Camlann. My two guardian angels. My only friends, now that I have lost my little brother.

The thought of losing Arthur lances through me. Where is he now? What is he doing? Is he safe? Merciful Gwenhael, I hope he's safe and warm. And nearby. Please, let him come our way. Despite these worries, I feel remarkably well-rested. There's only an echo of dizziness left when I stand up a little too quickly. Within a few seconds, it fades.

My stomach growls loudly. Food. Water. I decide not to fetch another meal from the garbage bins – not if we don't have to. Camlann is a harbour city, which means fishermen are at work.

Again I bend down, this time to brush Wolf's shaggy hair from his forehead. He looks up and finds my gaze. I notice that I momentarily forget to breathe. For a moment, we just look at each other.

'What are you going to do?'

'It's my turn to take care of you. I'll be back before dark.'

He doesn't tell me to be careful. He gets up and tears off a piece of his shirt. 'Tie this around your hair.'

He is right. With my red curls, I stand out like a goldfish among mackerel. I use a piece of string from one of the hay bales to tie my hair tightly back and then hide it under the not-so-clean cloth. The cloth may be dirty, but Wolf's scent clings to it. I smile.

'Make sure you're back before sunset, or I'll come looking for you.'

I nod and step out of the barn. The silvery grey morning light falls on my face and warms me up a little. I close my eyes and follow my nose. The smell of salt, brine and tar. The smell of fish.

Camlann is built on a hill. Narrow, cobbled streets and painted houses, which squeeze against each other, make me feel both sheltered and hemmed in. The people passing by seem to easily float past me. When one or two of them keep their gaze on me a bit too long, I manage to slip away quickly into one of the side alleys. The street between the houses goes down steeply. I stop for a moment. I now have an unobstructed view of the broad, blue streak of sea and the nearby horizon. The sight of it awakens something in me. It's as if I can hear the voice of the sea. Not just in my head, but in my whole body: *there you are.*

Yes, I answer without thinking. *I have come.*

Camlann Harbour is so big it would gobble up the whole of Gwennec. I look at the docks, where boats are moored like cows at the cattle market. Not just fishing boats. Sailing yachts, slender merchant ships, three-masted ships with colourfully painted hulls, heavy, flat barges that can bridge the distance of the rough open waters around Central Europe and the Periphery. I don't know what they are until I see the towering barrels lifted up by iron aerial work platforms. Oil, it occurs to me. The oil platforms, like the Oak Field which I grew up with, transport all their oil to this city, from where the oil barrels are then shipped via the open sea or inland rivers to other parts of Central Europe.

I peer over to my left, where I spot fishing boats more familiar to me. Simple sailing boats with one mast and a shallow hold, made to sail across the deep sea in calm water, the nets spread out on either side to catch schools of fish in their flight. Now all the masts pointedare upright without their sails, like a bunch of bare tree trunks.

I'm looking for a way down. The further I descend, the more hustle and bustle surrounds me. At the edge of the harbour, hawkers have put up their stalls. They're selling steaming, hot soup with large chunks of meat floating in it, cheap toys made of wood and tin, or freshly baked waffles, the smell of which almost makes me want to steal one. I suppress the thought and force myself to walk on.

It turns out to be more difficult than I thought to find a job for a day. Most of the fishermen have already left. Those who are still on shore look at me with an expression that makes it clear they expect little help from a girl like me. No wonder. My clothes are still sticky from the dried mud and my face must not be very clean either. When I propose to a stocky sailor's wife with three toddlers around her to help her clean her barrel of mackerel, I earn a few cents. It's probably just enough to buy two bottles of water. I slip the coins into my sock, out of reach for pickpockets and children I see running around. After a few hours, the woman sends me away and I wander through the harbour again.

I've only gotten more hungry. Just as I'm asking myself if it would be so wrong for me to spend a little of the money and buy one of those sweet waffles, I hear a scream. Automatically, I step back, away from the sound. A heartbeat later, a man-sized, wooden barrel falls down and smashes into the stones where I was standing just a moment ago. Startled, I stare upwards. The barrel was attached to a wrapper and a rope, but the rope has clearly snapped and the wrapper must have come loose.

A group of startled people gather around me. I see a couple of children slip between their legs and run off with handfuls of floundering fish, quick as rats. I open my mouth to shout and warn them – the black, rotting edges on their gills and fins show that the fish are infected.

'Out of the way! Rotten jellyfish, I have slaved away for this haul. Go away!'

The people around me are shoved aside and start walk away, shrugging their shoulders. I stay where I am.

'Damned rain.' The man who has come rushing towards me looks at me as if we have known each other for years and just happened to bump into each other. 'Bad for the ropes.'

He is heavily built, wearing sturdy shoes and trousers of good quality. His hair is bushy and grey, like his eyebrows, and his head is partly covered by a red crocheted hat. As he talks to me, he shifts something in his mouth with his tongue from one side to the other. Chewing tobacco, I guess. In Gwennec, it's rare and far too expensive, but here in Camlann I have seen several people chewing it.

He studies the scattered fish on the ground and touches them with his foot. 'A lot of rot. But that's a common occurrence these days, I'm afraid.'

'You have a lot of sorting out to do.' I glance up at the sky. The sun is a blurry orb behind the factory fumes rising from atop the hill behind the city. I'm estimating we still have a few hours of daylight left, before the same fumes usher in an early evening. 'If I help you, you will be ready before dark.'

The fisherman looks at me as if he's only now really noticing me. 'What would you know about that?'

'I'm a fisherwoman.'

'Are you hoping for a few cents? Too bad, lassie. I can't pay you anything.'

I already have some money, but that's for uncontaminated water. I lick the salty taste from my lips. 'Give me a small part of your catch, only enough to eat. I'm with my little sister and a friend.'

The fisherman takes me in for a moment. 'On a journey? In these trying times?'

I shrug my shoulders.

'Where to?'

'Far away,' I say vaguely.

'You're out of your mind, what with the Black Influenza lurking. But who am I to refuse a few hungry stomachs? Go on then, make sure I'm done before dark.' He drags an empty iron barrel off his ship and opens the lid. It has black burn marks on it. 'That one is for the rotten fish.'

His boat is not much bigger than *The Ragdoll*, just better maintained. I can't find any hastily patched-up holes in the hull, and the furled sail looks pristine. *The Herring Gull*, it says on the side in white paint.

I grab a couple of pitch-black fish by the tips of their fins and throw them into the empty barrel. They make a wet, floppy sound against the bottom. I don't feel like talking much. The catch has to be sorted, the infected fish burned and the good ones cut open and cleaned so they can be rubbed with brine. Things I could practically do blindfolded. Hunger urges me to work fast.

'Here.' The fisherman pushes a knife into my hands. I start gutting the healthy catch, one by one.

'Where are you from?' he asks.

'From far away,' I say, without looking up.

He grunts softly. 'I spent thirty years at this harbour, from morning to night. I know all the familiar faces and immediately pick out the strangers. Not many people here come from far away.'

It takes me a while to digest his words. Again, I lick my lips. 'Did you by any chance see three strangers dock here about fifteen years ago? A red-haired boy, and a girl with black hair? They must have looked disoriented...'

The fisherman takes his time. He must notice that I'm tense and performs a short spiel by frowning, scratching his forehead under his crocheted cap and stretching the silence to its limit. Finally, he peers at my arms, which are hanging idly in the fish barrel. I quickly snatch up a slowly thrashing cat-sized fish and slice it open with one smooth movement of my borrowed knife. The fisherman looks satisfied.

'I remember one couple. Half the town was dying of the Black Influenza and they wondered where they could spend the night. Black hair like a raven. A girl she was, hardly a woman yet. She was exhausted, pale, and almost starved to death. But there was something about her... Remarkable. Very remarkable. I showed them the way to the refectory, but I don't think they stuck around very long. Shark blood! Are you paying attention, las?'

I start and notice that I was about to throw a fish leaking with pus into the barrel of good fish. Just in time, I prevent the infected fish from ruining the healthy catch. 'Sorry,' I mutter, with a reddened face.

'You're not going to cost me wages and a hard day's work,' the fisherman growls. He lights a match and throws it into the second barrel. The fire starts slowly and then spreads. The smell is unbearable, but it has to be done. Like the fisherman, I pull the fabric of my jumper up over my nose to prevent breathing in too much of the dark smoke.

At home, I felt a growing distaste for fishery. That feeling is surreal to me now. For this *is* my life; these motions, these smells, the feeling of raw fish between my fingers. The slippery blood that gushes onto my hands when I push my knife into the soft fish belly, and the salt that somehow always ends up in my mouth. I would give everything to return to that simple life, when my biggest concerns were how much we would catch that day and how much it would earn us. Or whether we could get *The Ragdoll* to sail for another week before it really needed a new coat of tar, because that would mean extra days of unemployment.

'Lassie? Are you still listening?'

I mumble an answer without really listening.

'I saw her one more time, you know. Later.' He looks slightly offended that I do prick up my ears for that comment. But apparently he finds it worth putting his pride aside for, because he continues: 'That must have been about ten years ago now. She had no man by her side this time. And she looked as exhausted as when I first saw her. A strange whisp of a thing. But still beautiful.'

This sudden revelation takes my breath away. 'What was she doing here?'

He raises his grey, bushy eyebrows. 'Not much, if my memory serves me right. She staggered onto the pier like a drunk. But she looked happy. Or relieved. What a sight. White as a ghost fish, but eyes like that of a seal.'

'Did you speak to her at all?'

'No, I didn't.' He looks at me inquiringly. 'What do you care anyway?'

I swallow and throw a handful of entrails into the fire. 'She is my mother.'

'Well, I'll be darned.' He looks at me incredulously. His eyes take in my face and I know he's trying to determine whether I might also have night-black hair under my headscarf. 'Jellyfish and sharks, are you sure? You don't look like her at all.'

I manage to smile. 'Her name is Rona.'

'*Rona*.' He licks his lips, as if tasting her name. 'So where did she go?'

I shrug. 'I never saw her again.'

'Jellyfish and sharks,' he repeats, milder this time. He falls silent for a while, taking a heavy barrel of brine and gesturing for me to help. I grease the cut fish bellies, one by one. 'Well, wherever she went, she raised you a decent fisher girl.'

'My father taught me. In Gwennec.'

'Gwennec – huh. The Periphery? How is the price of fish there?'

I can't help laughing. Such an everyday question, things I haven't talked about for weeks. 'It's okay, it keeps us alive. What about up here?'

He spits out his chewing tobacco and shrugs. 'Up, down, up. Right now it's up. That's about the only good thing I can say about the new outbreaks. Black Influenza, storms – half the fishermen no longer risk going to sea every day. Only when it's smooth as a lake out there.'

'It's not storm season yet,' I say in surprise.

'Storm season has come early this year. Do you see that?' He points to the horizon, where threatening, black clouds rise up like a barricade. 'That one's been brewing for days. I have a cousin inland. After tomorrow's sail, I think I'll camp out there for a week or so. You and your sister better leave here too.' He nods at the storm clouds again. 'If that erupts, you don't want to be anywhere near the coast.'

I look at the horizon with a mixture of unease and despair. 'I've seen worse.'

'It will get worse. Believe me, las. When *this* storm season arrives, it'll be with a force that shatters the earth.'

When all the fish have been salted and put away, I collect my share of the fish into an old bucket he gives me, and exchange my coins for water at a stall further on. I try not to let his words evoke a fear in me that seems to grow as the sun is slowly smothered.

Fortunately, I notice the cars before the drivers have seen me. It's a small procession, just four or five cars with the shiny logo of the Asclepius Congregation on the doors. They trail after each other slowly like a black snake, along the uphill street I have to cross.

I stare at the cars for a while before I discreetly retreat from the open docks, fleeing into the area with the colourfully painted fishermen cottages. My heart is beating fast. If I run, I might have a chance to slip past them unnoticed, as long as my hair stays hidden under the headscarf. I could drop the heavy bucket of fish and make a quick run back to the barn. But then I'd lose our dinner.

I glance at the car closing the line, chewing my lower lip. Or I could go *around* the docks and find a way up through the south side of town, and return to Wolf and Katell through the narrow alleys winding between the rows of houses. But it will soon get dark, and I don't have a lamp – and it's not a pleasant prospect to be hopelessly lost in this town.

With a groan, I lift the bucket and walk past the stalls. The vendors are packing up their goods. I look around me. No one is paying attention to me. I take a few steps forward to cross the last open section of the docks and see the dark presence too late. He emerges from behind a stack of man-sized crates. The falling darkness and his black clothes and hood make it impossible to see who it is. He grabs me and pulls me backwards. A hand is clasped over my mouth, which prevents me from screaming. I let the bucket clatter to the ground. The dead fish spills onto the pavement as I struggle to escape like a freshly caught fish.

He turns me around and roughly shoves me into one of the alleys, out of sight of the harbour. My attempts to free myself work against me, because I stumble and hit the wall with my back. For a moment, pain shoots through my body like lightning. I gasp for breath.

The dark figure comes to stand in front of me. 'Nimue. It's me!' He pulls back the hood and reveals a head with dark hair and shadowy eyes. My mouth falls open. Will!

He grins at me and lets out a shrill whistle. 'Hey, Arthur. I found her.'

I turn around and there he is: uncombed curls, clean clothes and grinning like a skipper with money on shore. He hugs me until I gasp and push him away from me. 'You came back!'

'I've been lurking around here for hours, but I couldn't find you.' His gaze lands on the cloth around my head. 'I thought I'd find you easily, with your bunch of red hair. Is Katell still with you?'

'Katell and Wolf both. We're staying in a barn on the other side of town. Arthur, Detection is here. I just saw the cars drive off. It's not safe...'

'Sorry about that.' Even in the shadows of the alley, I see him chuckle uncomfortably. 'I'm afraid I led them here.'

'Excuse me?'

'Are you going to tell her how we got here?' Will asks teasingly.

'Another time, maybe. When she won't be able to hit me. That barn... how do we get there?'

'I was about to find a way there, before Will grabbed me.' I look from my little brother to the tall boy with his hood. 'Is everyone safe? Are Marci and Judika...?'

'In the Ark,' Arthur reassures me. 'With Mirna and Conn and the rest of the children. Safe.'

'Are they?' I look at Will. '*Will* they?'

His gaze hooks into mine and I see no anger in that look. 'On my life, Nimue.'

'And what about the others, the children who stayed behind...'

'There will be time for all of this later.' Arthur steps away from me and picks up the fish from the ground, putting it back into the bucket. 'Would be a waste to leave it here. Take us to that barn, Nim. Will doesn't want to stay long.'

It takes a while to get back to the barn via the backstreets, and when I open the door softly, there is a thin crescent moon in the sky already.

Wolf immediately grabs me by my arms and shakes me violently. 'Where were you?' he snarls. 'I've been waiting and looking!'

The force with which he grabs is so different from his exploratory touch last night that it shocks me. For a moment I'm lost for words. Arthur saves me.

'Detection is in town,' he says. 'Unless you want to be handed over to them, you let my sister go, now.'

He doesn't sound as if he is afraid to make good on his threat.

Wolf only now seems to realise how hard he's squeezing me. His hands pull away from me and I see him swallow hard. 'Nimue...'

'I am not your enemy,' I say, a little more hostile than I mean to. 'I had to hide. Arthur and Will found me. This is Will, from the Ark.'

Will flashes his crooked smile. Wolf nods before turning away from us to stoke the fire. I see that he's put Katell close to the flames. The sheepskin is back on her shoulders and her fluffy hair looks tidier and shinier than when I left. Seeing how well she's been taken care of soothes my indignation somewhat and I say: 'I have some fish with me, and clean water. If we are frugal, it'll be enough to feed everyone.'

Now that we have to share the fish with five people, there isn't much for each person. I give Katell an extra piece, which she stuffs into her mouth like a hungry animal, without chewing properly and without thanking me.

'The fisherman who gave me this told me about Rona,' I say.

Arthur looks at me perplexed. 'How can he know Mum?'

'He saw her leave port, ten years ago.'

He is silent for a moment as he processes this new information. 'Then we must do the same.'

For a while, I chew on my fish, licking the fat from my lips and throwing a leftover bone into the fire. 'We could be sailing the wrong way for days. That's to say, if we can even get a boat somewhere.'

'No, we wouldn't be sailing in the wrong direction,' Arthur says to my surprise. 'I've been looking for old atlases in the Ark library. There are islands west of Camlann, maybe a week's sail from here.'

'More than one island?'

'On the map, yes. It's assumed that they were all flooded when Britain disappeared under the sea.'

'I remember my grandfather telling me that there were dozens of islands to the north and west of our continent,' Will says thoughtfully. 'But if they were still there, we'd know about it.'

'I think there is one island left. Cut off by the ocean and forgotten by the world.' Arthur looks at me. 'Mum's island.'

'And that's a week's sailing from here?' I hesitate. 'We don't know the sea in this area. The currents could be...'

'It's doable,' Arthur interrupts me, looking at me with an intense gaze. 'With a good boat and enough supplies. Come on, Nim. You and me together? We can sail any sea we want.'

'Maybe so,' I admit. 'But even we can't live on seawater and raw fish for a whole week.'

'If you decide to go, you can take my backpack,' Will says unexpectedly. He speaks softly. 'It's not much, but if you ration well, it'll last you a few days. There's dried fish, some rusks, and plenty of water bottles.'

Arthur's eyes start to sparkle, but I let out a sigh. 'That won't get us anywhere. Without a boat we won't get far.'

'Nim, come on. This is a port city. There are hundreds of sailboats out there.'

'Which do *not* belong to us. Do you want to steal a boat?' When I get no response, I feel anger flare up. 'Have we become thieves now?'

'I don't *want* to steal, but we don't have money to rent anything either. And besides, we wouldn't be able to return a borrowed boat, would we?'

'If someone had stolen *The Ragdoll* back home, we'd have been ruined,' I snarl.

'This is a city. People are richer.'

'And there are also fishermen just like us!'

'Alright then.' Arthur doesn't sound nearly as out of sorts as I am. 'Maybe we can think of another solution.'

I get up and light the ship lamp. Again, the greenish light makes me feel like this barn is below sea level. We eat our meals and don't talk about boats or Mum's island any more.

Will decides to rest with us for a few hours before returning to the Ark before sunrise. We move the hay bales around to create more space. Katell quickly falls back into her slumber, her eyelids occasionally closing and fluttering open again. Will and Arthur are talking softly. I lie there listening to them for a while. Corentin's name is mentioned and I feel a stab through my heart. Arthur is talking about Taran and Marci, who have started building five permanent fish traps in the stream down in the swamp and about Judikael, who is making plans together with Mirna to cut down part of the forest to make the land suitable for growing vegetables. The Ark has many new mouths to feed.

Only when they too fall silent and the stillness in the barn feels like everyone's asleep do I roll over to move towards Wolf. His arms welcome me and I hide my head in his neck. I don't have to say anything – he just needs to embrace me. For a long time I listen to his breathing.

'Wolf? Do we have to steal a boat, you think?'

He waits a moment before answering. His voice is soft in my ear. 'That depends.'

'On what?'

'What you would be willing to give to find your mother.'

Now it's my turn to fall silent. For a long time, I lie staring into the twilight with my eyes open. Wolf drowsily circles my waist with his arms. I think he's falling asleep too. The hearth fire has died down, turning to a smouldering glow. I reach for Wolf's hand and wrap my fingers around his. He gives me a squeeze to let me know he's still awake.

'I saw a boat in the harbour,' I whisper. 'Arthur and I could sail her.'

Another squeeze of my hand, nothing more.

'Should we do it?'

'Yes,' his reply is a breath by my ear. 'The two of you should go.'

'And you will come with us?' When he keeps quiet, I move so that I can see his face. 'Wolf?' I whisper. 'You're coming with me, right?'

When he finally answers, it's almost impossible to hear. 'I'm not made for the sea.'

I'm immediately wide awake again. 'Do you want me to leave without you?'

He shakes his head. His smell penetrates my nose so strongly and I suddenly realise how much I want to hold him forever. As if he can hear my thoughts, he says: 'I want you to do what you always wanted to do. I don't fare well near the open sea and the taste of salt, Nimue. I need the trees, the shade, the smell of the forest.'

Like I always have to feel the vastness of the sea. Like Mum could never stay away from the pushing and pulling of the waves. I swallow hard. Like Sela was irrevocably called back to her existence under the waves. Yet I can't accept it. 'I don't want you to go.'

He kisses me on my forehead. 'You have freed me. Maybe I can free the children in my turn. Who knows what a shaman can do for the broken branches of the tree. I must try, in any case.'

'I wish I could go with you.' I swallow. 'But I can't.'

'I know that.' His arms pull me closer to him and I know we don't need to say anything more. The truth is that he's drawn to the trees and the marshes and I'm drawn to the tempting, thrusting sea.

Long before the sun illuminates the houses of Camlann, Arthur wakes me up. I see the look he gives me and Wolf, but he doesn't comment. He just states: 'Will is leaving now.'

With a heavy feeling of farewell, I allow Wolf to pull his arms away from me and scramble to my feet. I brush the bits of hay from my hair. 'Then we'll go too.'

Will seems wide awake, as if it were not the middle of the night. But he's used to keeping watch in the dark, I remember. Waiting for a sister who will never come back. 'The Ark's door is always open for you, if you ever change your mind,' he says.

Arthur looks at me. In that look I see resignation. He's leaving this decision to me, I realise with a shock. I don't know why. Maybe he sees me trying my best to hold back tears when Wolf puts a hand on my shoulder and caresses me for a moment before stepping past me to put on his boots. I rub my eyes hard to get rid of the stinging feeling. It's Arthur's acquiescence that wins me over. 'We can't go to the Ark. Arthur, I don't know any other way and I can't give up on Mum. There's a boat in the harbour we can sail. She's called *The Herring Gull*.'

Arthur nods solemnly.

'Then take this with you.' Will hands me his backpack, which contains the rations for a few days. 'And this too. They can be lifesavers – you never know.' He holds out a lighter and a pocket knife. Silently, I accept them from him.

'Before I forget...' He takes something out of his pocket and ties a leather cord around my neck. I look at what is now resting on my chest: the seal pendant. 'Mirna found it. She thought you'd like it back.'

'Will...'

'No need to thank me.' His smile seems a little weary. 'I hope we part as friends, Nimue. I hope I can make up for what I've done.' His eyes dart to Katell, who is being helped up and dressed by Arthur.

'Wolf will take care of her. Won't you, Wolf?' Standing by the extinguished hearth, he gives a short nod. I swallow hard and then suddenly feel tears well up in my eyes. I take a step towards Will and wrap my arms around him. Immediately, the smell of marsh and cigarette smoke surrounds me. A smell I found so attractive some weeks ago, and almost as repulsive shortly after. 'We part as friends. And as allies. Tell Mirna I miss her. Keep the Ark safe, okay? Make it the best place on earth.'

His arms squeeze me against him, then he lets go of me. 'Make sure you stay safe yourself. Both of you.'

'Can you tell Taran, Marci and Judikael something on my behalf?' I hesitate, but then say it anyway. 'Tell them not to give up on Gwennec just yet. That one day we'll all go back home together.'

Will looks doubtful, but he is kind enough not to say what I know he's thinking. He nods at me and gently takes Katell's hand in his.

I feel a hand on my neck. Silently I turn around and let myself sag against Wolf's body. He catches me and holds me up while I just want to disappear into him so we don't ever get separated. I can't – I don't want to leave without him.

As if he can sense my thoughts, he presses a kiss against my ear. 'You still have a journey to complete. Dear Nimue. Brave Nimue.' Another kiss, this time on my wet cheek. 'Be strong, and good luck to you.'

I restrain myself. One more week, one last time following in Mum's footsteps, and then our journey will be over. 'And once we have found her, I'll come back to you,' I hear myself calling out loud. 'This is not farewell.'

I kiss him and allow myself for the last time to enjoy the sweet, electric sensation of his warm mouth on mine, of his rough cheek against my skin. Then the moment is over and he lets me go.

Arthur is bending over to Katell to embrace her. When he slowly gets back up, he looks at me and then says: 'I don't want to leave her, Nim. She belongs to Gwennec – she belongs with us. We'll take Katell with us.'

16

THE HERRING GULL

The docks are silent and dark. The only burning lamps are near the houses, casting a yellow light on the stones of the harbour. Our shadows look like strange, elongated creatures that remind me of the Fisher King. A lighthouse is at the end of a pier that runs into the sea like a long arm. Its light flashes across the vast waters with the regularity of a slow heartbeat. Above us, the crescent moon has climbed higher.

Lamps, a beacon, and the moon – they all reveal the ships and sailing boats swaying in the water, firmly bound together. They'll give us just enough light to sail by. I show Arthur the small fishing boat that caught my eye this afternoon. *The Herring Gull* is at the end of a wooden jetty, standing in the sucking water on tall poles. It's low tide and the sea leaves part of the harbour bare. In another flash coming from the lighthouse, I can see oysters and the growth of algae and seaweed stuck to the jetty. The smell of iodine and salt hangs heavily in the air.

Another flash and I shift my gaze to the dark mass of water behind the boats. The sea is huge. Dark, and wide open.

Nimue, she calls, deep from her bottomless belly. *Arthur*.

And yes, here we are. Finally, we have arrived. Just as Rona finally returned here. I reach for Arthur's hand and he grabs my fingers for a moment. He feels cold, and I, too, shiver in the strong breeze. Katell is silent – a silence I've grown accustomed to. But when I take her hand and urge her to keep walking, I think I feel her shivering from more than just the nightly cold. Her face is tense and drawn taut in utter concentration.

'Did you miss the sea?' I ask softly.

Her eyes never leave the horizon. 'She breathes. In and out. *Wshh. Wshh.*' She mimics the sucking sound of the tide.

The Herring Gull is chained to the jetty. Arthur takes the pocket knife and sticks the point into the keyhole of the steel lock. It's as rusty as Will's blade and I know it won't hold out for too long. I push Katell across the wobbly gangway and lift her over the railing before helping Arthur cast off the mooring lines. The entire time I'm trying to ignore that nagging sense of guilt. That fisherman has family inland; he won't starve without his boat – at least that's what I tell myself, but I know that if he has to buy a new boat, we'll be forcing him into years of debt.

Arthur lets out a triumphant sound when the lock gives out. 'Lift the anchor.'

We grope our way to the other side of the boat. The anchor is on a thick chain that groans when we turn the windlass. I myself groan with exertion as we lift it.

Arthur gives a hard push and the anchor emerges from the water. *The Herring Gull* is ready to depart, and I can feel my heart thump in my chest. I'm not sure whether it's relief or fear that's spurring it on. As we push off, a shout suddenly erupts from the quay. Someone is running up the jetty with a lantern in his hand. Where the lantern lights up the darkness, I recognise the skipper's red hat.

The boat is already too far away from the jetty by the time he reaches the end. I stand by the railing as if petrified. His gaze bores into mine. I see his face, his eyes large and angry, his bushy eyebrows arched. For a moment I wonder if he's going to jump in after us. But what would that get him, except a useless dip in the cold water? *The Herring Gull* is a sturdy sailing boat, not a low sloop that a man could capsize with his bare hands. The same realisation must dawn on him, because he doesn't jump. He just opens his mouth and roars.

At first, I don't understand his words. Only when lights flash up behind him on the quay and I hear the heavy humming of engines do I realise the danger we're still in. He has called out for harbour patrol, and his call is being answered.

'Thieves! They're stealing my bloody boat!'

I curse and snatch Katell away from the railing. The boat has a small cabin, which can be reached through a low door and down a small staircase. I push her down the steps. 'Stay there. Arthur!' I'm already back on the foredeck. 'The sail! Let go of the sail!'

'It's too dark!' He's standing by the ship lamp on the mast and clicks it on with the lighter. I shout at him, but it's too late: like a star, the lamp lights up the deck and reveals us to the people on the quay. The rattling noise that follows is enough to make me fall to the ground, my knees weak with fear. Something pings off the metal railing. I hear Arthur scream, but my head is filled with only one nightmarish image: a leak in the keel, *The Herring Gull* capsizing and taking us all with her.

'Nim!' It's a sound somewhere between a scream and a groan. I crawl towards Arthur as two more loud bangs resound from the harbour. Arthur is lying flat on the deck, hidden behind an iron box which probably saved his life. I reach for him. There is blood on his leg and in the little light that the ship lamp casts on him, I see a wet, dark stain on the planks beneath him.

'Is it only your leg?' I ask with the small amount of breath I have left. The rest has been knocked out of my body, along with my courage.

'They're shooting...' He squeezes the words out, his face a twisted mask. '... leak.'

'Arthur! Your leg!' I almost shake him back and forth, but immediately regret it. He utters an agonised sound.

'Only my leg. Nim. Send...'

'I'll take you inside.' I hook my arms under his armpits and drag him to the cabin door. No other shots are heard. Are we too far away now? Are they coming after us with another boat? Is Detection already on its way to check out the noise and will someone tell them that Cormack wants us back alive? Or will he just...

I don't even want to finish that last thought. I drag Arthur into the cabin and roughly push Katell aside. The cabin isn't much bigger than my old cell in Platform Zero. There is a chest against the wall with an oil lamp on top of it, and there's a wooden chair in the other corner. Most of the space is taken up by a pallet with a straw mattress. I lay Arthur down on it. He's gasping for breath, clearly making an effort not to make too much noise.

'Medicine kit, medicine kit...' I know it must be somewhere, every decent boat should have one. I rummage around in the chest. An extra woollen blanket, half a pack of dried rusks, an unopened water bottle – somewhere in the back of my mind, I register that we're lucky to have that – and a heavy pair of binoculars that must have cost a lot of money. Fishhooks, spools of rolled-up rope, a box that I first think is the medicine kit, but which turns out to contain only sewing thread and needles, a star chart ... 'Here! Don't move, Arthur, I've got it.'

It's a stainless steel box that hasn't been locked. 'Katell, kindle the lamp. Give me some light.'

The girl obeys. I'm relieved that the cabin is below deck, where the light from the oil lamp can't penetrate to the outside. Although I don't know if it matters; they could be right on our heels. There's no one on deck steering *The Herring Gull*, hoisting the sails or operating the jib.

Don't think about it. Arthur is losing blood.

I reach for a roll of bandages and a glass bottle. When I unscrew the cap, the smell tells me what I already suspected.

'Katell, hold the lamp up to here.' I turn around and roll up Arthur's trouser leg. It doesn't go up far enough. 'Where's the knife?' When I get no answer, I look up. 'Arthur, the knife?'

'On deck.'

Damn. I hesitate for a moment. Then I hurry up and peek outside. The dark of night envelops us. Except for the lamp on the mast, it's pitch black all around us. Dark as death. I try to shake off the frightening image as I reach for the knife he dropped. In any case, there's no sign of anyone chasing us. When I risk glancing over the railing, I catch just a glimpse of the harbour – and of the car headlights staring at us like deathly eyes. They're letting us go, I realise. Because in front of us only endless water awaits, without a coastline in sight.

My hand finds the handle of the knife and I grab it. *The Herring Gull* hits a wave and leans dangerously far to portside. I slide across the deck and only just manage to hook my arm around a rope to prevent smacking painfully hard against the other railing. The boat is adrift on the waves, which are getting higher and higher the further away we get from the coast. Someone needs to hoist the sail and put their hands around the rudder, but I don't have time for that. With the knife in my hand, I return to my little brother, who has rolled off the pallet and is now dragging himself back onto the mattress. That little effort seems to suck up all his energy, because he's now lying on his back with a pale face. Without wasting time on more words, I cut his trouser leg open, up to his thigh. The wound is near his knee. I make a choking noise and he raises his head a few inches to peer down.

'How bad...?'

'Be quiet.' I can't really see it and I have to do my best to stay calm. The sight of Arthur's fresh blood is almost too much for me. 'Katell, see if there's a clean rag in that box. Leave the lamp here.'

The girl has turned completely white. I don't know if she has enough of her soul left to feel concerned, but when she hands me a soft cloth, I think I can see fear in her wide-open eyes. I use the cloth to wipe the blood from Arthur's leg. Very quickly, the cloth is soaked and I have to put it aside. The bullet wound is just above his knee, on the left side of his leg. I take a deep breath and pull the lamp closer to me. The bullet has penetrated deep into his flesh. I see a glimpse of white bone.

'Clean knives.' My voice is shaking. 'I need clean knives and needle and thread and ...'

'Nim?' Arthur's own voice is weak. 'What are you going to do?'

'That bullet has to be taken out.' I bite my lip as I bend over to get a closer look at his wound. The sour bile in my stomach rises up; I swallow it back down with gritted teeth. 'Katell, hand me a clean knife.'

'There are no knives.'

'A pair of scissors, then.'

She hands me a pair of scissors, but as soon as I hold them up to the light I see that they're tainted with rust. 'That won't do. Shark blood! Let me see that kit!' I don't wait for Katell to make room for me, so I grab the medicine kit and turn it over on the floor. A few more rolls of bandages, cotton wool, and a box with a few pills that I'm not sure about what they're for. Nothing suitable for a procedure like this. I curse again and try to decide what to do. The only knife I have is Will's pocket knife. But that too is rusty and blackened with dirt. I wouldn't even think of sticking it into Arthur's flesh, let alone digging out a bullet.

The boat gives another lurch. I hold Arthur to the floor while the contents of the medicine kit scatter criss-cross across the floor.

'Nim!' my little brother hisses. 'Steer the damn ship!'

'You're losing too much blood!' I hesitate for a moment, then unbuckle the belt of his trousers. 'If you lose more blood, you will faint. Katell, help me.' Katell crawls closer. 'Lift his leg. No further than a few inches... That's it.' Arthur bites his lip at that slight movement. I slip the belt under his leg and buckle it firmly around his thigh, quite a bit above the wound. I pull the belt so tightly that my little brother lets out another scream under his breath and grinds out a few harsh curses.

'A real skipper you are,' I comment weakly. 'Now lie still. Katell, you come with me.'

I grab her by her jumper when *The Herring Gull* crashes down on the waves and rears up again. Sea foam splashes up around us like snowflakes. 'Keep looking at your feet once we're on deck,' I instruct her. 'Follow the light of the lamp. You and I are going to sail the boat, Katell. You think you can do that?' Meanwhile, I push her across the back deck towards the rudder.

'I think I'm scared.'

'I understand you are.' I'm secretly relieved. Fear is an emotion I can make sense of. Anything will be better than the silent, blank stares she was giving me earlier. 'But the most important thing is that you have to be brave now. Stand up straight. Chin up. Here's the rudder. Can you feel the ship moving around the helm? Put your hands around it, Katell. Tighter.' I'm standing behind her, my hands folded around hers.

'I can't see anything.'

'That's alright, you have to feel it. Do you notice how the waves are hitting the bow? Do you feel on which side? You just have to stand here and feel, that's all. Steer the boat – more to port. That's it. Now we're going with the flow, do you notice that?'

I think she's giving me a hesitant nod. I moisten my lips. 'You don't do anything else, you understand? You don't run across the ship, you don't get close to the railing. You just stand here and maintain course. If you get scared, you have to sing.' I clear my throat and conjure up the tune of the Sailors' Mass from somewhere within my body. The words we both know from the church service in Gwennec. '*Gwenhael, lord of the endless sea, we ask of you our lives to keep, and aid us* ... Katell, sing along.'

Instead of singing, I hear her make a choking sound. She whispers: '*When the seas are deep.*'

I press a kiss to the back of her head and let go. Katell bravely remains where I put her, and it dawns on me how improbable the whole situation is when I glance over my shoulder and see this frail, bird-like girl facing the full strength of the ocean.

The foresail is flapping in the wind. I secure it firmly to prevent it from slamming into me or Katell. In a few hours the sun will rise. By that time I can use the morning light to set a true course, so we can hoist the sail and use the wind to drive us forward. Now I'm in more of a hurry than ever; I need to take that bullet out of Arthur's leg and without the right tools, I can't do anything for him. I take the ship lamp from the mast and walk along the railing. My fingers skim it. I can't see bullet holes anywhere and *The Herring Gull* doesn't seem to make any water. At least that's a small consolation.

Katell's voice reaches me all the way to the foredeck. She's singing, and the sound of the melody scatters and is blown away by the wind.

Gwenhael, please let Katell hold the rudder firmly. With that little prayer on my lips, I descend the steps into the cabin. Arthur breathes in with a large gulp of air, then exhales sharply. I kneel down by his side and stroke his hair. 'I'm going to clean and bandage the wound. Brace yourself, this is going to hurt.'

He gives a nod. I unscrew the cap of the glass bottle and pour some alcohol onto the wound. Arthur hisses like oil on fire. I start to unroll a roll of bandage to put it around his thigh.

'The ... the bullet?' he pants.

'We'll have to wait until we get there.' I speak more calmly than I'm feeling. 'I can't operate on you until we reach Avalon.'

'Nim...'

'Shh. Don't say anything. It's only a few days; you'll have to hold on until then.' I'm not saying what we're both thinking: that there's no certainty we'll ever reach Mum's island, or that there are still people there who can help us.

And I know about something else, something I'm afraid to tell Arthur right now: that growing, brewing storm on the horizon. If it erupts while we are still at sea, not even Saint Gwenhael will be able to save us.

'Nim. I don't feel so good.'

I put my arms around him and hug his upper body, careful not to touch him anywhere else. 'Try to sleep – it will ease the pain too.'

Arthur lets out a weary laugh. 'A bit hard to fall asleep with a bullet in your leg.'

I pick up the scattered items from the medicine kit and put them away again. The pillbox attracts my attention. I open the cover and sniff it. 'Smells a bit sour.'

'Yuck. I don't want it.'

'But it might be anti-inflammatory. Or a painkiller.'

'Or rat poison. I don't want it.'

I sigh and tighten the cap again. 'I'd better go back up to Katell to see if she's alright. I left her on the back deck.'

'Gwenhael's grave.' Arthur settles on his palette with a groan. 'Go and help her. Make sure we don't drown.'

'Sleep,' I say again, urgently. I cover him with a woollen blanket, but leave his injured leg uncovered. 'Call if you need anything.'

'I can tell you've... never had a bullet ... in your body ...' He rolls his head to the side a little to show me a weak grin. 'Sail fast and get us to that damn island.'

'Aye, Captain.'

Dawn creeps in with gentle, grey stripes on the horizon. The sun slowly rises above the distant line of the sea, and the crescent moon fades in the early morning light. I'm standing on the deck of *The Herring Gull* with my compass and follow the trembling needle to the west. The restless night has taken us far off course. *The Herring Gull* is a boat keen to respond to her master: she reacts to even the smallest corrections at the helm and rides the waves more smoothly than The Ragdoll ever did. As if she were a living creature, she seems to sense that her new skippers are in a hurry to find a safe haven.

I stare longingly at the horizon, but I know that it's no use imagining the peaks of an unknown island there. We're still too far away. The clouds are tricking my eyes. Still, I stand at the helm and stare ahead, until the sunlight on the gleaming water becomes too bright and I have to avert my gaze. Katell is on the foredeck, her hands on either side of the railing. She doesn't care about the salty splashes of water hitting her face – she stares in motionless fascination at the bow cutting through the water. I call her to me and look at the dark rings under her eyes, the sickly pallor of her skin.

'Did you sleep last night?'

She shrugs her skinny shoulders. It's such a small gesture. 'I don't know.'

'How much have you slept since you became... since you left the Institute?'

'I don't know,' she says again, then pauses. 'I did sleep in the barn.'

I smile at the memory of that night, but not because Katell finally got some sleep. 'It's not good for you to sleep so little.'

'I can't help it. When I sleep, everything is black. And sometimes...' Katell visibly hesitates. 'Sometimes I think I'm somewhere else. But I'm not really. In the barn I did sleep,' she says again.

'You were very tired, then.' Maybe that's the solution, it occurs to me. To exhaust the girl so much that her body automatically falls asleep as soon as she lies down. I could start trying out that theory that right now. I take a step back and say: 'Take over the ship's wheel. Look carefully at the needle of the compass. We must keep sailing west at all times.'

Katell obeys. I watch her for a moment as she puts her hands around it, how the wooden wheel is almost as tall as she is. 'Maybe you should stand on a box.' I give her a kiss on the head.

I spend the rest of the morning sitting cross-legged on deck examining and rationing our supplies. The food in Will's rucksack and the water bottles are our greatest treasure. I put them to my left. The contents of the medicine kit I put on the right, and the extra stuff I found in the fisherman's box in the middle. When I go to check on Arthur, I discover that his forehead is burning hot. I hold a bottle of water to his lips and he drinks like a parched animal. He almost empties the entire bottle of water, but I don't comment. After all, he needs it more than Katell and I do. I carefully peel the bandage off his leg. His skin is hot there, too. A swollen, bright red circle has appeared around the wound. I carefully touch it with my fingertips. And yet Arthur hisses, as if I have pricked him with a thousand needles. I guiltily withdraw my hand.

'How does it look?' he asks, once he has recovered from the pain.

Bad, despite my attempt to disinfect the wound. I lick my dry lips. 'The sooner that bullet gets taken out, the better.'

He lifts his head slightly in an attempt to peer at his own leg. 'And if we can't?'

'We can. We will. We're sailing with a strong wind in our sails. You'll be fine.'

I don't know if he believes my forced lie, but he doesn't say another word. He rests his head on the straw mattress again and closes his eyes. I dress his wound with clean bandages and let him sleep, hoping the fever will drop and his body will be able to fight the infection.

Later in the afternoon, the sun disappears behind smothering clouds and the wind picks up. The sea, which was playful but not rough until now, turns restless. The water grows dark. I feel an unpleasant tingle running down my spine and make sure that everything that's loose is firmly latched to the boat. But the night doesn't usher in the storm I was fearing, even though *The Herring Gull* bobs restlessly up and down. The morning light reveals those threatening storm heads, still gathering on the horizon. Is it my imagination, or have they come closer?

Arthur's fever is rising, and when I go down to feed him some breakfast, he refuses all food. Yesterday he was so greedy with the water, but today I have trouble getting him to take even a few sips.

With another day passing uneventfully, a dullness descends on the ship. Katell becomes more tired and silent than she already was. I try to keep her mind occupied with all the little chores that have to be done to keep a fishing boat running. Not that we're catching any fish. If Arthur were healthier, it would be a good way to supplement our provisions, but with the little food we have and lack of adequate rest, I don't have the strength to cast heavy nets or lift them out of the ocean.

Arthur sinks deeper into his feverish sleep. The infection has already doubled in size, the flesh around the bullet hole growing unnaturally soft and puffy. The colour of the wound has also changed, from bright red to almost black. The stench coming from it is unbearable.

I try to ignore my nagging fear as I change the bandages. I may never have been trained as a full medical caretaker like Yannick, or as a doctor like Cormack, but I'm not so ignorant that I can't recognise blood poisoning. The bullet has nested itself deep in Arthur's leg, and from there, it's killing the healthy flesh like a cancer.

Without clean tools, I cannot remove the cause of the infection. All I can do is try not to let the poisoning spread through his whole leg. Because if it does, it will eventually reach his heart. I put my hands on the wound, suppressing a shudder when the foul smell meets my nostrils. Arthur groans in his sleep. His leg spasms. The pain must be a constant companion, I think, even in his sleep. I dismiss the thought and concentrate solely on my intention. Just as I once sucked the Black Influenza out of Katell, I suck the black, impure substances from the wound into my own body.

It's not the same. I gag and barely manage to keep down the acidic bile bubbling up. I'm very aware of the iron intruder, the bullet – how it has torn away muscle and flesh. I can sense the piece of bone that has splintered off. I feel it all, but can do nothing to repair the shattered body parts. Instead, I try to isolate the infection, to stop it from spreading. I breathe in and out slowly.

Fresh blood in my nose, whispers the voice of the Hunter somewhere in my mind. For a moment I can see him: a flash of his elongated face and his blood-red tongue sliding out past his shark teeth.

'Go away!' I say in a panic.

I hear him laugh. *Above or below, I know his scent. The King who Must Come is slipping through the door.*

'Get lost!' My scream bounces through the cabin, echoing off the walls and jolting Arthur awake. I shake him off and without another word I go outside, where I lean over the railing and empty my stomach into the water. The Hunter has grown silent.

Was Wolf right? Can I banish him, simply by demanding him to go away? I wipe my mouth with my sleeve and stare out across the water. On this side it may be possible to banish him, but I know that he'll always be ready on the other side of that door he was talking about.

I try not to think about his impending prophecy.

To calm myself, I take the wheel from Katell and send her to the foredeck. The sky is a patchwork of clouds, which sometimes allows the sunlight to hit the deck, but most times obscures the sun's glow. I no longer want to go back down there; I'm too afraid to look at Arthur's wound. I feel helpless and useless and clench my cold hands around the wheel, more tightly than necessary.

Night falls and reveals a bright, cold moon. Again, she has grown. I tell Katell to eat two pieces of rusk and drink a few sips of water; that's all. I'm not hungry yet. At night, when the wide sphere of darkness makes it impossible for me to see the spinning arrow of the compass, I simply look up and navigate by the stars.

The fourth night at sea is so hard that I almost don't believe we'll make it through until the morning light. The wind and the waves shake the little boat mercilessly, like a child holding a rattle. In the suffocating darkness, I fight my way from the cabin to the quarterdeck with pouring rain in my face. I throw all my strength into steering the boat and pray to all the spirits that might be watching over us from the Other World. Every time a wave hits the railing and douses me with cold water , I gasp. Perhaps some creature will hear my pleas – perhaps Saint Gwenhael himself. Again, it's the sunrise that saves us and calms the brutal gusts of wind.

I share the last rusks with Katell and force Arthur to take a few sips of water. He's barely awake now. I hold his head back and press down on his throat to make him swallow. Arthur coughs and weakly tries to resist by turning his head away and pushing my hand holding the bottle away. I shove his arm down and tighten my grip, which is enough to make him drink until the bottle is half empty.

Only one full bottle left in the rucksack, and a horizon that is still so distant. For a moment, fear overwhelms me. Have we taken too much risk? If I'd listened to Will, we'd all be safe in the Ark now. Arthur would've been healthy and I wouldn't have been separated from Wolf...

I could turn *The Herring Gull* around. Back to Camlann – back to Cormack if necessary, if that will save Arthur's life.

I look up at Katell, or the half-empty shell that is left of her. Sometimes I catch a glimpse of the old Katell, the girl I knew in Gwennec. I know with a deep certainty that if I forced her to live within the walls of the Asclepius Congregation again, that last glimmer of Katell would be extinguished. No. For better or for worse, this is the path we have chosen. *The Herring Gull* dances across the sea, towards an island that will eventually appear on that illusive horizon. The compass is showing us the way. We just have to keep going.

Katell is on the quarterdeck the moment when the first raindrops mingle with the salty water splashing up from the sea. I inhale deeply. The air is heavy with salt and iron and iodine. I stand beside her, my hood pulled over my head. It will offer little protection against the burning blisters, for the fabric is a simple woven cotton, not the oiled cloth I had back home. If the fisherman ever had a rainproof anorak on board, he brought it home with him after he docked.

I glance at Katell. 'Get into the cabin. This is going to be another downpour.'

'Is Arthur going to die?'

A question I don't want to answer. A question I don't even dare to ask myself. I fold my arms over the steering wheel. A splashing sound surprises me. I look aside, past the railing. 'Katell, look! Dolphins!' I'm relieved and take the opportunity to change the subject. 'How many can you see?'

She bends dangerously far forward and counts. 'One, two, three. There were no dolphins in Gwennec.'

'No, not usually. Do you remember that whale that once washed up on the beach, under the big cliff?'

She shakes her head, all her attention caught by the wet, grey backs rising above the water and disappearing again.

'You were still small back then. It was the hottest summer evening I ever experienced. Our fresh catch went rotten before we could even drive it to town. And the whale took up half the beach. A mountain of bacon and fat and skin.'

The image is still fresh in my memory. The trembling air, the overwhelming smell of decay coming off the unwieldy animal. Arthur and I, together with Dad. The sand burning hot under the soles of my bare feet. The dead whale was an impressive monster to me, even more so when I imagined how it had once moved through the depths of the ocean. I even believed it could've swallowed a boat the size of *The Ragdoll*. Despite the stench, I approached it, together with the other children of the village. Yannick had drawn a line in the rubbery skin with the point of her pocket knife. Ripples had passed through it when she did it, sending her right back to her father like a pebble from a catapult. I can still hear Dad's laughter echoing in my ears.

'What happened to it?'

'It exploded.' I can still hear the dull bang it made and think about the pieces of the carcass lying on the beach for weeks, used as bait for all the seabirds scavenging for food.

The wind separates the clouds, then drives them back together again. Whenever there's a hole in the cloud cover, the moon appears for a moment. And then, it starts to rain really hard and I send Katell inside. I can't bring myself to sit with Arthur, so I take shelter under the narrow roof of the cabin, which is no more than a ledge.

I already know I wouldn't be able to sleep. I'd just be sitting by Arthur's side, brooding. I'd rather stay out here in the pouring rain and daydream about the old days, when Dad and Grandma were still with us, and my world was small and safe. Sometimes it was hard and sometimes it was cold, sometimes we were hungry when we had a poor catch and didn't sell enough at the market, but it was never so bad that I feared for my life. I stare out at the sea and let all the thoughts and worries wash over me, and they burn me like the rain and chill me like the cold waves crashing against the bow of *The Herring Gull*.

The strong wind eventually makes the clouds drift away and clears the sky again. I'm glad that the rainstorm was brief, because the evening light is magnificent. It bathes the sea and the foredeck in a golden glow. For a long time, I sit there completely motionless, even when the temperature drops a few more degrees.

The stars always shine brighter at sea. Dad once said that to me. I look up and count them like Katell counted the dolphins.

I see them before I realise what I'm looking at: an arc of five bright dots in the sky. Slightly to the left of our course. The constellation doesn't look familiar. That's strange – that's not right. Don't I know the sky almost as well as I know the currents of the sea? And yet, there is something inexplicably familiar about that sign in the sky. It tugs at my mind, like a vaguely familiar scent whose origin I can no longer recall.

Whenever I see these stars ...

I jump up and look for the diary, which I kept stowed high and dry in the big chest. Despite the moonlight, it's dark on deck and I have to hold the book close to the ship lamp to read the curly letters. My hands tremble excitedly as I breathlessly turn the pages. There, yes, there it is: the rough sketch in the margin of the page, Mum's melancholy words, her memory of a song from long ago ...

'*So farewell and adieu, my well-beloved land... Whenever I see these stars in the sky, I'll be sure that they are twinkling in the heavens above the hills of my homeland.*'

With a pounding heart, filled with newfound hope, I adjust the course of *The Herring Gull*. To follow the compass in the sky, towards those stars that will lead me to Avalon like lighthouses in the night.

17

ISLAND OF APPLES

The Herring Gull scours across the beach in the shadow of a high cliff. I hear the shuffling and groaning sound of the boat, but hardly have the energy to get up from the floor. Like Katell, I'm sleeping on the bare floor of the cabin, next to Arthur's motionless form. My little brother gives no sign of life other than the rhythmic rise and fall of his chest. My head is throbbing painfully. It's from dehydration, I know that, but I'm not in a position to do anything about it. Yesterday I squeezed the last drops from the plastic bottle to moisten Arthur's lips.

The moment I get up and open the cabin door, a loud bang resounds. The ship tilts heavily to starboard. In order to stay upright, I grab the railing with both hands and find my balance. From there, I take in the situation outside.

We're lying still. Water is licking the lowest part of the ship, but a large part of the bow is sticking out above the sucking current. Ahead of me, the view is taken up by the towering walls of the island, where the beach forms a natural cove. It's no wider than ten large steps to either side. Further up on the cliffs, I can see the green of trees and shrubbery. The wind howls against the bare rockface. It creates a high, lilting sound that travels far and wide and blends in with the sounds of the sea. I can't see people anywhere.

I call out to Katell and when she obediently comes towards me, I lift her over the railing so that she can lower herself onto the beach. It's not far to jump, but my knees are weak. My ankle twists in the process and I stumble forward. The sand is littered with razor clams and dried-up flakes of sea foam. The broken shells cut painfully into my palms.

'Stinging jellyfish,' I mutter grumpily as I get up and wipe my trousers. Not that I have any chance of getting them truly clean. The dirt of two weeks of constant flight sticks to the fabric of the trousers, my jumper, and even my hair. I turn around to *The Herring Gull* and regret my hasty jump down, because I suddenly feel shaky. More than a week of sailing on the small boat has allowed my legs to get used to the rocking deck, but now that I'm back on solid ground, I sway awkwardly back and forth, almost losing my balance again.

The boat is bobbing in the surf and I fear she'll actually capsize. I suspect that currents and treacherous cliffs have pulled her closer to land and then pushed her sideways. I curse myself for not having paid better attention. I should've been on the quarterdeck, alert and agile, sailing *The Herring Gull* into the cove. Exhaustion, however, had forced me to lie down at last.

There is no point in complaining about the awkward position of the boat. Arthur is still in the cabin. And I realise that I don't have enough strength to carry him off the boat like I did Katell. I consider pulling him out to the foredeck, but shudder at the thought of having to drag his unconscious body across the rough planks of the deck. I don't know what it would do to him if I moved him now. It might open his barely-healed wound, and he's already so weak that he shouldn't lose any more blood.

I'll have to get help.

A drizzle begins to fall from the sky, causing small, stinging pinpricks on my face. I flip my hair forward like a protective veil, and grab Katell by the hand.

To the right of the beach, a sandy track seems to lead up the cliff. Further up, it seems that path turns into a barely passable road, no wider than two feet. We're halfway up the slope when I see them: a man holding a young girl by the hand. I shout at them. Even from this distance, I can see the bewilderment on their faces. Less than a minute later, they're standing in front of me, their heads protected from the rain by colourful hoods.

The man has a golden-blond beard with streaks of grey interspersing the blond hair. He's wearing a baggy anorak, which covers his upper body down to his knees. He has sturdy leather boots on his feet. When he moves, I hear a soft tinkling sound.

The girl can't be older than five. She, too, is dressed from head to toe in an anorak. Her long, blonde hair falls forward, out of the hood and onto her shoulders, and I notice that it's plaited in many tiny braids. At the tips, she's wearing small shell beads that bounce against each other with every movement of her head.

I know that they're taking us both in like we are observing them. The puzzlement leaves us all speechless for a moment before I point at *The Herring Gull*. 'Please help us. My brother is on board and he's injured.'

The man lets his gaze drift from me to the boat. He turns to the girl. His voice is low and warm, and for a moment I find it hard to understand what he's saying. In his mouth, the words sound like a foreign language. 'Tillie, run uphill and send people down. Tell Enja to come. Go!'

Tillie obeys and runs up the long path snaking across the cliff. Relief flows through me. The man looks at me before speaking again. 'Where are you from?'

'I came from far away.' Now that I know that help is on the way, I can hardly keep still. Only when I know that Arthur is safely and securely disembarked will I be able to relax. 'From Camlann and even further.'

I see no recognition on his face when I mention Camlann. He looks shamelessly curious. I awkwardly avert my gaze. He must have noticed, because with sincere apology in his voice he says: 'Excuse me. Until a few years ago we weren't sure that land still existed beyond the sea. Shipwrecked people never wash up here. Did you get you lost in a storm? There's a big storm brewing in the distance. Thank the spirits that you came to shore before it will erupt.'

'We're not lost,' I reply. Katell is partly hiding behind me like a frightened hare. 'We're not shipwrecked. We were looking for...'

Suddenly, a few shouts are heard from the top of the cliff. Six or seven men and women in coloured anoraks descend down the path, their wide eyes fixed on *The Herring Gull*. They rush onto the beach. A few are touching the bow, as if they can't believe that the boat is really there. A young woman with long, blonde hair passes me and her startled gaze hooks into mine before she joins the people standing around the boat.

'Careful,' I exclaim, as soon as two men climb on board via the tilted side. 'My brother is sleeping. He's got a bullet in his leg, I'm afraid he's going to bleed again when we move him, and he won't wake up. I think he has blood poisoning and...'

'Calm down.' A tall woman grabs me by the shoulder and turns me around to face her. Her single braid hangs across her shoulder like a thick, grey rope. Like all the others, she's braided a strand of shell beads through her locks. 'We'll move your brother carefully. Where is he? In the cabin?'

I nod.

The woman gives a few orders to the assembled group. Only now do I see the stretcher they brought: a woven mat suspended between two sturdy branches.

'He has a bullet in his leg,' I repeat.

'Bullet?'

It dawns on me that these people may not have known about bullets on their island for several generations. 'Big iron marbles. From a weapon... Meant to kill.'

The woman looks horrified for a moment before nodding. 'And how long has he been unconscious for?'

I try to count back the days. Everything seems to be a single, long chain of events, like the strand of beads in her braid. 'He was still awake when I cleaned the wound. Then he caught a fever. I think he's been asleep for a few days,' I end weakly. 'I don't know if I did it right. There was only a small medicine kit.'

'We'll see soon enough. I'm Enja, the healer.' She presses her fingers into my shoulder reassuringly, then lets go of me and joins the rescue team. I can only watch helplessly and nervously as strangers lift my brother onto the deck and carefully lower him onto the stretcher. Without waking him, they manage to get him onto the beach. It's only in the bright daylight that I notice how pale he actually is. His skin is waxen and covered with an unhealthy-looking sheen of sweat. His face is so sunken, making his cheekbones stand out sharply. I want to rush over to him and hug him tight. Only Katell's hand in mine keeps me from actually doing it.

Enja heads the troupe and they carry Arthur up the cliff path. The man grabs me by my arm again. 'Are you alright? Can you walk?'

I nod.

'Then come with me.'

'The boat...'

'Don't worry about the boat. We'll see what we can do with it later. Come.' He hooks his arm through mine. I'm grateful for the stability and strength he's giving me as we continue to climb the steep path.

'My name is Tomas. This is my daughter, Tillie.'

The girl who ran to the village earlier is back and is following us at a short distance. She's looking at us as if we landed here coming straight from the moon.

'Nimue,' I mutter. 'And this is Katell.'

He nods and doesn't ask any further questions for now. I'm glad, because I need all my energy to just put one foot in front of the other.

The path ends where the cliff starts – in a field of wildflowers, which have now closed to protect themselves from the drizzling rain. A few trees and their wide canopy offer natural shelters. Behind them, the first houses of the village loom up.

They're not like the houses I know from Camlann – the red-painted fishermen's houses by the harbour – nor like the stately homes in Brevalaer. I can't even see a resemblance with the clay fishermen's houses in Gwennec. Here, the houses are round, like snail shells. The walls are inlaid with coloured seashells, which give each house a shade of soft pink or fragile white. I can't detect any streets or other infrastructure. Surrounding the gardens are low walls or fences cobbled together from random pieces of wreckage. And there are crooked, gnarly apple trees everywhere. The sight of all that white blossom is overwhelming. The rain makes the pungent, sweet smell even stronger.

We pass a car that's parked out in the grass. It looks like it has been there for a long time. The wheels are missing and there are plants growing all over the bonnet.

'Bring him to my house,' I hear Enja say from up front. A young, blonde woman leans towards her and says a few words, but too quietly for me to understand. Enja mumbles something in reply.

'Please,' the woman says. Enja responds with a nod.

They take us into one of the shell houses. Immediately we find ourselves in a circular living room. In various corners are large looms, covered with colourful cloths, some of which have only just been stretched, whereas others are almost finished. In another corner is a simple spinning wheel. I think we had a wheel just like that in the attic.

The thought of that attic, and all the things that have disappeared, lances through my heart.

The blonde woman takes off her anorak and shakes out her many braids. the shells tinkling against each other. 'Clear that stuff off the table and bring it here.'

Enja gives instructions and moves Arthur from his stretcher to the table. It's not that he's white as a sheet, but the fact that he hasn't opened his eyes after all this lugging around makes fear stab my heart like a knife. He looks dead in every way possible. I would've believed it too, had I not heard his wheezing breath just now. In his feverish sleep, my little brother struggles to take every single breath.

I shuffle closer and take his hand. It's burning hot. On the other side of the table, Enja leans over him and takes off the bandages. I wrapped the last piece of clean bandage around his leg the day before yesterday, but by now it's very dirty. What is sticking to the fabric isn't clean, red blood. It's dark pus, which also sticks to the frayed edges of the wound. The stench is wafting towards me. I clench my jaws to keep from gagging. Enja's face remains impassive, but I see a flicker of unease in her eyes.

'I need a few people to help me. Collum, Dermid, Tomas, you are strong, you can stay. The rest of you: out.' She talks easily, as if she's used to giving such orders. 'Tillie, bring my tools and the white bottle that says "poppy milk" on it. You know where to find it. No shillyshallying!'

Tillie dashes out of the house.

Enja turns to the blonde woman. 'I need water and cloths. Do you have a supply of devil's claw somewhere?'

'A few dried strands, that's all… And I doubt it'll be enough.' The look both women then give my brother only makes me more anxious.

When Tillie comes back, I refuse to let go of Arthur's hand. Enja tries to be gentle at first, carefully prying my fingers off his hand. When that doesn't work, she roughly pushes me aside. 'I need space, girl. Take her upstairs, please.' The latter is directed at the blonde woman.

'You don't understand,' I say. 'That's my brother! I have to stay with him. I have to know how bad it is. Whether he will… when he will wake up again.'

'Come now, step aside.' The blonde woman's voice is gentle. 'Enja knows what she's doing, you best help her by letting her do her job. Let me look at your face.'

Unwillingly, I turn to her and allow her to cup my face between both hands. I flinch a little when her fingers run over the newly formed blisters.

'Fortunately, it was only a gentle rain. This will ease the burn.' She applies an ointment that immediately numbs the stabbing pain. I recognise the smell of chamomile. 'You must be exhausted. When was the last time you slept?'

What does it matter? I turn to Arthur again. 'What are they going to do with him?'

Enja makes an annoyed movement, as if to swat away a fly. She pulls the bandage away again and, with the help of one of the men, strips down what remains of Arthur's trousers.

The blonde woman hesitates. 'The infection has nestled deep inside his leg.'

'I already know that.' I lick my lips in an attempt to moisten my parched mouth. 'I tried to help him. I couldn't operate on him...'

'What you did made a difference,' Enja says unexpectedly. She doesn't look back. 'But to stay alive, he'll probably have to give up his leg.'

Shock reverberates through my body. After temporarily being rendered speechless, I start to shake my head. 'That cannot happen! There must be another way to...'

'Come.' This time, the blonde woman is firmer, her grip on my arm stronger. 'You've done everything you could. Let Enja take over now. Meanwhile, you need to rest and eat.'

'Then let me stay with him! Please!' To my horror, I start to blubber like a child. The blonde woman grabs Katell's hand and pulls us both towards a wooden staircase, using all her strength. For a few moments, I try to resist, but the horror and my weakened state soon force me to give up. She takes is to an upper room. There is a small table in there as well as a bed.

'Wait here.' She disappears and soon returns with bread, a pot of honey and fresh water. My stomach immediately starts to growl. Katell stares at all the food without moving. I follow the blonde woman's gaze. Suddenly I realise what we must look like – how incredibly dirty and bony we must both be. I stop crying and wipe my face. Automatically I walk over to the table and break off a piece of bread, shoving it into Katell's hands. 'Eat,' I say, as I've had to do so many times by now. 'I know you're hungry.'

'Is she your sister?'

'No. I'm Arthur's sister.'

'Arthur?' Her voice falters and fear suddenly flickers in her eyes. 'And what is your name?'

'Nimue,' I reply slowly.

All of a sudden, she looks as pale as Arthur. She steadies herself on the edge of the table. 'I thought I saw something familiar in your face. I was telling myself it was just my imagination. A wish, nothing more... Oh, spirits.'

Perhaps it's still the shock that stuns me as I struggle to understand the stream of words coming out of her mouth. Like the other village people, she speaks the same language as I do, but in their mouths the words seem so elongated and lilting. 'I don't understand.'

'Of course not. I beg your pardon. If it's true... if it's true what I think, then you are Rona's children.'

Now it's my turn to stare at her wide-eyed. Due to my anxiety, I had almost forgotten where we have ended up. That someone might know us – even recognise us – hadn't even occurred to me. Sweet Gwenhael! 'We've lost her a long time ago! How do you know my mother? Who are you?'

She puts a hand on her chest, above her heart, either to calm herself or to point to herself. 'My name is Ana.'

It dawns on me that I know who she is. 'Mum's friend.'

She takes me in as if she's afraid that she's dreaming. Her eyes have the colour of a cloudless summer sky. 'How did you get here?'

'We sailed here.' I realise how obvious that is and almost laugh. 'We travelled across half of Central Europe to find her.'

'But your father...'

'Is dead. He's been dead for years.' I look around, as if the small room could be hiding my mother somewhere. 'Mum must be here. Everything points to... She *is* here, isn't she?'

Ana turns even paler. 'Oh, sweet spirits.'

'What does that mean? Is she here, yes or no?'

'Rona is gone, Nimue.'

'Has she left again?' My last bit of courage washes away like water in dry earth. I sink down onto the bed. The hope I've been clinging to in the past few weeks is replaced with bitterness. 'Did she ever come back here?'

'She came here,' Ana confirmed softly. 'And she never sailed away again. But she is no longer with us, Nimue. I'm terribly sorry.'

'If you mean she's dead, just say she is dead!'

Ana shakes her head. 'Gone. Not dead. Though it makes little difference to those who are left behind. Nimue, you look as if you might faint at any moment. We shouldn't speak about such difficult topics right now. Come, eat and rest. Be secure in the knowledge that Arthur is in the most capable hands.' As if to prove that I am also in good hands, she kneels down at my side and puts her hands on my shoulders. 'Rona was like a sister to me. I'm glad to finally meet you.' Her hands on my shoulders turn into an embrace and I do nothing to stop her. I'm so exhausted. And it's been so long since I felt safe. I wish I could be happier that I've found a trace of my mother again. But I feel empty, like a hollowed-out shell.

Ana gets up. 'Eat and rest,' she says again. She closes the door behind her and I hear the sound of her footsteps retreating on the stairs. I could go after her. No one can forbid me to stay by Arthur's side when the healer puts a sharp knife into his soft flesh, and with expertise and cold determination, will cut the living flesh away from his fevered body...

Dizziness makes me not want to get up from the bed. I can't see clearly. After all I have done for Arthur and myself, I can't bear to watch him lose his leg. With a burning sense of shame, I force myself to eat some bread with honey. I hardly notice how sweet it is, or how fresh the water tastes, as if it didn't come from a plastic bottle. Exhaustion finally makes me pull Katell onto the bed beside me. I fall into a dreamless sleep, with my arms around her, as if her warmth can protect me from the nightmare unfolding downstairs.

***

I look at Arthur's resting form and listen to his breathing. His face is as white as the sheet that covers him. I don't know how long I've been standing next to him like this, only that he hasn't moved in all that time. Only his eyes blink every now and then, as if he's having a restless dream.

I know that Ana and Enja are worried. Enja says he has been in this state for too long and too deep. Her herbs have almost driven the fever out of his body, but he still won't wake up. I have heard her say that it's as if he's hiding. As if he *wants* to be somewhere else.

A small part of me can understand that he doesn't want to wake up. Not now that his body has been mutilated beyond repair. Unwillingly, my gaze drifts downwards. To his stump.

Because that's what it is. Not a wound, not a scar, and certainly not a leg. They took off the leg a hand's width above his knee. Enja has done it perfectly. She has sawed clean through the bone and saved a flap of skin, which she has sewn around the stump with thin, strong thread. I get nauseous if I look at it for too long. The wound at the end of his stump is clean. It will heal well, Enja has assured me. But I can't look at it. Horrified, I avert my eyes.

A soft footfall alerts me to someone's presence. Ana enters with a basket full of unwashed, unkempt sheep's wool. I've learned that she is a weaver. She glances at my pale face, puts her basket down and says: 'Come out with me. It's dry now, and the air will do you good.'

'Nothing will do me good,' I complain, discouraged.

She takes me in with a critical gaze. 'I would at least like to see some blush returning to those cheeks.' Ana grabs my arm and ignores my feeble protest.

The island sits high above the sea, rising up in steep cliffs and cradled by low sandy beaches. Those cliffs must have preserved Avalon when all the other islands disappeared under the waves. There is a harbour, Ana tells us, a place further away from the village where the hills roll down in gentle slopes and where a wide cart path allows the inhabitants to drive back and forth with their cargo. How many inhabitants are left she cannot say exactly, but there are fewer than before. She tells me about her childhood, when there were five villages, all a stone's throw away from each other. Three of them now remain abandoned between the hills like deserted memories. Only the voice of the wind can be heard there now. We walk between an arc of blossoming apple trees. When she sees me staring at them, she smiles. 'Avalon is an old name. It means *island of apples.*'

'When Mum, Benji and Esoldi lived in Central Europe, they had a house called Avalon,' I tell her. 'They missed the apple trees. Every spring they thought back to all the blossoms on the island.'

'I'm glad she missed something from the island,' Ana says softly.

I give her a sideways glance. 'She missed you.'

Ana smiles sadly.

One through the orchard, we pass the last house of the village. The persistent sea wind and the other elements have had free rein, because the shell walls look dilapidated. The window shutters are closed, and parts of the roof have clearly been repaired several times, yet show fresh signs of decay. Next to the house is the carcass of a smaller building, overgrown with plants and the sprouts of young trees. Ana slows down. It's as if she's hesitating.

'What is it?' I ask, somehow fascinated by the scene.

'That's an evil place. We have many bad memories of it.'

'Was that *their* house?' I inquire, my voice fading to a whisper. 'Is it still inhabited?'

'Someone lives there still, yes. But it wouldn't do you any good to go and look.' With new determination she marches past the house. I hesitate and glance over my shoulder. Did I just see movement in the rear garden? Did I hear the creaking of a door? Ana isn't waiting for me and I hurry to catch up with her.

When we have walked far enough to leave the village behind and the hills abruptly end at the steep abyss of the cliffs, she stops. Ana shocks me by turning towards me with tears in her eyes. 'There. The last time I saw Rona, she went over there.'

I peer in the direction she's pointing at. A thick mist rises from the sea, obscuring the far horizon. But I can see the beach below us, where the tide is retreating, and behind it, the shadow of another island, much smaller than the one we are on now.

'That's Gull Island,' Ana says.

'The beach where she freed Sela.' I can still vividly recall Rona's first entry in her diary. That grey shape in the sea is where it all began. Now that I'm so close to it, I can feel my blood tingle.

'It's both a place of imprisonment and freedom.' Ana doesn't look at me. She's staring in the same direction as me, though I have a feeling she's remembering events from long ago. 'You have the right to know the whole story, Nimue. And I have to tell you, even if it hurts my heart. When Rona returned, she didn't stay for long. Long enough to make sure I understood what was going on, that I understood what she *needed* to do. Not long enough to comfort me.' Ana sighs deeply. 'She left this with me before she went out there. I know she left the book with her husband, so her children could read it as soon as they were old enough. She desperately hoped that you would be safe. And that one day you might understand. But here you are now. Not as safe as she wanted you to be. And sweet spirits, not nearly as unscathed...' She looks at me as if she's about to say more, but then falls silent. She reaches into the pocket of her honey-coloured dress and hands me a carefully folded piece of paper. 'This page she kept with her on her return journey. To remember, she said. To hold on to, whenever she was feeling scared. And then she gave it to me so she could allow herself to leave.' When I do nothing, she presses it into the palm of my hand. 'Read it, Nimue.'

Speechless, I unfold the piece of paper and see my mother's familiar, swirling handwriting.

So soon the end will come. A life for a life. I'll stand before the mighty sea and call to the seals until they swim up to the surface to be my witnesses. I'll step into the waves and let myself be carried away – my air, my light, my memories.

Soon, the sun will fade and my time will be over. I know that I will cling to the images of Arthur and Nimue in my mind until my humanity is completely wiped away. And though it's strange, I'm not so afraid anymore. So here I come, sea. I am ready.

My hands tremble. I can only just prevent my feeble fingers from letting go of the paper and letting the wind take it away. I whisper: 'Was she expecting to die?'

'I believe she was.'

'But you said she wasn't dead!'

'Nimue, let me have my say. Rona expected she would die – but that's not what happened. Her mother emerged from the waves. I was standing on the rocks, hiding. I saw it all happen.' Ana swallows again. 'The sea took her human life. Sela seized it. She saved her daughter. Changed her ...'

'*Changed* her?' I can no longer keep up with the hurricane of emotions and unsuccessfully grasp for logical thoughts. 'How...?'

She looks at me. Her voice trembles slightly, but her eyes are so calm. 'You know how. Think, Nimue. Think about what Sela is. Think of what flowed through Rona's blood ... the same that flows through yours. The magic of the spirits.'

Slowly I shake my head. This cannot be the whole truth. This cannot be the end of the story – not now that Arthur and I have finally arrived on Avalon. But Ana's words are like the bells of Saint Gwenhael – they chime the truth in my head, and it's a sound I cannot escape. And I hear myself speaking: 'Sela brought Mum to the bottom of the ocean. Her sight changed... her skin... her eyes...'

I fall silent, but I can't deny the truth. I have felt it all in my dreams. *Swim deeper. Come to us.* Those words were never meant for me.

'Is she still there? Is she on Gull Island together with Sela, like a...' I'm almost unable to pronounce the word. 'A seal?'

'Maybe.' When Ana looks at me, I see a reflection of my own helplessness on her face. 'After the transformation, I often rowed over to the island. I watched the seals on the sandbanks ... I thought I'd recognise her. How could I not pick her out of that group of seals, her being my best friend? And by their own magic, maybe they could take on human form again. If Sela could do it, why not Rona?' Ana shakes her head sadly. 'They never changed, Nimue. In the end, I gave up. There are no humans on Gull Island.'

'I have to see it for myself. I have to see *her*!'

'You wouldn't recognise her.'

'I still have to go there. Please, Ana.'

'Then I will row you there. But we must wait until high tide, or the boat will smash into the rocks. The currents will pull you down as soon as you capsize.'

I nod. For a while we're both silent. 'A life for a life,' I say softly. I still don't understand. Or maybe I just don't want to understand. With difficulty, I say: 'Ten years ago, Benji died on the floor of his laboratory.'

'Yes.'

'Ten years ago, Mum came back to Avalon...'

'You know what it means, Nimue.'

I shake my head. I open my mouth but cannot manage to speak. My eyes burn and my cheeks are suddenly wet with tears. *Don't say it*, I beg Ana with my gaze. *I don't want to hear it.*

But she is ruthless. Ana wraps her fingers around my hand and prevents me from letting go of the paper. When she speaks, it is a quiet sound. 'She traded her life with the spirits to make her brother's life disappear. She killed Benji.' Her light blue eyes are looking for mine while she pronounces this terrible truth so easily. 'It was the only way she could think of to prevent him from ever getting his hands on you.'

The cliffs suddenly seem dangerously close. I pull my hand away, stumble backwards and sink through my knees. Ana says something else, but all I can hear is the whooshing of blood in my ears, as if the sea is in my head and waking up full of rage.

'Nimue?' Ana leans over me. I lift my hands to ward her off. I need space. 'She did it because she loved you.'

I force a sound past my lips. 'She loved Benji too.'

'Of course she did.' I blink through a mist of tears and see Ana's face nearby. Her blonde hair dances wildly in the sea breeze running free on these cliffs. 'Just as he loved her. Never doubt that! Whatever else happened... He was her brother and she was his sister.'

'And they destroyed each other.'

'Because she loved you more...'

'How can you kill your brother? I would never do anything to hurt Arthur!' My sudden scream startles her. Ana flinches. But in my mind is a deep, black voice that wonders if what I say is true. Am I not somehow to blame for Arthur's deep sleep? For the fact that Camlann's harbour guards fired those bullets at us? I should've paid more attention. I should've been more careful. Faster. I'm his big sister and Rona only gave me a single task before she left: *Take care of your brother. Never let him out of your sight. You and Arthur must always stay together.*

And I have failed.

I bury my face in my hands and curl up into a ball. 'Please leave me alone.'

If she hesitates, if she's about to say something or pull me up, I'm not able to see it. I stay in the same position until I hear her soft footsteps retreating. Then only the wind remains, howling as loudly as I do.

The sun simmers out, swallowed up by the rising mists and suffocating clouds hugging the sea. I'm cold, my tears dried up on my face. I scramble to my feet in order to get warmer. I don't want to go back to Ana's house – not yet. As darkness falls, I wander around the island until I find a path that takes me back to the ruined house where my mother and uncle spent their unhappy childhoods. A thin plume of smoke billows up from the chimney. I look at it with narrowed eyes and feel the horror of all that Benji and Rona have done culminate in this one place: this house, this history, that shadow of a man I see walking around through the cracks in the ragged shutters – slowly, as if every step hurts him. It can all be traced back to this place, to the father who did so much damage to his children.

While my head is still questioning the wisdom of my decision, my legs are already carrying me forward. I walk to the front door. My heart begins to beat more wildly, warning me that danger is near. I take a deep breath and let my fist pound on the weathered wood of the door.

A silence descends like a suffocating net. Then something creaks and the door is pulled open. From the opening, a streak of yellow lamp light falls out. That light reveals a man, bent over and leaning on a stick. His hair is thin and grey, his mouth pressed in a thin line. His skin is sunburnt and leathery, like that of the old fishermen in Gwennec. Everything about him shows traces of neglect: the stains in his clothes that make me suspect he's been wearing the same jumper and trousers for weeks on end, his calloused, unwashed hands, his crocheted cap, which looks limp on his head and has been patched up several times. But underneath that cap, his sea-blue eyes stare at me with a suspicious sort of intelligence. Those are Benji's eyes, as I saw them in Cormack's photograph. A reflection of my own eyes, equally blue, and at this moment, probably equally suspicious.

For a few moments I'm unable to move. I stare at the old man in front of me and try to remember why I was banging on that door again.

He breaks the silence. 'I'm not standing here waiting for the sun to set! What do you want?'

That growl wakes me from my trance. 'Fergus Cairn,' I say. 'Do you know who I am?'

His gaze dances across my face, or across whatever he can make out in the sparse light. I know he's looking at my red curls, at the freckles on my cheeks, at my sea-blue eyes. For a moment I think I see a shiver go through him, a flash of superstitious discomfort.

'I have never seen you, wench. What do you want from me?' He takes a step back inside and I follow him so that I'm standing on the threshold.

'I am Nimue Pesketaer,' I hear myself say. 'I came to Avalon with my brother Arthur. We were born in Gwennec by the sea. My father was Bertram the fisherman. My mother is Rona.'

Fergus shoves the door in my face, but I have more strength in my body than he has. I push the man backwards and step past him, straight into the room.

It's messy and dirty inside. The room is filled with a heavy, unpleasant odour. There is a table pushed against the wall, under the window with the broken shutter. The other shutter is closed. In the hearth, a fire struggles to stay alive, but the ash residue from previous evenings is smothering the flames. It generates more smoke than heat. The only lamp that's lit is on the table, spreading a yellow glow and revealing a door to a room in the back. It's dark there – an uninviting sight. On the walls are strings of shells and pieces of washed-up wood, polished by the sea, smoothed out into rounded shapes. Once, this must have brightened up the room and the shells must have gleamed in the light. Now, threads of dust and cobwebs disgrace the decorations. I boldly step over a heap of clothes on the floor and take in the room. I feel no hesitation intruding on him like this. Now that I'm here, even the fear has slipped away from me. I have only a dull, sickly feeling as I look around this house, this place where Mum and Benji once lived, and observe the man standing at the front door taking me in. I know he's staring at me. I feel his burning gaze in my back. I deliberately take my time to look at everything before I turn around to face him.

Fergus follows my movements with a strange look in his eyes. Fear? Is he afraid I'll attack him? My lip curls up into something more of an animal-like grimace than a smile. 'Do you know what happened to my mother?'

'I never saw Rona again.' He narrows his eyes. 'Your mother didn't come back.'

I laugh briefly and joylessly. 'You are wrong. Do you know why she left? Do you know what happened to Benji? Did Ana never tell you anything?'

'Ana?' Now it's Fergus's turn to let out a bitter laugh. His voice is as rough as sandpaper on wood and when he gets closer, I can smell alcohol on his breath. He gives me the shivers. I lift my chin in an attempt not to show him what I feel. 'No one ever tells me anything. I have two children.' He peers at me from underneath his cap and his furrowed brows. 'A faithless daughter and a worthless son. Stinking fish gods! And what are you doing here, child of Rona? Were you expecting to find my daughter in my house?'

I clench my fist and want to knock his teeth out, struggling to control my anger and disgust. I understand this is not a man who realises what he has done. But he has to know. I *want* him to know. I take a deep breath and let it out slowly through my nose. 'I have come to tell you the truth. You are like poison in the sea, Fergus Cairn. Everyone who has dealt with you has fallen ill. Benji is dead. You tortured and beat him and in his turn, he mutilated dozens of children.' I walked closer to him. He is a head shorter than me. 'You made your son like yourself while he tried to become the opposite. What remained was a mutilated life.'

Fergus is silent for a long time. When he finally speaks again, his voice is soft. 'Benji didn't know when to obey. He was rebellious, brash and stubborn. I tried to correct him. As befits a father.'

'You're not a father.' The words tumble from my lips in a soft hiss. 'You're a coward. You were afraid that Sela wouldn't stay with you, so you hid her fur. You were afraid you couldn't control your son, so you beat him like a mutt. And my mother? What did she ever do to you?'

'Rona was foolish.' Fergus's face becomes a mere shadow as he walks away from me and steps outside the circle of light cast by the lamp. 'She believed I would purposely kill my son.'

'What are you talking about?' I ask coldly.

He gestures towards the night, which is visible through the open door. The cold air is whooshing over the already struggling flames. 'She thought I'd pushed him into the barn when it was burning. And then she jumped into the flames. Silly las. Wasn't it enough that her brother was trapped in there?'

'They escaped,' I say softly. 'Rona saved Benji and you did nothing to help them.'

'I brought water. I extinguished the fire!' Suddenly he sounds furious and his fist hits the table top. I almost jump out of my skin in fright and take a hasty step towards the door. Fergus doesn't seem to notice. 'I wanted to see my children come out of the flames alive, but they were fools to go in there in the first place! Maybe I wasn't a perfect father, but I'm not the monster Rona made me out to be. She betrayed me. Sela betrayed me.' He grits his teeth. 'All those years I provided them with food and a roof over their heads. Blood is blood. And you, granddaughter? Have you come to see what a monster I am? Have you heard enough?' He approaches me again and I take a few more steps back. 'Oh, leaving so soon?'

The hairs on the back of my neck stand up when he laughs softly, bitterly.

'You have nothing left,' I observe. 'And I have nothing left to say to you. You can stay here with your regret or your bitterness or your love, whatever it is. You are my blood, but not my family.' I step across the threshold and breathe in the chilly sea air. After the suffocating smoke inside, it's a relief to breathe in the saltiness.

'Wait.' His voice breaks when he comes after me and hesitates in the doorway. That sound startles me – it's a sob and a snarl at the same time. 'How did he die?'

I speak to the night in front of me. 'Rona killed him.'

I decide not to wait for a reaction. I don't think I can bear to hear him curse or laugh. Or, spirits forbid, cry. I flee down the path, into the protection of the darkness.

18

BY MOON AND TIDE

The rowing boat cuts through the water between Avalon and Gull Island. Calm waves are licking the bow. From where I'm sitting, I feel the strong current pulling at the hull, but Ana steadily mans the oars and keeps us on course.

Then the boat scrapes a flat beach, littered with small and large pebbles. I jump off board and help Ana pull the rowing boat onto land, away from the surf. The bottoms of my trouser legs suck up the seawater.

Like the small cove where Arthur and I washed up, this beach almost immediately gives way to towering cliffs. I look up at the sky, which is a clear, deep blue. The sun flickers on the surging sea and the dancing spots of light on the water still clutter my vision when I avert my gaze. Gull Island lives up to its name. Silver-grey birds perch on anything high enough to protrude above the water. They fly across the beach and cliffs, their cries mingling with the whistling of the wind and the low voice of the ocean.

'The beach surrounds the whole island,' Ana says. 'If we walk along the cliffs on the west side, we'll reach the inlet where we can see the seals.' She hesitates and then shrugs apologetically. 'I wish I could promise you more.'

But there is simply no more to promise. I feel strangely hollow inside as I follow her. The beach first narrows, then widens. In the lee of two protruding cliffs is a crescent-shaped inlet, where Ana finally comes to a stop. The sand under the soles of my boots is packed and damp. With every step, shells and strands of seaweed crunch under my feet.

Ana points to a sloping cliff in front of us, which disappears into the sea. 'There's the cave.'

I look at it silently. It's not as high up as I'd imagined from Rona's descriptions. I can't see an opening, but then I remember it's high tide now. The cave must be under the water at the moment. Later, when the sea retreats, it will be accessible again for a few hours. I avert my gaze. The tide washes over the beach, the water almost reaching our feet. I look out over the sea. It's empty all the way to the horizon. 'When will the seals come?'

'They'll be here before sunset,' Ana says softly. 'We don't have long. It will be dark soon and we have to row back while the water is still high enough.'

I nod and find a seat on a protruding piece of rock, flattened at the top, perhaps by centuries of rising and retreating water. It's not a comfortable spot. Nevertheless, I pull my legs up and lean against the cliff. Good enough. I fold my arms and wait. Ana is standing next to me. I know she's watching me and I'm grateful that she doesn't break the silence.

I'm trying to find out exactly what I'm feeling. There is a hard knot in my stomach. As the minutes slip by, that knot tightens. I'm scared, I realise. Anxious for the moment when the seals will come out of the water to rest on the beach, because then I'll finally have to face what Ana has told me. This is not how it should've been. After all we have endured to get to this island, the reunion with Rona should've been a triumphant ending of our journey. But Arthur is in a coma, permanently mutilated, and my mother is a seal. It's still hard to digest and I could almost have a laugh about it. Mum, an animal with no human characteristics, who will soon not even recognise her own daughter anymore!

No, there is nothing triumphant about that. We are the ones who have lost.

The sun dips lower towards the horizon. I clasp my arms tighter around my waist and shiver in the anorak I borrowed from Ana. The collar, hood and sleeves are lined with sheep's wool and colourful stitched edges. At home, all our clothes were practical and unadorned. I study the pattern of fish and shells running along the sleeves and across the chest. In Gwennec or Brevalaer, I bet this anorak would fetch quite a lot of money.

The soft sound of Ana gasping for breath wakes me from my trance. I look up and she points. Not necessary; my gaze is automatically drawn to the sea that's starting to retreat by now. A little while longer and Ana and I will have to row back to Avalon.

I defiantly push that thought aside. Dark blobs rise up out of the water and drag themselves onto the beach. The seals are leaving the waves for the shell-filled sand. There are more of them than I can count, and some approach so closely that I can distinguish the dark and lighter patches on their fur and see the last bits of sunlight reflected in their eyes. I hardly dare to breathe. When I glance aside, I see a sad smile on Ana's lips.

The seals don't care about us. They spread out on the sand. Somewhere among them is my mother. I know it's true, yet I find it hard to believe. No matter how gently their eyes take us in, I don't detect even a spark of humanity in those dark, shining pools. And of course Ana is right, I think, disheartened: there's no point in standing here. Even if my mother would be lying here at my feet, I have no way of recognising her, and she won't remember me either.

But knowing and accepting this are two different things. I sink through my knees and lean my back against the cliff face.

'Nimue.' Ana's hand rests gently on my shoulder. 'The tide will not wait.'

'If you want to leave, you should go.'

'I won't leave you here by yourself.'

'You can pick me up later.'

'Nimue, if I leave now, you'll be stuck here until the next high tide.'

'Maybe I want to.' It takes effort to turn my eyes away from the dark animals on the beach. Although I know Ana is right, I want nothing more than to sit here. I don't care about the cold. I'm not ready to leave yet, tide or no tide. 'Maybe I should stay here and try to come to terms with everything. Give me this one night, Ana. Please.'

Ana visibly hesitates.

'I can take it,' I say. 'I'm tough and I'm used to being outside.' I smile with little joy. 'What I don't think I can take is to go back into that room and see Arthur lying there as he is now. With his leg chopped off. Unconscious. Too much has happened at once...' I suddenly find myself out of words, like a well that has dried up. Ana kneels down next to me and wraps me in her embrace.

'At the next high tide I'll come back for you. Make a fire, it'll be cold at night. And find some shelter near the rocks. There are plenty of inlets in the rockface.' She hands me two flints which, by the looks of it, have been used countless times. I wonder if she had them with her by chance or if she deliberately slipped them into her pockets, knowing that I might want to stay behind.

'Thank you,' I say sincerely.

She studies my face for a few moments. 'May the spirits be with you, Nimue.' With these words, she leaves me alone on the beach.

For a long time I sit motionless, my gaze fixed on the resting seals. The sun sets behind the edge of the world. The rock against my back still retains some warmth, but soon, it turns cold and dark.

I wasn't lying when I said I didn't mind a night in the open air. But still, I'd rather be warm while sitting out this daunting vigil. So I hoist up my cold body and start a slow stroll along the beach. There are plenty of washed-up branches and pieces of wreckage scattered among the protruding rocks. Some are saturated with salt water, only recently left behind by the sea. Other pieces are tangled in seaweed and dried out by the sun.

With my arms full of wood that is more or less dry, I walk a meandering route through the pod of seals. They move aside for me. A few look startled, most don't seem to be so impressed. In the sparse light of the rising moon, the creatures are no more than shadows with gleaming eyes. I look at every seal I pass from up close. *Is it her?* Even if our eyes met, I wouldn't know. This harsh thought encourages me to keep walking until I discover a hollow in the rocky cliffs that gives me just enough shelter from the wind. With my bare hands, I dig a shallow hole in the sand. A damp smell rises up from the sand: a mixture of earth and sea. I build a fire and use Ana's flints to light it.

I creep closer to the warmth provided by the flames. The flickering light and the wafting smoke form a barrier between me and the seals. I decide to resign myself to it. By the fire, I can see them better, even if they crawl further away. I rest my head against the rock and realise how tired I am. All my limbs are aching. But that pain isn't nearly as sharp compared to what I feel inside, where the image of Arthur keeps forcing itself upon me. He should be here with me.

I do my best to think of something else. My eyes flicker shut and I give in. In the darkness, I listen to all the sounds surrounding me. The fire crackles and hisses nearby, the slow, rhythmic melody of the surf rising above it. It's the sound I have fallen asleep to all my life. I hear wingbeats as a seagull flies across the beach near me. Most of the birds have taken shelter on the rocks. The seals shuffle and scrape across the sand as they move, but their silence deepens too.

I doze off for a moment and am startled awake again when I slide down the cliff. To keep myself awake, I start singing. I sing softly and hoarsely and the melody melts away with the sounds of fire, wind and the sea.

'Will you, will you follow me
Breaking the waves and braving the sea
Come from Camlann, lift anchor, set sail
If death won't withhold you, then nothing else will
Hold fast the helm through the mist all those miles
Sail past the cliffs to that sweet, secret isle

Will you, will you follow me
Breaking the waves and braving the sea
The wind turns west, then turns nevermore
The broken boat has run fast ashore
Hold fast the helm through the mist all those miles
I'll stay 'neath the cliffs of that sweet, secret isle.'

I never realised how much truth was hidden within those lyrics. Now it dawns on me that Mum had given us the key to her abode. If only we'd understood the words of this simple song earlier ...

I feel goosebumps erupting on my arms and move closer to the flames.

A sound pulls me out of my trance. It's not the shuffling of a seal's belly across the beach – it's unmistakably a soft footfall on the sand. I open my heavy eyelids and watch through a screen of flames and smoke as a shadow approaches me. She has the delicate shape of a woman: long limbs and black hair, waving with every step with the grace of swaying seaweed. Her pale skin reflects the white moonlight. I can't tell if she's wearing clothes or fur, but whatever it is, it ripples smoothly around her belly and legs.

I sit rigidly by the fire as as she approaches with graceful step. My heart is thundering in my chest. *She has come after all*, it occurs through me and I feel another leap in my chest, this time of hope and joy. My mother has given up her seal appearance to come find me.

Then she takes another step forward and I know that it isn't Rona. Her face is so similar to my mother's that it's easy to recognise her in those features.

Disappointment takes away everything I've wanted to say. Then I swallow and manage to squeeze out one word: 'Sela?'

Behind her, something moves. Only now do I see that she has not come alone. I'm surrounded by tall, pale creatures. They are partly absorbed by the darkness.

Spirits are with you.

My mouth goes dry and my gaze flits up at the apparitions that have gathered in a semi-circle around me and my campfire. The sallow Fisher King is not one of them. He must still be chained to his throne, alone in that tower room, endlessly yearning for the King Who Must Come to deliver him from the consuming corruption in his decaying body. I know now how it feels, having that black hunter inside your soul.

As if my memory alone were enough to summon him, I feel my hands shaking. A dizzy feeling runs through my whole body. I take a deep breath and try to suppress the feeling while I still stare at the spirits. *Others*, Wolf called them. Maybe that's a better name for them, because they are undeniably different.

There are beings who, like Sela, have a human appearance, although their limbs and faces are oddly elongated. I see a woman with small, round breasts. Her skin is white like sea foam. Her nakedness is such a natural part of her beauty that it doesn't embarrass me for even a moment.

There are men with glittering eyes and moonlight in their hair, which remind me of the story of the White Prophet. They have pale, blue spirals on their bodies, which cover their limbs in intricate patterns. I think I recognise some of these patterns: the eye and beak of a crow, making its way from the forehead and cheek of an elongated face to a sharp point at the side of the nose. Or the antlers of a stag, the tusks of a boar, interlaced leaves of oak and willow. Other patterns are too muddled for me to understand, but all are beautiful and emphasise the strangeness of the Others.

Other creatures have nothing human about them at all. In the corner of my left eye I catch a glimpse of a giant bear. Its fur is dark and wet, as if it has just emerged from the sea. Its skull is as big as a ship's figurehead, its teeth are as long as my entire forearm. A grey wolf trails the circle of ghosts behind him, like a guard on duty. My heart speeds up at a fast, nervous pace. With those jaws, it could easily break me in two if it wanted to.

Close to the flames is a yellow-brown hare, its long ears flattened against its back. He looks up at me with beady eyes that sparkle in the light of the fire. Although it's far from a human gaze, I'm struck by the intelligence shining through when I look him in the eye. There are large, silver gulls and gannets; something I mistook for a piece of protruding rock suddenly moves and slides forward, leaving a trail in the sand.

But none of those creatures is as beautiful or as sad as my own grandmother.

It suddenly occurs to me that I shouldn't sit on the ground like a disrespectful fool. I scramble to my feet and, a little embarrassed, wipe the sticky sand off my clothes. I'm painfully aware of the dirt under my nails and how the salty wind has made my curls stiff and tangled up. Things that have been usual business for me all my life, but in the presence of these pure beings suddenly feel terribly earthly.

Sela holds out a hand. Her fingers are long and feel cold as she runs them first through my hair and then across my face. A shiver goes through me. Not because her touch chills me, but because I feel a deep connection. Skin touches skin, and under that skin, blood flows close to my blood. This being I know from folktales, Sela the seal woman, the selkie, is my mother's mother. Where she touches me, my skin tingles. I know that her magic is also alive within me. I have known it since I've read Rona's diary, but for the first time I can look at the face of the woman who has shaped my life so deeply. Her hand slides further upwards, until the fingers come to rest on the seal chain on my chest. There is so much palpable loss in her gaze that I feel the urge to wrap my arms around her narrow body. But I wouldn't dare.

Sela lets the air escape from her lungs. 'I see so much of him in you.'

For a moment, these words upset me. I want her to talk about Rona, to bring my mother back to me. Then it dawns on me who she's talking about and I feel embarrassed. I force my gaze to meet hers. 'Your son is dead. Benji... is dead.'

She gives me the saddest smile. 'I can't change what I am: the mother of a son, even if that son is no longer alive. I made this pendant out of pebbles from the beach, when I was still carrying Rona in my lap. I impregnated the stone with a few drops of my own blood. I hung it above her cot when she slept and when Benji was born, I hung it above his. I hoped it would protect them...'

'I'm sorry,' I say with a gasp. 'Oh, Sela, I know the whole story now. What Fergus did to you – what he did to Benji. My mother and her brother... All the misery, all the grief. And me...' I lift my hands to my face. 'I feel polluted.'

'It's true,' Sela admits softly. 'Pain is what you have inherited.'

'It should never have happened. Fergus shouldn't have taken you. Rona should not have killed Benji...'

'Then you would never have been born. And we would never have had our King That Must Come. Oh, Nimue, is that really what you believe? Do you see only the anger and the hatred that bind our story together?'

'What else is there?' I ask, desperately longing for something to relieve the razor-sharp pain in my chest.

'Love. As true as the north star.' Sela's simple words make me lower my hands and look at her again. She continues: 'Even though I didn't love my prison, I loved the children it gave me. And you – do you really believe that you're born of something other than love?'

'No,' I admit slowly. I remember the way Mum wrote about Dad. 'She loved him passionately.'

'As she loves you too.' She takes my trembling hands in hers. Again, her touch awakens something deep inside me. 'You have inherited pain, but pain is the twin of love. The kind of love that strikes like lightning and digs deep into the core, like a knife cutting the trunk of a beech tree. You have inherited my gift for healing, my magic flows through you like it flows through Rona. Finally, my dear, you inherited the power to break chains and regain freedom.'

I remain silent while I let her words sink in. It could all be true what she says. I could love as fiercely as lightning and as deeply as a knife might cut the trunk of a beech tree. I might even have broken the first links of the strangling chain of the Asclepius Congregation, but is that enough? Was it enough for Katell? Enough for Arthur? And lastly, the question I hardly dare ask myself … I tremble even worse as I swallow and fix my gaze on Sela. 'I don't know if it's enough for me. I needed my mother so much. She was never there.'

The selkie woman takes me in. She doesn't seem angry or upset. She keeps her hands around mine as she turns and speaks softly: 'Come.'

The semicircle of Others silently disperses and then follows us, while Sela leads me along the beach. We dodge the seals crossing our path until we reach a tongue of sand that disappears into the foamy surf. A lone seal has chosen this spot to rest, on the boundary between salt water and damp earth. Her fur is a mottled patchwork of black and grey. So far away from the campfire, I have only the moon to help my eyes. I take in her almost motionless form. There is something ragged about her. Her fins are frayed at the tips, the dark flesh torn by small and larger wounds or scars. She hardly seems to have enough fat reserves to get through another winter. If I had come across such a seal at home, I wouldn't have even bothered to kill and skin her for the meat and the fur. I would've simply left her where she was and let the sea or the changing seasons determine the animal's fate.

Now, entirely different thoughts cross my mind. I can hardly breathe while looking down at the seal. I don't doubt for a moment who this is. Yet I'm suddenly afraid to say it out loud.

Sela lets go of my hand. The corners of her mouth tilt up into that small, sad smile. 'She doesn't want to change. Or maybe she can't. I'm afraid guilt and despair have affected her far more than my spell. Every day she forgets more of who she is.'

I drop to my knees beside the seal, in which I can recognise nothing of my mother. She starts and makes an attempt to crawl away on her belly. After a few weak movements, she gives up and stays still, her round eyes fixed on me with suspicion. My throat squeezes shut. 'What's wrong with her?'

'She is weak,' Sela says. 'The tide brings her to the beach and pulls her back to the water. I fear that soon she won't even be able to swim.'

She doesn't have to say what that would mean. I look at the emaciated animal form of my mother and feel warm tears running down my cheeks. 'I have to save her.'

Sela is silent. I run my hand over Rona's body. I feel the bones under the fur, the dark hair dull instead of shiny. My mother shivers at my touch. More tears spring to my eyes and I whisper: 'I want to break the spell.'

The bear is suddenly close by. He is even bigger than I thought. I cower when I feel his hot breath on my face and do my utmost best to stay where I am. His voice is like the low rumble of thunder. 'A life for a life is what she promised. A life for a life is what was taken. This exchange is sealed and settled.'

'But look at her!' A hysterical tone enters my voice. 'She's weak. She's unhappy. She doesn't even know who she was anymore.' My voice breaks and I begin to cry. I look up at my grandmother, begging her. 'Don't let her die like this! I need my mother... Arthur needs her.'

Even through the haze of my tears, I can see the pain that's marked her face. 'Perhaps death is the gentlest of gifts, Nimue. When Rona came to this beach ten years ago, she was determined to give herself to the waves. I couldn't let her go like that. So I took her life in my hands and moulded her into something equal to me. Now I know better... I know that she can never be completely like me. She doesn't straddle the border between worlds, she can't travel between the two like a true selkie. Maybe...' Her pretty face twists in pain. 'Maybe that was the most selfish thing I've ever done. I was never a good mother. I tried to save her and as always, I was only cruel to her. Oh, Nimue. Maybe my daughter was always destined to die.'

'No!' I'm surprised at how furious I sound. My fingers dig into the sand and I clench my fists. 'I refuse to let her go. Not now that I've found her. I refuse to let her die because she should never have been turned into a seal. You hear?' I shout and hurl the words at the Others. 'I *demand* my mother back! I don't care how you do it. I don't care what I have to do! Bring her back to me the way she was!'

'You can't reverse the agreement she made with us.' The man with the crow pattern on his face throws me a solemn look. 'Even if we were willing to reverse it.'

'Then I want a new agreement.' I don't really know what I'm saying. All I know is that there must be a way out and I must find it before it's too late. I blink violently to clear my vision and stare up at the pale-skinned Other. 'Tell me what you want in order to let my mother go.'

A murmur of voices rises like a rushing wind. I don't understand what the Others are saying to each other, probably because the blood is pounding in my ears so loudly. Sela is standing ramrod straight and stock still. I don't know whether I should continue with my pleas. I open my mouth, but then my grandmother makes a tiny gesture with her hand: *be quiet*. I clench my jaws.

Finally, the man with the crow pattern raises his hands. The moonlight lights up the other half of his face like a silver mask. The ghostly whispers ebb away and I hold my breath.

'You are asking for a new agreement. But it is still a life for a life. A life is what we would ask again. Who would pay the price? You?' He takes a step closer and I automatically lean closer to Rona, as if my mother could protect me even in her weakened, unaware state. 'Your little brother who has crossed the threshold?'

'No,' I answer and I feel fear rising. That's the one price I don't want to pay. 'You leave him out of this. I want Arthur and me both to live.' When the Others don't respond, I desperately blurt out: 'There must be something else I can give you!'

'That's it.' The grey wolf creeps forward silently. I stiffen as its maw presses against my body. One bite and I'll bleed out on the beach. 'There's life in your womb. I can smell it.' As if to reinforce his words, the wolf inhales deeply, his head pressed against my belly.

I don't think I heard him right. I shake my head. 'There is no life there.'

The wolf curls up his upper lip and lets out a soft growl. My whole body trembles. 'You are wrong.'

'You are lying!' I say.

'The blood of a shaman from the north and a descendant of the selkies,' says the man with the crow pattern. 'It would be a good combination.'

The Others start mumbling again.

'Look at her. Pale as moonlight. She didn't know she was carrying the child inside.'

'It's still young. It can still die easily.'

'But it could live. Every day the odds are more favourable.'

'Then we will take it. A life for a life.'

'You have your agreement, child of the sea.'

'Stop!' The world is spinning around me. I press my hands to my ears to shut out their shocking words. It's as if I can still hear their voices inside me. 'I haven't agreed to it yet!'

It's the grey wolf who answers: 'But you will. This is the agreement you asked for, which we're giving you. Your mother in exchange for the child in your womb. Not immediately... When he has reached the right age.'

If he thinks these words reassure me, he's wrong. I can hardly string two sensible thoughts together. I want to think clearly, but with my emaciated seal mother next to me and Sela silently by my side, that's completely impossible. My wide-open eyes scan the circle of Others, who are now all looking at me expectantly. Were they expecting me to try to bargain for Rona's life, and did they know what they would ask for in return? Is that why they came to the beach?

I have to think. My heart is beating so fast it almost makes me feel sick. Thinking is impossible – I feel like a fish caught in a net. In an attempt to shut out the Others and the whole beach, I squeeze my eyes shut.

Breathe in and out, Nimue. Just in and out. Ignore their eager looks. Figure this out.

Could it be that the spirits are lying? I consider the possibility, but I know that that's not the case. They have no reason to deceive me. So it must be true then – I'm pregnant with Wolf's child.

In a flash, I remember what Mum wrote in her diary about being pregnant with me. I wish I could be as thrilled as her, but all I feel is the depressing urge to hide my head in my arms and curl up in a corner. Instead, my hands fly to my flat stomach. My ribs are still protruding, but I'm not as skinny as I was back in the Ark. Those few short days of being taken care of by Cormack have made my body curvier. Still – it's impossible to imagine a *child* growing inside me. If it's true, what has it had to endure these past weeks? Hunger, dehydration, the rough conditions of the constantly rocking boat. If the child has survived all this time, it must be a miracle.

But it could indeed be a miracle. And every day I spend in the safety of the island increases the chance of the child being born alive.

My child.

Mine and Wolf's, the man with his rough hands and his electric kisses. The man with whom I don't need to exchange words to be understood. Slowly, I feel a warmth rising in my body. I open my eyes and notice that the Others haven't left their positions. I take a deep breath and force my fists to relax. When I speak, I can only just keep my voice under control. 'You give me back Rona and I will give you my child. But only under these conditions.' I take another deep breath, as if I'm about to jump into cold water. The Others are silent; their silence makes me nervous. 'Rona never died. That's not a life for a life... not the way she meant it. So you will never get the life of my child. My mother was stuck between two worlds... so, my child will live on the threshold between two worlds, like his father. Let him be a bridge builder.' With my tongue I lick my dry lips. Still, they remain silent. When I risk peeking at Sela for a second, her facial expression is unreadable. 'Well? Isn't that what you all want? The King Who Must Come? Someone to mend the rift between the worlds?'

'Do you propose that your child will also free the coming king from his task?' The man with the crow pattern sounds disapproving. 'You, child of the sea, are trying to cancel two debts at once. No.' He shakes his head gravely. 'Your brother is not part of this agreement. This is our promise: Rona will be freed from her spell and your child will be ours, when the right time comes.'

I blink and struggle to find an appropriate answer, but as soon as I open my mouth to say something, the creatures fade away like fog in the sun. The beach is deserted, except for the seals and Sela. A deep sense of loss overwhelms me. What have I done? I have traded the life of my child for that of my mother. I lean far forward and support myself with my hands on the sand, preventing myself from tumbling over. 'I wasn't ready to decide this!'

'For better or worse, the deal is done,' Sela says softly. She must sense the desperation in me, because she continues: 'Don't be too anxious, Nimue. You were clever when you said that Rona never died. My people are desperate, not cruel.' Her cool hand rests on my shoulder. 'Come. Your task is not done yet. Even if my daughter is free to break her chains, it doesn't mean she's capable of doing so.'

'Then how do I help her?' I ask, trying to push aside my anxious feelings. Sela's right: for now, I need to concentrate on Rona.

'You have to reach that part of her heart that can still remember she is Rona. I don't know how to help you.'

Discouraged, I look at the sad shape of the seal. There must still be something of my mother that remains, something I can find. I sigh. 'I wish Arthur were here.'

'He can't be here. The King Who Must Come is on his way to us on the other side.'

'Does that mean he's going to be asleep forever?' I ask weakly.

'It means he's waking up on the other side.' Sela pulls her hand back. 'Nimue, I know how much you have already lost. I'm ashamed of the grief I have caused you. Listen, my dear. You can no longer wake Arthur up, but you *can* see him.'

I look up at her. 'How?'

'In the cave where my skin was hidden is a pool. Climb up to it and drink.'

'I ... I don't understand. Why?'

'The water from the Whispering Pool can make you see the other side. That's my gift for you: so that you may continue to see Arthur, even if he's far away. That's all I can give you, Nimue. Perhaps... if you're lucky, our wounded king will help you. Speak to him, if you can reach him. Call out: Fisher King, Fisher King! If he can, he may answer.'

'Alright,' I say in a composed tone of voice. 'If that will help. He's my only hope.'

'Now climb up there first. Perhaps it will give you time to think. Let thoughts of Arthur strengthen your heart.' Sela bends down to me and kisses me tenderly on my sandy forehead.

I allow her to gently push me away from my mother, but only because I'm too exhausted to protest. Here on the beach there's nothing that can help me save Rona. I don't know if the Others don't have the power to help me or if they simply don't feel like it, but clearly, I can't rely on them. All I can do is go up to that cave and find out what magic is hidden there. Maybe it will be useful. Maybe the Fisher King will hear me.

Speechless, I get up. My clothes are heavy with mud, my anorak is flapping in the relentless wind and my trousers are sticking uncomfortably to my legs. The water has retreated even further, revealing a whole new section of the cliff. The rockface is rough and full of sharp edges. Higher up, I can see the dark cave. It's not wide, but just wide enough for a person to squeeze through.

'Not a safe climb,' I hear myself muttering.

'Are you afraid of it?' my grandmother asks softly. There is no blame in her voice.

'No. Mum climbed that rock when she was not much older than me. She did it to save you.' I shift my gaze to look at Sela. 'Now I want to save her. Do your people ever pray?'

'There are no gods beneath the waves.' A smile tugs at the corner of her mouth. 'But I learned it when I was trapped on the shore.'

'Could you please stay with her when I'm gone?'

'Of course,' she whispers. 'Don't delay, Nimue. Don't let the tide change and carry her away.'

With one last look at my forlorn seal mother, I cross the beach until I'm standing in front of the tall cliff. I look up and study the rocks in an attempt to determine a route, to discover the safest places to grab with my hands and to plant my feet. The anorak is baggy and long, so I take it off.

Then I take hold of the rock that my mother climbed so many years before me. Now it's my turn.

19

BLOOD MAGIC

A heavy smell pervades the cave – salt water, seaweed, and fish. There is barely enough light coming through the narrow opening to see anything, but in the twilight I study my new surroundings as well as I can. The ground is littered with shellfish, strands of weed, and sea drift. In many places, the stone floor has been eroded by the rising and falling tides, and pits have formed in which stagnant seawater has collected in smelly pools. I hear the splashing of my feet in the shallow water.

I have to be careful where I put my feet. Like the wall that I'm resting my probing hand against, the ground is slippery with algae. Peaks and protrusions rise from the rock like cancerous growths. Mum once mistook them for creatures that could come to life at any moment, and I can't really blame her. With a superstitious shudder, I walk past them, following a track that I'm not even sure is one, partially relying on my memories of Rona's description, partly trusting my own intuition.

Soon the cave makes a slight turn to the left and the opening disappears from sight. The light doesn't touch this part of the cave, so I'm swallowed whole by the darkness. I stand and listen to a dripping sound coming from up ahead. My eyes don't adapt to this new darkness, so I'll have to keep going by touch.

The open space turns into a narrow passageway, which slopes down after a few more minutes of walking. I drop to my knees and crawl forward and upwards, as the ground rises slightly again. The darkness and the enclosed walls hem me in, and it's as if I'm encased underground. If something happens to me now, it will be hours or maybe days before Ana finds me – if looking inside the cave even occurs to her. My screams would be swallowed up by the stones of the cliff.

I push away the thought. What's the point of scaring myself? I feel secure in the knowledge that Mum has also managed to squeeze through this narrow gap and return safely at one point. I struggle on, gritting my teeth, until suddenly the walls fall away and I'm able to stand upright. I see a faint flicker of light in front of me. I run the last few steps towards a huge space, where I can hear the murmur of the sea again. The ceiling arches up high. At the very top is an opening in the roof, where a pale moon and a few stars are visible, shining down on me.

I take a moment to recover, relieved that the stench and utter darkness are now behind me. So this is where Fergus was hiding Sela's seal skin all these years. I wish I'd climbed up earlier so that sunlight would be falling through the opening right now. The moon lights up some rubbish and stones scattered on the ground. I walk around, carefully and alert. There is no sign of a pool or spring here – I can only smell the salty air of the ocean, but much less pungent than below, and the muddy rocks around me. If there had been fresh water around, I would've picked up the scent. I would've seen a reflection of stars, at least.

Discouraged, I let myself fall to the ground. There is no magical water here that can give me a glimpse of the Other World, let alone let me speak to the chained king in his tower room.

I have to face it. As soon as the sea washes over the beach again, it will take Rona with it. Eventually she'll die in that cold water. Every moment I spend in this cave is a moment I didn't spend with my mother before I have to let her go. With heavy limbs and an even heavier heart, I get up.

I don't see the hole in the ground until I have almost passed it. Like the entrance to the cave, the opening isn't very large. I drop to my knees and stick my head in. It's as if I'm suddenly going blind. I blink and it makes no difference: the darkness remains impenetrable.

I hesitate. There's no telling how deep the tunnel is or where it will lead, but it's my last hope. The alternative is to go back to the beach and accept that I have lost both my mother and my brother.

With clenched teeth, I lower myself into the narrow opening. At least the space is big enough for my body to pass through and the tunnel doesn't abruptly end with a barricade of stone. I hold out my arms like antennae and slowly move forward. My knees scrape the ground and it won't be long before my trousers finally start to tear. Breathing is difficult. I have just enough room to move my head to the left and to the right, but I can't turn around.

The air is thick and stale. I have the feeling that with every breath I take, I'm sucking more oxygen out of this narrow space and leaving less for the next breath I take. My heart is pounding uncomfortably loud and my ears are ringing.

I don't know how long I'll still have to crawl forward like this, blind as a mole in the earth. At least a mole would know where it was, I think sourly. A mole can push the earth aside and create its own paths; I depend on the benevolence of the rocks and a healthy dose of dumb luck.

I'm on the verge of a claustrophobic panic when the ground suddenly slopes down sharply. I slip and scramble for purchase, but by then it's too late to stop myself from falling. My own weight pulls me down. I bump into something hard and sharp and I feel pain in my cheek, as well as a sharp stab in my shoulder. But then, I notice that the walls on either side are widening. Suddenly I have room to move. I stretch out my arms and manage to stop my fall. I sit up, panting, and don't move.

There is some light here, though I can't yet discover its source. It's certainly not daylight – this faint glow, which allows me to see the shadows of my hands and the cave walls, is too dull and greenish to come from outside. Besides, the narrow tunnel ran downwards, so I suspect that I'm now far underground.

It doesn't take long before I discover the source of the glow. Pointy crystals are growing against the walls, phosphorescent like the sea sometimes lights up at night after a sweltering summer's day. It gives me enough light to take in the space. The ceiling is like the vaulted roof of the cathedral in Saint-Thonan, only lower. The amounts of stone and earth above me muffle all sounds coming from the beach. Yet it's not completely silent in the underground vault. I can hear it clearly: the babbling of a small brook, water trickling down stone. I follow the sound, crawl forward on my knees to feel the floor with my hands. Finally I hit the water – a stream as wide as my hand.

And there, further down, is a moon-shaped pool. Like stone sentinels, the pointy crystals on either side of the pool rise up. The light reflects in the water, giving it the greenish glow of the sea. I bend down and bring my face close to the surface. My breath makes the water ripple.

'Arthur?'

For something called the Whispering Pool, the water remains awfully silent. With a sigh, I scoop up a handful of water and rub it onto my face. My forehead and cheeks are covered with a fine dust. It sticks to my eyebrows and eyelashes and I taste it in my mouth. Sela has told me to drink. I scoop up another handful and bring it to my lips. Gwenhael's grave, I hadn't realised how thirsty I was!

I wipe my mouth when I see the change in the water. Immediately I stare at the pool again.

What I see is not the reflection of crystals or my own dusty face.

I see Arthur. He's lying on moss, surrounded by towering trees, full of leaves. Ferns are growing around him, as if the plants are shielding him from the rest of the forest. One arm is folded protectively across his chest, the other serves as a pillow for his head. I lean in as close to the water as I can without dipping my face into it. My eyes scan the image of my little brother, trying to discover whether he's injured, whether he's bleeding, whether he's breathing...

His cheeks have lost the unhealthy pallor of the past few days and instead have a healthy blush. His eyes are closed, his sweet face smooth as a child's. As I breathlessly and confusedly stare at this scene, I realise that he has two legs. I'm so relieved that for a moment I cannot speak. I don't know where he is, or how real his unharmed body is in the Other World, but he is safe.

'Oh, Arthur,' I whisper. My breath ripples the water and the image moves with it. It seems as if Arthur is moving at the same time. Can he hear me?

'Arthur? Arthur, wake up! I'm here, I'm near you!' No matter how long I call and beg him, my voice doesn't seem to penetrate the surface of the water and reach the other side. In despair, I bang my fist on the ground. 'Open your eyes! Where are you, Arthur? Where are you going?'

As if to taunt me, the image suddenly fades. I let out a frustrated, hoarse scream, but even though he couldn't hear me, it was comforting to be able to look at my little brother.

'Come back!' I beg, but the Whispering Pool shows nothing more than my own reflection. Disappointment fills my eyes with tears.

I wipe them away and whisper: 'Fisher King, Fisher King.'

For a moment, nothing happens. Then the Whispering Pool slowly reveals the image of the wounded king.

Only a translucent trace of him remains: his seated form on the throne is wavering like a ghost on the water, even whiter than I remember it. He's thinner too, almost transparent. His cloak hangs off his body like an oversized piece of cloth, the crown on his head seems to be sucking in the light instead of reflecting it. His face, hair and beard are as white as dry seal bones, and the rest of his body is black and hard. Like stone. Even the heavy chains holding him down look dull and made of stone. I feel that my breath alone is enough to break him.

'Fisher King,' I whisper again. 'Please help me.'

His voice drifts towards me like a soft wind. 'Is he coming?'

I discover that I can hardly speak louder than him. 'Arthur is asleep.'

'He'll wake up soon.' The Fisher King barely moves, but a satisfied expression appears on his face.

'I want him beside me,' I say defiantly. 'I need him.'

'He has his way to go and you have yours.' When I remain silent, he heaves a wispy sigh. 'Well, child of the sea? What is it that saddens you so?'

'I'm about to give up.'

'Why? Has your faith left you?'

'Yes,' I say sourly. 'I set my mother free, but now she doesn't want to change.'

'Don't you think you can change her mind, sea child?'

'Then tell me how!' Part of me is ashamed to shout at such a fragile figure. 'I don't know how, that's why you have to help me!'

'I can't do that. I'm too weak and too far away. Help yourself. Find the magic within you.'

'Where inside me?'

'What made you undertake this journey? What pushed you through the night, knowing that you might never reach Rona – was it not the call of your blood?'

I close my eyes. Suddenly I'm so very tired. My limbs hurt, they're tired to the bone. 'I think I just couldn't accept the alternative. That Mum would be gone forever.'

'Ah, you see?' His white lips curve upwards into an echo of a smile. 'Your confidence is stronger than your doubt.'

'I don't think it's enough.'

'Maybe not. But if you can regain your confidence, then maybe you can summon your own magic, from your body, your blood. It's simple...' His voice weakens. I see no more than a flickering of him now. 'Blood passes on. Blood connects. Blood remembers. Close your eyes and breathe. Remember...'

Like an extinguished flame, he disappeared.

'Wait!' My voice echoes through the cave. There is no reply.

I shudder. The way he spoke of blood reminds me sharply of the Hunter's rasping voice in my ear: *fresh blood in my nose. I know you, child of the sea. Above or below, I'll know your scent...*

Blood and smell and memories. Is that the answer? My thoughts are a swirling tide of half-formed ideas and a little bit of hope that I almost don't want to say out loud. No, I'll have no hope yet, I won't even pray, I won't do anything that could break this fragile new thought. But I will hurry.

The way back seems like a much longer journey. A few times, I'm afraid that I'm lost – that I'll never be able to pry myself loose from the insides of the earth. But at last I crawl out through the crack in the cliff face and am greeted by the wind blowing in my face. After the silence in the cave, the ocean around the island is roaring with overwhelming force. I can't see much as I reach for crevices and protrusions in the rocky wall to lower myself safely to the beach, but I hear the waves breaking against the cliffs.

As soon as my feet reach solid ground, my knees start to tremble. I clench my fingers harder around the bit of rock I'm still holding onto and force my body to stay upright. No time for weakness, no time for rest. I'm driven by an urgent feeling. My heart is beating out an insistent tattoo: *do it now, or never again. Do it now, or lose your only chance.* Somehow I have the presence of mind to put my discarded anorak back on. When Sela emerges from the darkness, I have no energy to say anything to her. It doesn't seem necessary. Silently, she takes me by the arm. In the short time it takes us to get to Rona, my eyes have become accustomed to the night again. The moon has moved across the sky. How long have I been underground? It feels like an eternity. Yet it can't have been more than an hour.

Sela is still holding me. Despite her delicate body, her grip on my arm is surprisingly strong.

'It's alright,' I say. 'You can let go of me.'

I immediately kneel down next to the seal. My heart stutters when my mother makes another attempt to move away from me, then gives up and lies still, breathing heavily. She really is at the end of her tether.

'Give me something sharp,' I say to Sela, without looking up. 'A knife, a shell, whatever.'

I hear her soft footfalls on the sand. A moment later, she pushes a broken razor clam into my outstretched hand. The point is sharp and thick, like the blade of a knife. Without hesitation, I grab the point with such force that it bores into my palm and makes my blood spill. The pain comes as a shock, but I force myself to watch as the blood gushes out of the cut. Warm, dark blood, like that of a felled animal. I turn my hand around and press the palm against Rona's head. I smear the blood onto her fur. A shudder goes through her emaciated body.

'Mum,' I whisper. 'It's me, Nimue. I know you're scared, and tired, but try to listen to me. Let me tell you a story.'

My voice falters and I hesitate to speak again. What if this doesn't work? No – I've already hesitated for long enough. The Fisher King was right about that: doubt won't get me anywhere, but confidence might.

Blood connects. Blood remembers. I cling to those words as if they were lifelines.

'When your mother gave you the name Rona, she named you after the glimmering seals that always lie on vast sandbanks between Gull Island and the cliffs. She told your father that it was a word from the old language; a language that no longer exists on the island...'

The moon continues its journey through the heavens while I tell my mum everything I know about her journey. I leave nothing unsaid. I tell her about her shell house, about the pink and yellow shells hanging in strands on the walls, the big fireplace, and the furniture made from pieces of wreckage. I talk about Ana, demanding that my mother remember her faithful friend. I tell my mother about rowing to Gull Island, to the very beach where we are now, how she climbed the rough, tall cliff to enter the cave that held Sela's secret. I don't hesitate to talk about Benji, and I describe his fiery curls and freckled face as confidentially as if I had known my uncle personally. I tell the story of Sela, naked and silent on the sandy beach, with the wind whipping up her coal-black locks and ruffling them, how that sad creature was set free again by wrapping her frail body in a long neglected fur.

'Like a fairy tale, Mum. And look how she's keeping watch over us now. Do you remember how she watched over you all those long years?'

I talk about leaving the island behind. About the swaying boat, the wind almost ripping the canvas, the sun and the stars their only compass. I describe the shipyards and the many boats in Camlann harbour, the smell of the oil tanks moving slowly through the deep channels, and I tell about the fisherman who showed them the way. I dig up from memory every detail in her diary, everything I can remember from all those hours spent reading it. Around us, the night progresses.

Sela remains perfectly still. She stands beside us like a guardian, her eyes like pools of the deepest water. My mouth dries up and my throat begins to ache, but I continue.

I describe all the little houses of our beloved fishing village. The smell of salt and iodine that you could never escape, no matter which way you turned. The cliffs growing out of the foaming sea, just like the cliffs here; the small, sandy beaches full of shells and crabs and other crawling creatures. The fishing nets, strung up between the houses to be repaired, the best nets that Jost had to offer. The glow of the lamps behind the shutters of those houses, and the glow of the distant lights of Gwennec. The rolling hills behind us, and the beach in front of our house. And I tell her about Grandma and Dad and *The Ragdoll*, floating on the waves while the sun made the whole sea glow like glass.

I tell her about myself, reaching for the few memories I have of my time with her. When I'm through with that, I go on to tell her about her blonde son, and how Arthur and I grew up with the sea as our constant companion.

I'm so tired. My body is shaking and the wind that seems determined to blow me over isn't helping. I pull my anorak tightly around me and keep going, clearing my throat again and again. I should've remembered to bring fresh water and build a new fire. But no – Mum would only have become more frightened because of the flames. I push away all my discomfort and resume my story. I tell Rona about our search in Central Europe, how we followed in her footsteps. Does she remember the menhirs? The one that looked like a face, the one that lay almost completely crumbled on the ground? Does she remember the house with the red facade in Brevalaer, the sweet smell of the blossoming apple tree that Esoldi planted in front of it?

'We've got it all back, Mum. Me and Arthur. Oh, we searched for so long! Please, please, remember it. Listen to my words. Please.'

And then, sweet Gwenhael, my mother raises her seal eyes to mine. For the first time, she really looks at me. I stare back, my breath caught in my lungs. For a long moment I cannot speak.

Then I say, my voice breaking: 'Mum?'

Something cold and wet washes over my lap. I automatically look down and what I see chills me. The sea is changing. The tide is claiming the beach and is steadily closing in on us. My head starts to spin when I realise how little time we have left.

'Change – change now! Mum, I beg you!' I shake her back and forth. The waves washing over us turn the sand soft and muddy and slippery, making it far too easy for my mother to slip away into that hungry sea.

Her eyes stay fixed on me. I really believe that she can hear me. Then why doesn't she do what I beg her so desperately to do?

It doesn't matter, I think lightheadedly. It doesn't matter – if she can't do it, I will. Because I have magic. Sela had the power to turn Mum into a seal, so why shouldn't I have the power to bring her back? I remember the first time I healed Katell. The deep connection I felt then with Sela and Rona, connecting the three of us – that's where I got my strength from. Blood passes on. Blood connects. Blood remembers. I think I finally understand the Fisher King. Spirits help me, even the words of the Hunter echo through my head. The magic that flows inside me is my own blood.

I grab the shell and force myself not to hesitate. Before Sela can protest, before my mother can see what I'm up to, I ruthlessly put the point into her back and press hard. The cut I make is not deep, but definitely as long as my hand. Rona lets out a high, tormented wail. The blood wells up. I press my cut palm against it, forcing her blood to mix with mine. Her writhing body digs a hole in the sand and makes it easier for the sea to claim her. I fling my arms around her and hold her desperately against me. The power she suddenly summons up astounds me. With all my weight, I let myself fall forward, half on top of her.

'Listen, Mum. Listen!' I hear how desperate I sound. 'You left us with a final message in your diary: no storm, no darkness could separate us. Well, we braved storms and darkness to track you down and now I've finally found you! I know what you did to Benji, Mum. I know that decision has haunted you every day of the rest of your life. I know how it burns your heart and that it's easier to forget everything about that life. But now it's time to come back. Your son is sleeping too deeply. And I... I can't spend another moment without you!'

I bend over and rest my face against her round head, my lips against her skin. She suddenly stops her attempts to escape and lies motionless in my arms. With my body against hers, I'm aware of every fast, heavy breath she's taking.

'Mum, can you hear me? The morning light is already cresting the horizon. The tide is beginning to rise. Time to change, my selkie mother.'

A movement distracts me. Opposite me, Sela kneels down in the sand. I'm deeply shocked by the pain radiating from her black eyes. The first grey of the morning illuminates her wet cheeks. She puts one hand on Rona's back, the other on my cold fingers.

'Don't look at me,' she says. 'Look at your mother.'

What I see halts my breath. Mum's grey fur is discolouring in the rising light, but it's not the wavering sun that makes her look paler. No, the change comes from within. The grey spots on her skin are disappearing. Before my eyes, her fur coat turns a soft pink. Pale and sickly, yes, but clearly human flesh. Her body grows longer, the tail stretches and splits, forming two legs. Her belly, neck, chest, and head grow like an emerging flower suddenly budding. I'm only able to stare motionlessly at the metamorphosis that my mother is undergoing, until at long last, nothing remains of her seal form, except the large, black eyes, surrounded by a messy bunch of jet-black hair.

There she lies, naked and skinny in the cold wind, while the sea water mercilessly crashes over her. Her hair is sticking to the bloody gash between her shoulder blades. Rona stares into nothingness. A new wave arrives; it washes over my lap and rinses the sand from Rona's bare legs. The cold seems to bring her to life: a deep shiver runs through her. Her naked skin, stripped of the fat and fur that protects a seal from the cold, is trembling. I hear her exhale. Then her eyes turn and catch my gaze.

She knows me. I know it the moment we look at each other. Something goes through me that is difficult to describe with words. A shock, a shudder, a landslide turning everything upside down and then rearranging it with a blow. I fold my hands tightly and press them to my chest, against my painfully pounding heart. I'm not sure if I'm making any sound, if I'm crying out loud or in silence. All I'm aware of are her eyes exploring my face, hungrily taking in my whole sodden and soiled appearance – and the light that slowly begins to dawn in those eyes. That careful, awkward curling of her pale lips that transforms her face into the lantern that will show me the way home.

She raises her arms, so rail-thin that I can see all the bones under her skin. But just as the strength of her seal form surprised me, her embrace is also more powerful than I expected. I feel all her bones against me like sticks in a bag. She is as cold as I am when she presses herself against me, but her breath is so warm against my cheek and her kiss on my head so tender that it dispels the fear of the sea washing over us. The sea is just a cold mass of water, jealous that she can never take Rona away from me now.

'Mum,' I hear myself whisper, as I embrace her tightly.

'My girl.' Her voice is barely audible above the sounds of the beach, and hoarse, as if her throat no longer knows how to form words. It's the most beautiful sound in the world. 'Oh, my girl.'

When I finally break free from her arms and look over her shoulder, I notice that Sela is no longer next to us. There are no tracks in the sand, except my own footprints and the hole that Rona dug while still in her seal form.

'She's gone,' I mutter.

Mum strokes my cheeks with her long fingers, as if she has found a treasure and still can't believe how beautiful it is. 'Who's gone?'

I return my gaze to her and shake my head, smiling. She didn't realise that her mother was sitting next to her when the spell broke. 'It doesn't matter, Mum. She let you go. And I... I found you.'

I cover her quivering body with my anorak and walk her to the spot where my campfire is struggling to survive. She lingers for a moment before she approaches the flames. I see an animalistic distrust shining in her eyes, although her lips part longingly. I hold her and silently let her get used to the heat on her skin.

As soon as she dares to take a seat, I feed the fire with a piece of driftwood that spatters blue-green sparks into the clearing sky. I let Mum lean against me and hold her in my arms, determined to give her every bit of body heat I can.

We don't speak. During all those months since we left Gwennec, I thought that I'd have a thousand things to say to her if I ever saw her again. Now I discover that our silence is a softer balm on my heart than all the stories Mum and I have to share. We sit together and watch the golden disc of the sun rise above the sea. The seagulls, awakened by the light, let their cries ring over the island. My mother's regular breaths, her warming body in my arms, the salty smell of her hair – these are the threads weaving my torn world back together. I sit completely still and experience how that torn world is mended, stitch by stitch. The nagging discomfort I feel when I think about my agreement with the Others and what price I'll have to pay for it is best ignored. For now.

20

TIME FOR THE FUTURE

We're in Ana's small, round room, so full of colour with the half-finished tapestries on their looms. Even though sunlight is coming through the windows, she has lit the fire. My mother is wearing a dress she's borrowed from her friend. The waist is too wide around her hips and the bodice is baggy around her torso. It's the feeling of fabric against her skin that makes her uncomfortable, she tells us. No matter how soft the garment is, it seems to rub against her like a prison. And it's true – she looks like a stranded creature that doesn't feel at home in this man-made room with its furniture and walls.

I can hardly take my eyes off her. The glow of the fire has finally brought a blush to her white face and the flames are reflecting in her black eyes. There's something timorous in those eyes, something wild that I don't remember ever having seen before. I wonder if that frightened look on her face will ever disappear. Her hair falls like tangled seaweed past her shoulders. She lifts a hand and thoughtlessly brushes some hair away from her forehead. I smile: she hasn't realised it, but that's the first human gesture I have seen her make so far.

Ana must have noticed it too, because something as bright as the firelight flickers across her face. For the past few hours she looked just as pale as my mother. Their reunion was one of shock and disbelief. Only now does the joy of this reunion seem to get through to her, like rainwater slowly seeping through the cracks and crevices of a roof.

It was a perilous journey back, with the three of us crammed into the small rowing boat. In that sense, it was almost a blessing that my mother is so frail that she barely weighs more than a child.

200

Ana pours steaming water from a kettle boiling above the fire into three handmade stone cups. Life on Avalon reminds me of the fact that this island and its people exist by the grace of the sea: the cups are inlaid with tiny shells, the kettle is an iron jug that once washed up on the beach, the table where bread, cheese and a sweet apple pie are laid out is constructed from two types of driftwood – one dark and smooth, the other light and full of holes and curves.

Mum puts the tea carefully to her lips as if she's afraid the cup might explode. After a first, tentative sip, her eyes blink and a strange smile comes to her lips. 'What a pleasant pleasure,' she whispers. 'I didn't think I'd ever taste this again.'

'Had you forgotten how much you like chamomile tea?' Ana asks with a smile on her lips. 'You used to drink it with honey, whenever my mother would give you a jar. Sometimes I would bring it to you to cheer you up ...'

'Oh, Ana,' Mum says softly. 'I've let you down.'

'You've left me behind. I don't think I ever stopped missing you, although time eventually dulled the pain.' Her smile fades. 'And I have been so angry with you. For never asking me to come with you ... I would've come with you, Rona.'

'You belonged on Avalon. I couldn't take you away from your family, Ana.'

Ana shrugs. 'And I was angry when you came back. You didn't come back to *me*, you came back just to throw your life away. I was so furious...' Her hands clench into fists. 'So furious about what you did to your brother. It broke my heart.'

The light seems to disappear from Mum's eyes at once. She remains silent for a long time. In that silence, she cradles her head in her hands until the knuckles turn white and tight. When she finally speaks, it is so quietly that I lean in to pick up her words. 'It broke my heart too. It's a crime that has no excuse. Ana, the prospect of death was... a relief. I knew I couldn't drag you into it and I knew I couldn't live with myself, so I gave my life away freely.'

'I forgave you years ago,' Ana sighs. 'I'm glad you didn't follow him in death. And I'm so grateful you're here – that this time it's not a dream. Oh, Rona.' She takes her friend's hands in hers and kisses them. I get up quietly and leave Mum and Ana by themselves.

Arthur is lying in the exact same position as I left him. Someone has taken the trouble to run a comb through his curls and wash his face. A sheet covers him, and his hands are folded on his chest. In many ways, he looks more like a dead man lying in state than a boy who is resting. I sit on the edge of the bed and stroke his cheek. There's some stubble on his jaw. Despite everything, I feel myself smile. My little brother Arthur donning a beard? I can't imagine it, but if no one shaves him, it won't be long before it becomes a reality.

'I have seen you, little brother,' I tell him. 'You're sleeping in the woods among the ferns. I hope someone's watching over you there. I hope you're not afraid and will wake up soon.' The lump in my throat makes it harder to speak. 'I'll watch over you in my dreams, Arthur. I'll be with you on your journey, wherever it takes you. I promise.' I kiss him on the mouth and feel his breath on my face. 'Remember – we do it together, or not at all.'

A creaking sound of floorboards and soft footsteps tell me I'm no longer alone. Mum slowly approaches the bed. It must have taken up almost all her energy to climb the stairs, but she refuses my outstretched hand with a smile. She bends over Arthur.

'Oh, my son. My little prince.' She cries and she laughs. Mum kisses him on the mouth, like I just did, and then on his cheeks. I don't know if Arthur, somewhere in his forest, notices anything in this wonderful moment, because he doesn't give us any signs of life. His breath continues uninterrupted, rising and falling the same gentle rhythm. I feel an unexpected surge of pain and bitter disappointment. What was I expecting? That my brother would open his eyes and wake up as soon as Mum touched him?

Yes, I think reluctantly. Part of me has always believed that Mum's return would put things right. While staring at Arthur's resting face, I almost want to beat him up and yell at him. *Wake up, you weakling, you idiot! Can you really not try harder to look our mother in the eye after all we've been through?*

Mum turns around. Her eyes look straight into my heart and I feel exposed. Before I know it, I'm in her arms again and her hand is running through my curls.

'You've been so strong,' Rona says. 'So breathtakingly strong.'

'We have lost so much,' I sob.

Mum holds me for a while longer, then pulls out a stool to sit at Arthur's bedside. I know that she still has trouble standing upright and on two legs. Every step she takes is shaky and tentative. She's told me that her knees and ankles hurt a lot.

I nestle against her sitting down on the floor, my back against her legs. Her hand ruffles my hair again, but she says nothing. Her silence is inviting. She hasn't told me how much she still remembers of the long story I told her during the night. Even if she did remember everything, it is far from the whole story. I take a deep breath and try to organise my thoughts. And then I start again.

Dad's accident with *The Ragdoll* and the wave that devastated the village make her face twitch with grief. I tell about Yannick in Saint Gwenhael, the man with the fishhook in his shoulder, my ice-cold hands and how I cured him of a fatal wound to my own surprise. Now that I've started talking, I can't stop. I tell her about our journey from Gwennec to Saint-Thonan, about the train where we first caught a glimpse of the men with the snake emblem on their uniforms. Mum's fingers clutch my hair and I hear her breath catch, but I don't give her a chance to ask any questions. I talk about Mirna in the cell, about Will and his Ark, about Katell, whom I have come to love as if she were my own sister. Mum's hand slips out of my hair and into my hand. Her grip is reassuring. When I get to the part about Cormack, she turns very quiet. I peek over my shoulder to fathom what she's thinking. In her eyes, fresh tears well up. Maybe she's thinking about Benji's first son and feels the flame of guilt in her heart. If so, she doesn't mention it. When she squeezes my hand, it tells me that she wants me to keep talking. Only when I'm about to tell her about Wolf do I hesitate. That one sweet night in the barn belongs only to us; a warm memory, like a blanket on a cold night. But...

'Oh, Mum, I'm with child. The spirits wouldn't let you go until I gave him to them. I didn't know what to do, I didn't even know I was pregnant! I don't want to think about what will happen...' Suddenly I choke on my own words and let my face sink into my hands. Rona sits there, frozen. Her hand goes cold around mine and I feel her shiver when she finally bends down to me.

'Whatever you do,' she whispers in my ear, 'don't let them take your child away from you. Whatever you do, Nimue: you must never let that happen.'

I look up and she gently turns me around to face her. Mum takes my tear-soaked face in her hands. 'By now you should know what happens when a mother leaves her child,' she says and I hear both self-reproach and sadness in her voice. 'Our family was the victim of heartbreak after heartbreak, and it has torn us apart. Don't do that to yourself once more. Don't do it to your son or daughter.'

'What should I do?' It is the question of a child, and I speak in a forlorn, high-pitched voice.

Rona presses her lips to the crown of my hair before letting go of my face. 'When you're ready, you will leave Avalon. Find that lover of yours and bring him home to us.'

'He hates the sea. He refused to go when we offered to take him.' A hopeless, sinking feeling floods my body. I put my hands on my belly, where I cannot sense any trace of life.

'Tell me this. Do you love him?'

'Maybe.' The memory of his safe arms sends a pleasant tingle through me. 'I could love him.'

'And does he love you?'

'I don't know. It was so brief. He'd just been released from his cell and everything was so uncertain, and...'

'Would he love his child?' Mum interrupts me quietly.

His child. I think of his hands around mine, how he shaped my fingers into the branches of a tree and let his own fingers wander over them. 'I think so. Yes, I am sure.'

'Then you need him. Promise me you'll find him, Nimue.'

'I promise,' I say, and I can hardly believe I'm saying it. Back to Central Europe, where all kinds of dangers await me, while a child is growing in my belly – and this time *without* Arthur? I must be stark-raving mad! But at the same time, I have this mental image of Wolf embracing me again while I take in his scent. And then I imagine the surprised and delighted expression on his face when he hears that he'll become a father... 'Yes, I'll find him. When the time is right.'

The air is pleasant in the orchard when I take my mother out, supporting her by her arm. The first real summer day won't be far away now. We walk slowly, in order to give Rona the opportunity to regain her balance after each step. She leans on me the whole time. It would be a burden if she were heavier, but as light as she is now, I could lift her up and carry her to the beach myself.

'You are strong,' Mum remarks.

I smile at the admiration I can hear in those words. 'I had to become strong.'

'I'm sorry you had to endure all these hardships. But when I look at you, I'm also relieved.' Rona pauses and I give her a moment to catch her breath. 'You have what I ultimately lacked, Nimue: everything you need to live in this world. Not just on Avalon, but far beyond.'

We walk away from the orchard along the winding path that leads up to the cliffs. Mum tells me some small things about the village: about the pointy rock where somewhere, the faded letters of her name are still written in red paint, about the crooked apple tree where she and Benji used to build huts when life was simpler. How Ana hid in the car overgrown with flowes outside the village, when her mother was looking for her and she didn't feel like helping with the carding and weaving of the wool. We pass her old house. Mum freezes. The colour drains from her face and her hand digs into the flesh of my arm so tightly that I feel a bruise coming on.

'He's home.'

'He's an old man,' I reassure her. 'He can't hurt you.'

Nevertheless, I feel her trembling. For a moment I'm afraid that she'll fall to the ground. But then Mum lifts her chin up and straightens her back. 'I'll go to him at some point. I have to face him. But not yet.'

We walk until the even terrain ends in a steep cliff plummeting down in front of us. The sea wind beats down on us mercilessly and makes our clothes flap like sails on a ship. Below us is a white beach.

'This is where I stood when I was secretly watching my mother. There, she danced on the sand right into the surf. Always so impetuous... I was always afraid she'd fall...'

I'm afraid she'll fall herself if she hovers so close to the edge. I tighten my grip on her arm and pull her back. 'The past is the past,' I tell her firmly. 'Now it's time for the future.'

I take my eyes off my mother to look at the horizon. There, the storm heads are gathering, about to shake up the world.

21

EPILOGUE

THE AWAKENING OF THE KING

Surrounded by a wall of ferns and trees, the boy wakes up. Leaves crunch in his hair and he has grass stains on his shirt.

His body is supple and willing. He remembers a stiffness in his joints and a pain in his leg once, as if he is now an old man. He looks down at his body and shakes his head, dazed by dreams.

He doesn't know where he is, but he doesn't mind. The scents of the forest surround him – a comforting smell of trees bathing in sunlight, of white flowers growing close to the forest floor, making his makeshift bed soft and fit for a prince.

Where he came from or why he's here are things he remembers only vaguely. The world he has left behind is a blur in his mind. The lapping of the waves and the smell of salt belong to the same dreamlike haze as the fiery pain in his leg and how exhausted he always felt. All those things he can now simply forget. His mind is getting clearer. He rises and stretches his body like a young wolf, delighting in the strength of his own muscles, the suppleness of his limbs and the keenness of his senses.

Something rustles in the bushes behind him. He stands perfectly straight, his face turned towards the sound – not afraid, just alert. The leaves are pushed aside and a girl steps into the circle of sunlight. She is small and slender, with a halo of blonde hair that dances around her head like spun gold. He recognises her face from a dream, but when he tries to put a name to that image, it slips away from him.

The girl takes him in with big, pale blue eyes, as clear as a forest lake. Then she bends her knees in a strange gesture – a curtsy, perhaps – and as soon as she speaks, her voice meets him like a sweet, clear bell. 'You have arrived at last, Arthur, the King Who Must Come. Greetings and welcome.'

'Who are you?' he asks, intrigued by her beauty and mysterious words.

'I don't know how long I've been here or who I was before I started waiting for you,' the girl says. 'All I know is that my name is Goldilocks, and my job is to take you to the Tower of the Fisher King.'